CL16

or

Matters of Trust

*Pamela Oldfield titles available from
Severn House Large Print*

All Our Tomorrows
Changing Fortunes
Early One Morning
New Beginnings
Riding the Storm

Matters of Trust

Pamela Oldfield

Severn House Large Print
London & New York

This first large print edition published in Great Britain 2004 by
SEVERN HOUSE LARGE PRINT BOOKS LTD of
9-15 High Street, Sutton, Surrey, SM1 1DF.
First world regular print edition published 2003 by
Severn House Publishers, London and New York.
This first large print edition published in the USA 2004 by
SEVERN HOUSE PUBLISHERS INC of
595 Madison Avenue, New York, NY 10022.

British Library Cataloguing in Publication Data

Oldfield, Pamela, 1934 -
    Matters of trust. - Large print ed.
    1.   Hotels - England - Chester - Employees - Fiction
    2.   Large type books
    I.   Title
    823.9'14 [F]

    ISBN 0-7278-7335-0

Except where actual historical events or characters are being described
for the storyline of this novel, all situations in this publication are
fictitious and any resemblance to living persons is purely coincidental.

Printed and bound in Great Britain by
MPG Books Ltd, Bodmin, Cornwall.

For Ellie and Arnold,
Bill and Eve,
with love

One

Wednesday July 5th, 1905

Alice straightened her back, wishing as usual that she were a little taller, and a little prettier. She took a deep breath and squared her shoulders. Her right hand moved irresolutely towards the door then stopped. She took another deep breath. With nervous fingers she smoothed her dark skirt, checked the hairpins that held her dark wavy hair in place and ran a finger around the inside of her high collar.

'Don't be such a fool!' she told herself. 'You're not a schoolgirl and Miss Lightfoot is not your headmistress!'

But she *was* her employer's sister and a summons from her was most unusual. Fortunately Alice's conscience was clear – at least with regard to the hotel and her own area of work. She had worked her way up to her present position of assistant manager by dint of hard, conscientious work and good behaviour. The other matter, which *was* on her conscience, was still very much a secret which she had shared with nobody.

'Get on with it, Alice!' she told herself.

Before she could change her mind she rapped on Miss Lightfoot's door and waited breathlessly. Her heart was beating so loudly that she was afraid it would be heard.

'Come in!'

Alice closed her eyes, muttered a quick prayer for help, and opened them again. She stared at the brass numbers on the door as though she had never seen them before. Twenty eight. At last she turned the handle and stepped inside.

Nervousness slowed Alice's tongue and the old lady was the first to speak.

'Good morning, Mrs Meredith.'

'Good morning, ma'am. You wanted to see me.'

It was not a question. The summons yesterday had been explicit. *Please come to my room tomorrow morning at eight thirty. Hester Lightfoot.*

At seventy-five Hester Lightfoot was a heavily built woman but her cheekbones were still clearly defined and a long straight nose gave her an austere appearance. Although the year was 1905 and England had a king, Miss Lightfoot was still very much a product of the late Queen Victoria's reign. In spite of her age her mind was as sharp as ever and Alice knew from bitter experience that very little in the hotel escaped her sharp eyes. She was dressed in her outdated grey bombazine and her thinning hair was tucked away beneath a lace cap. Black velvet slippers comforted her feet and a woollen shawl was draped carefully around her broad shoulders. She was sitting in a chair beside her bed and a second chair had been placed nearby.

'Sit there, please, Mrs Meredith.' She indicated the spare chair with an elegant wave of her hand. 'I have something to say to you which you may not wish to hear.'

Alice hoped that she was not revealing her increasing nervousness. She sat down and folded her hands in her lap. Something she may not wish to hear? As she forced herself to look at Miss Lightfoot she was deeply puzzled now as well as apprehensive, for the old woman's manner was not hostile.

Alice said, 'I shouldn't be more than ten minutes, Miss Lightfoot. The church group is coming at ten and I have to prepare the room...'

'Reverend Tanner can wait if needs be,' the old lady replied. 'What I have to say to you is more important than the vicar's committee meeting.'

Alice remained silent, hiding her surprise. With her right hand she stroked the skirt of her own black dress, aware of the older

9

woman's head-to-toe scrutiny of her appearance, and was thankful she had given her black button boots an extra polish. What on earth had inspired this summons, she wondered. It would hardly be a complaint about the room service for, as the owner's sister, Hester Lightfoot received preferential treatment. Henry Lightfoot had made it clear when she first arrived at the hotel that his sister was to be treated as an honoured guest at all times and had put her in room twenty-eight, which had by far the best view. She had occupied the room for the past nine years and had rarely complained.

'Mrs Meredith, I have to tell you that certain facts have come to my notice. About your state of health.' She leaned forward slightly. 'About what I will call your "condition".'

Alice felt an immediate tightness in her throat as the last few words struck home and her composure faltered. Her *condition*! She stared at Miss Lightfoot, her throat dry with shock. Hester Lightfoot *knew*.

'My ... My condition?' Her voice was little more than a whisper. 'I don't think I understand...'

'I think you know what I mean.' Hester Lightfoot watched her closely and Alice thought she saw a glimmer of sympathy in her eyes. 'Mrs Meredith, a little bird tells me that you might be in the family way.'

For a moment Alice couldn't rally her thoughts. She felt dizzy with fear. It was early days and she had thought the pregnancy undetected, clutching the secret to her. She had expected another month or two before she had to declare it and had intended to think carefully about her situation before making any rash decisions.

'But how ... ?' she stammered. 'The doctor? He had no right to discuss my condition with anyone!' For a moment anger flared. 'That was a breach of trust...'

Hester Lightfoot was shaking her head. 'Don't blame the doctor, Mrs Meredith. I used my own eyes. There is a certain haunted look in those wonderful eyes of yours. I have seen it many times in women who are expecting a child. I saw it in my sister years ago. As for the doctor, he is a personal friend. He plays chess with my brother. I brought pressure to bear and he finally agreed that I had guessed correctly. You must blame me. I can be very stubborn.'

Alice was filled with a wild despair. Her employer knew. It was all over.

Hester Lightfoot went on. 'And, of course, you look tired. Sleepless nights spent worrying about what to do. All those changes your body is making. All the adjustments necessary to create a new life.' She smiled suddenly. 'Plus a certain air of distraction lately.'

'I haven't shirked my work!' Alice protested with a flash of anger.

'No, but yesterday you forgot to check the bookings with the manager.'

'He told you?' She felt betrayed. She had always counted Mr Warner a friend.

'Only because I asked. I've been keeping an eye on you, you see, with good reason.'

Alice's anger left her and she found herself drained of energy. What was the point of arguing? The secret was out and Hester Lightfoot was preparing to sack her. But if so, why the smiles. Confused, she waited, speechless with anxiety.

'You must forgive me, Mrs Meredith.' The old woman regarded her intently. 'I hope when you hear what I have to say – when you understand – you will forgive this intrusion into your private life. You are a widow, are you not?'

Alice hesitated, unsure how best to answer. Was she making things more difficult for herself? No, she thought bitterly. She could hardly be in worse trouble. She glanced down at her hands and said nothing.

'Mr Lester asked me about you one day,' Hester Lightfoot continued. 'I suddenly realized how little we know about you.'

'Mr Lester?'

He was one of the hotel's occasional guests.

'Yes. He asked if you were married.'

How was Mr Lester involved, Alice wondered, thoroughly confused. What on earth was all this about? Still recovering from the shock of knowing her secret was out, Alice considered her answer. She had used the married woman's title for years, avoiding the *Miss* that would proclaim her a spinster at the age of twenty-six.

Tempted to lie she heard herself stammer truthfully. 'I have never been married. I ... I believe the title gives me a certain status in the eyes of the staff.'

'Ah yes. I see.' Again the tentative smile. 'Mrs Meredith, I have to ask you a very personal question – several, in fact. About the father of your child.'

'I'm not prepared to talk about it!' The words were sharp but Alice no longer cared. This intrusion into her private life was unacceptable. If she was going to lose her job she would like to know. There was no need to—

Hester Lightfoot held up her hand by way of interruption.

'My dear, you must save your protests until you have heard me out. Let me ask my questions and explain the thinking behind them. Only then will you know if protests are in order. Believe me, my dear, I don't intend you any harm. Will you hear me out?'

Alice nodded doubtfully. This was the end

of everything. She was about to lose her job and with it her home.

'Mrs Meredith, I want you to tell me about the father of your child. Will you do that? Could you bear it?'

'Oh no! I can't ... It's too...' Alice's eyes filled with unexpected tears. The truth was too ugly. Too sad. She shook her head.

'You have to trust me, Mrs Meredith.'

Again Alice shook her head. She could never explain about Sebastian and her own gullibility. As to trust – that was a word that no longer held any real meaning for her.

Seeing that Hester Lighfoot was still waiting for her to speak she felt a renewed rush of anger. 'Isn't it enough that I find myself in this dreadful fix?' she demanded. 'Without having to humiliate myself by...' She swallowed hard. 'By dwelling on my mistakes!'

'Mrs Meredith, it's very important that I understand how this child came into being.' Hester Lightfoot produced a large neatly folded handkerchief and pressed it into Alice's hand. 'Dry your tears, my dear, and tell me how this happened.'

Alice was determined to refuse but she quickly found herself in tears again and suddenly the desire to tell all, to share the burden, began to overcome her fear. She reminded herself that the Lightfoots would have to know eventually so why not now?

14

She had made up her mind to keep the child and she couldn't expect to hide the pregnancy in the later months. There really was no alternative.

Reluctantly she began. 'I have always loved Seb. Sebastian Callard. Ever since we were children together. We planned to be together always as you do when you're young ... It simply didn't occur to me that as he grew older he'd find anyone else.' As she spoke she could see him clearly in her mind's eye. A proud figure, resplendent in his soldier's uniform. 'He and my brother, Eddie—'

'You have a brother, then? Any other close family?'

Alice nodded. 'My father is dead but my mother lives with her sister in Ireland.' She hesitated, wondering how much to tell.

'And you couldn't confide in your mother?'

'I didn't want to hurt her. She would be so ashamed.'

'Were you planning to go home to Ireland?'

'I hadn't thought that far, to be honest.'

Hester Lightfoot nodded. 'Do please go on.'

'Eddie and Seb enlisted together – the 1st Battalion, Cheshires – and their regiment was sent to India. Seb hadn't asked me to marry him. I was broken-hearted.'

'But you had other suitors, surely? You're not unattractive.'

Startled by the compliment, Alice said, 'But I was in love with Sebastian. No one else would do.'

Hester Lightfoot raised her eyebrows. 'You're not talking of "true love", I hope, Mrs Meredith. My mother married twice and didn't love either of them but she was happy with both. There are always men who can make a woman happy. My dear, the "one and only man for me" is a myth. It's important that you realize that. But please go on.'

This well-intentioned homily left Alice unconvinced but she forced herself to continue. 'There was another man who proposed but I was waiting for Seb to...' Choked by the memories, Alice closed her eyes against the compassion she now saw in the other woman's eyes. 'Then a few months ago Seb came to Chester on his own to tell me my brother had been wounded and was still in the hospital.'

'Oh dear! Not seriously, I hope.'

'No, thank the Lord!' Alice's voice grew stronger. 'He was late meeting me and I knew at once he'd been drinking. Dutch courage he always called it. He said we should go for a walk because we had to talk. I imagined he had come to propose but he seemed so nervous – and somehow downcast. Not his usual self at all. We went to some woods where we'd spent half our childhood and...' She stopped. 'I expect you can guess what happened.' She lowered her voice. 'He wanted to ... I thought that if I allowed him to...'

Hester Lightfoot tutted. 'Men! They can't be trusted, most of them. Old or young ... You trusted this Sebastian to make an honest woman of you. Because you loved him. Natural enough but most unwise. You must see that now with hindsight.'

Alice wondered how an elderly spinster could possibly know so much about men but kept that thought to herself. 'Yes, I trusted him but ... afterwards he confessed. He'd asked me out so that he could confess. He had married someone else. Nellie somebody. A whirlwind romance he called it.'

To Alice's surprise, Hester Lightfoot reached out and patted her knee with a thin hand. 'How terrible for you.' She regarded Alice intently. 'The man's a cad!'

'Oh no! He—'

'Face it, my dear. You've had a lucky escape. Suppose you had already been wed when this Nellie Somebody appeared on the scene.'

'It would have been different.' Even as she said it Alice was aware of a small doubt. 'At least I would be a married woman with a child instead of...'

'You would have been in a worse position,' the old lady insisted. 'Because you wouldn't have been free to marry when a *thoroughly decent* man wanted to marry you.' Before Alice could counter this rather odd remark Hester continued. 'So was that the first and only time? For you and him, I mean.'

'The first and only time with any man,' Alice whispered then lifted her head. 'But at least I am not an old maid ... Whatever happens I shall have my child.' She realized she was trembling and stared down fixedly at the black velvet slippers with a feeling of growing despair. Retelling the story had been a mistake. Sharing it had robbed it of any vestige of honesty and romance and had turned it into something tawdry. Sebastian was *not* a cad. He had told her so many times that he loved and adored her and she had believed him. Surely she could not have misjudged him so completely.

Hester Lightfoot frowned. 'There are people who know how to – how to remove an unborn child. Did you never think of that?'

'Never!' This time Alice's head snapped up and she glared at her inquisitor. 'I already love this child.'

'Good. That's what I wanted to hear.'

'It's Sebastian's child. I couldn't harm him – or her. I intend to keep the baby but I haven't yet decided—'

'Does the father know?'

'I wrote to him but then tore up the letter. How can I tell him? It wouldn't help, and think what it would do to his wife. She's not to blame for what we did and it might ruin their marriage. I can't do that to Sebastian.'

'And your brother? Does he know about your predicament?'

Alice shook her head. 'I suppose he'll have to know sometime.'

The old lady regarded her steadily and Alice grew uneasy. 'Perhaps not. I have a solution for you, Mrs Meredith. A trifle unconventional, perhaps, but if you agree you will be able to keep your child *and* be supported. It means you can be a married woman and your child will be born in wedlock.'

Alice stared at her, bewildered. What on earth was she talking about?

Hester leaned forward. 'Listen to me and think very carefully before you give me your answer. It will only take a few minutes and then you can take the rest of the day to think it over before you decide.'

Alice glanced at the alarm clock on the bedside table. In ten minutes the vicar and his nine ladies would be arriving for their meeting in the small function room and she hadn't checked that the room was ready. The vicar did so hate the smell of stale cigars and the window had to be opened to disperse the smoke.

Hester Lightfoot sat back and squared her shoulders. 'I want you to marry my brother,' she said. 'He's too old for you but he is a thoroughly decent man and will make you a good husband. I know it's a rather surprising suggestion but...'

Alice blinked in surprise then frowned. Had she heard the woman correctly? 'Your brother, ma'am?' she stammered. 'Have I met your brother?'

'Of course you have! He's your employer.'

Alice's eyes widened. *That* brother? You mean *our* Mr Lightfoot?' Alice stared at her in disbelief. Henry Lightfoot, owner of the Mere Hotel, was at least sixty years old and had been married to his wife Marion for thirty-six years until her death three years ago.

Hester smiled. *'Our* Mr Lightfoot. Yes, that's who I mean. And before you start to list your objections, Mrs Meredith, I will finish what I have to say. Henry is a lonely man. He needs a wife. He also needs an heir. You need a husband. Your child needs a father. I think I have made my point.'

The silence lengthened as Alice struggled to make sense of what she had heard. This woman wanted her to wed her employer – the elderly owner of the Mere Hotel. Incredible but true.

'Whose idea was it?' she stammered. It

20

seemed unlikely that Henry Lightfoot had even noticed her existence. She was simply one of a large staff.

'Mine – and Henry must never know that. He must think it's your idea.'

'Mine! But that's … that's impossible.'

'You'll think of a way. He will die one day and without an heir the hotel will pass to Donald Lightfoot, his nephew – a man we both heartily detest.' She leaned forward earnestly. 'You will have to convince Henry that this is your idea and that no one else knows anything about it. Not even me. It must seem to him that the story will be believed by everyone or he will never see the advantages of such a union.'

'The story?' Alice frowned. Had she missed something?

'Yes. Everyone has to think that the child is Henry's. That's why you have to act fast. When the child arrives people must think it is premature. You must see that for yourself. And the child must think of Henry as his natural father. The son, incidentally, who will inherit everything.'

Alice considered this for a moment. 'But if there was another child your brother might well—'

'There will be no other children. It isn't possible. I needn't go into detail but the fact remains. My brother cannot have a child of his own. Your child will inherit.'

Baffled by Hester's insistence, Alice stared at her. She had obviously given the idea a lot of serious thought and Alice found that unnerving. 'But if I *did* agree, and I won't, who will run the hotel when your brother dies and the baby is still too young?'

'*You* will, Mrs Meredith. Don't shake your head like that! You *will* agree because the alternative is too dreadful for both you and Sebastian's child. Imagine. An unmarried mother! You will be an object of pity, not to mention scorn. Your son will grow up with a terrible shadow over his life. You will be poor. You will both struggle against a shameful secret.'

Alice felt a shiver of apprehension at the bleak prospect being outlined for them. For herself she thought she could bear it but the child was blameless. Damn Hester Lightfoot! She closed her eyes, daring a single tear to find its way between her eyelids.

Her tormentor went on relentlessly. 'You will have no employment. No money. No home. I'm sure I don't need to continue. I am offering you a great chance to turn your mistake into a triumph.' She poured herself some water and sipped it, never once taking her eyes from Alice's stricken face. 'You will run the hotel, Mrs Meredith, because you have to. You have a sensible head on your shoulders and you're a quick learner. I've been watching you for some weeks and I will be around for a few more years, God willing, and Cecil Warner is an excellent manager. You can learn from him and I will help you.'

'But I'm only an assistant manager,' Alice protested. 'I was only promoted eight months ago. The staff wouldn't listen to me.'

'They would if you were Mrs Henry Lightfoot. As Henry's wife you would have power. You would have authority. It comes with the position. Look at Henry. A quiet, shy man who avoids confrontation like the plague! But he is respected and obeyed because he is the owner and that gives him authority.' Hester Lightfoot regarded her triumphantly. 'No buts, Mrs Meredith. Go away and think about it. I want your answer by tonight so that you can tackle Henry in the morning. We have to move quickly if the plan is going to work. Now get along to the vicar.' She smiled briefly. 'And please tell Maggie to bring me a cup of warm milk. All this talking has tired me.'

In a daze Alice left the room. The woman was quite mad, she told herself with growing irritation. Marry Henry Lightfoot? The idea was impossible.

Ahead of her she saw the Reverend Tanner's large form emerging from the function room. There was a scowl on the round florid face.

'Good morning, Reverend,' she called,

with forced cheerfulness. 'I'm so sorry I'm a minute or two late. I'll just open the windows for you and then you can start your meeting.'

Preposterous, she muttered as she pushed up the large sash window. She was rapidly revising her opinion of her employer's sister. Only a crackpot could come up with such a wild idea and expect her, Alice, to obediently fall into line.

Behind her, other members of the committee were drifting in and taking their places around the large rectangular table. Alice turned from the window with a brief greeting for each one of them. They were fortunate to have such a pleasant room at such a low price but Henry Lightfoot was a very religious man and obviously felt it his duty to offer the church committee a discounted rate.

Leaving them to their meeting Alice hurried downstairs to check that the tea and biscuits would be taken up on time. In the large airy kitchen the chef was in deep conversation with the maître d' and Maggie was setting up the trays. A small portly woman in her early twenties, she was inclined to be forgetful. She smiled at Alice and then narrowed her eyes.

'You all right, Mrs Meredith? You're looking a bit peaky this morning.'

'Quite all right, thank you, Maggie.' Alice

inspected the trays. 'Better not give them Nice biscuits again. They had them last week – and white sugar lumps, not brown. And Miss Lightfoot would like a cup of hot milk.'

So she looked peaky, thought Alice. Not surprising in the circumstances. Very few women could have had such a bizarre conversation before nine o'clock on a Wednesday morning. She made her way to the ladies' cloakroom and stared at herself in the mirror then pinched her cheeks vigorously until two spots of colour appeared. What was the phrase for women in her predicament? Pale and interesting. In a certain condition. In the family way ... How on earth had Hester Lightfoot guessed that she was pregnant. *It's in the eyes.* Suddenly her mother's words came back to her. *Something in the eyes. A looking inward.*

Alice looked at her own eyes with interest. Had they betrayed her? Hester Lightfoot had called them 'wonderful' and they certainly were her best feature. Somewhere between a deep blue and green. She sighed. Why hadn't Sebastian found them irresistible if they were so wonderful? She went into the lavatory and closed the door but she didn't sit down. Automatically her eyes checked the cubicle for cleanliness. Reasonable – and there was a spare toilet roll. She ran a finger along the window sill. That was dusty and she tutted. She would have to have a word with Miss Scarpe ... Leaning back against the door she tried to visualize her employer.

A lonely old man. Well, that was sad but it was nothing to do with her. He was a rich man, presumably, and could find himself a new wife without help from his meddling sister.

'I wouldn't make you happy,' she told her absent employer. 'And you would be no match for Sebastian.'

But there was the child to think about. Reluctantly Alice considered a son being brought up in comfort and with glittering prospects. He would go to a good school. He would mingle with the right people. *He would eventually own the hotel.*

Alice felt breathless as her excitement grew at this glittering prospect. Sebastian's son would eventually be accepted in the town as a man of some standing. A man of distinction. What right had she to refuse her son such a future? It was her fault he was being brought into the world – hers and Sebastian's – but since Sebastian had no knowledge of her condition the responsibility lay with her. When he was old enough the child might well blame her – *if* the truth were ever to come out. If she had insisted on a life of poverty and shame instead of...

'No!' she muttered. 'I won't be forced into a loveless marriage. Almost at once her conscience pricked her. Her own folly had allowed the child's conception and now she was being offered a chance to make amends and didn't want to take it. Or was afraid.

'What sort of mother are you?' she demanded but at that moment she heard the door to the ladies' room open.

'Mrs Meredith? Are you in here?'

Alice recognized the voice. 'I'm just coming.' Hastily she pulled the chain, waited as the toilet was flushed and opened the door.

Miss Maine, the receptionist, turned towards her. 'Oh, Mrs Meredith! Mr Warner wants to see you. We have another runner!' Her blue eyes flashed with excitement.

'Oh no!' Alice's personal problems were immediately relegated to a corner of her mind as the business of the hotel reasserted itself.

'Room thirty-four has left without paying his bill and—'

Alice stared at her. 'Room thirty-four? Not that nice Dr Stewart? I don't believe it.'

'Honestly! He has.'

Alice shook her head in dismay. He had seemed such a kind man, visiting Chester to be near his mother who was dying in the hospital. All lies, presumably. What had Hester Lightfoot told her? Most men can't be trusted. Alice didn't want to believe that.

27

'I liked him,' she said, meaning Dr Stewart...

'We all did.' Miss Maine shrugged slim shoulders. 'He slipped me a tanner once for fetching a package from the post office.' Seeing Alice's expression change she clapped a hand to her mouth. 'I'm sorry. I was only gone a minute or two.'

'You know the rules.' Alice bit back a sterner rebuke. It worried her sometimes that she might be a little hard on the young woman simply because she had everything Alice lacked. Blonde curls, a creamy complexion...

'Mr Warner was there,' Miss Maine explained hastily. 'While I was at the post office, I mean.'

'And where is Mr Warner now?'

'He's gone to the police station now to report to Sergeant Flint. He'll probably have to give a description. You're to take over in the office while he's gone.'

Alice finished washing her hands while Miss Maine filled in the details.

'Dr Stewart didn't come down to breakfast, which was odd because he's a hefty eater. Maggie says he must have hollow legs! Always a full breakfast with an extra egg and so we wondered if he was ill and Mr Warner said to send Connie – I mean Miss Bates – to go upstairs and knock on his door and there was no answer so she thought he *was* ill and went in and found him gone but his suitcase was there but it was empty!' She paused for breath. 'But the cunning wretch must have been wearing all his clothes at once! I mean to say, he's been here for three weeks and he must have looked very fat so maybe that's why no one recognized him.' Alice sighed. 'That's a new one on me. I suppose he owes all three weeks.' She dried her hands on the towel.

'Not all three. He paid the first one.'

'So that we would trust him.' She cursed under her breath. 'Three weeks for the price of one. So much for nice Dr Stewart. A false name probably.' She sighed. 'I'll come to the office at once.'

'Never a dull moment, eh?' Miss Maine beamed as they prepared to return to the reception area.

'I think you could say that!' Alice's reply was heartfelt.

Twenty minutes later she was seated at the desk in the office compiling a list of additional items for which the so-called Dr Stewart had failed to pay. A bottle of malt whisky, a ticket for the theatre, a loan from the desk of five guineas and an unpaid taxi fare costing one pound two shillings and sixpence.

'Mrs Meredith?'

Alice looked up with a start to find Henry

Lightfoot in the doorway to the office. Ridiculously she felt herself blushing and jumped awkwardly to her feet.

'Hear we've had another one,' he said in his quiet voice. 'Wanted to speak to Warner.'

'I'm sorry, Mr Lightfoot, but he's still at the police station.'

'Ah! The police station.' He glanced round helplessly but made no move to come into the office. 'I abhor this kind of thing, you know. Leaves a sour taste in the mouth. And a doctor, of all people. Still, it makes a change. Last time it was ... Let me see now ... It was a bogus colonel. Colonel Bardsley, wasn't it?' He sighed. 'Is he a doctor, I wonder, this Stewart fellow? Doubt it very much. A thoroughly rotten apple!'

'I'm very sorry, Mr Lightfoot.' It was all Alice could do to look him in the eye as she recalled his sister's monstrous plan. How could she ever share this man's bed?

Henry Lightfoot was a tall, spare man, with a voice that hinted at a good education and a refined background. Was the family newly rich, Alice wondered, or did they boast aristocratic connections somewhere in their past. He was dressed as always in a fine wool suit with a matching waistcoat, a high white collar and a paisley cravat. His hair was white but plentiful, his face chalky white with milky blue eyes. His hands were large but fragile and Alice tried to imagine how it would feel to be touched by them and felt an immediate frisson of distaste.

'I'm not blaming you, Mrs Meredith,' he went on. 'Not blaming anyone. These things happen from time to time and have to be taken into account. Remind Mr Warner to put it into the log book.' He smiled sadly. 'The damnedest thing is that people like him always get away with it. He won't dare come here again and when he goes elsewhere he'll use another name.'

Alice could almost pity him. A fraudulent guest and a determined sister plotting behind his back. She stole a quick glance at him. Was he lonely? Probably – for Marion had been his companion for most of his adult life. Alice remembered how her grandfather had reacted when her grandmother passed away. He had stopped eating and lost interest in the world around him. The doctor diagnosed extreme melancholy and prescribed pills but the old man died three months to the day after his wife's death.

Presumably Marion Lightfoot had loved her husband. Alice glanced surreptitiously in Henry Lightfoot's direction, hoping to see what the other woman had found lovable. Had he ever been as handsome as Sebastian? But then Marion had married Henry when he was younger and presumably more full of life and they had grown into old age together. Alice couldn't imagine

31

any woman falling in love with Henry Light-foot today. He wasn't unattractive but he *was* elderly.

At that moment the manager returned and he and Henry Lightfoot were soon deep in conversation, so Alice felt able to slip away from the office. She hadn't checked the fresh linen in the bedrooms and also wanted to speak with Edith Brightling, one of their few permanent residents.

Armed with a copy of the new menu, Alice knocked on the door of room forty.

'Come in.'

Edith was lying on her chaise longue with a magazine in her hand. She was thin with pale freckled skin but her large brown eyes were a redeeming feature.

'Oh it's you, dear heart!' Smiling broadly, she waved the magazine. *Ladies' Weekly Journal*. I found it in the foyer. I'm just reading this wonderful article by someone-or-other about Colrose Hall in Wiltshire. I played there, you know, years ago. It was an invitation from Lord Colrose's nephew. I did two of my monologues and after the first the guests had tears in their eyes. It was so moving.'

This happy memory brought a bright flush to her face and Alice smiled at her with real affection. 'I can imagine,' she said. 'Colrose Hall! Quite a compliment. Look. I've brought you next week's menu.'

Edith Brightling, who had pursued her stage career under the name Edith Ellway, had been immensely kind to Alice when she first came to the Mere as a young waitress. Although much older than Alice, Edith had taken pity on her. Alice, for her part, had quickly understood that beneath the woman's theatricality there was a warm human being. Edith's bid for fame on the stage had been short-lived. After a promising start she had somehow failed to capture a leading role and was forced to rely on understudies and second-rate parts until eventually she found herself a wealthy young 'stage-door Johnny' by the name of Gordon. He had persuaded her to abandon her unsuccessful career and marry him. Scorned by his family, the pair then fled to Paris, where Gordon gambled and drank himself to death. He left her penniless.

His wealthy parents bought Edith's silence with a sum of money which was just enough to keep body and soul together and she had returned to Chester, where she had started her stage career. The Royalty Theatre no longer needed her but she stayed on in the town, living in the Mere Hotel. Here she played out the role of a distressed actress with a certain style which Alice admired and over the years the two women had become firm friends.

Now Alice fought back the temptation to

tell Edith of Hester Lightfoot's proposal. The need to confide was overpowering but somehow Alice resisted it. She had, instead, to break bad news. Smiling, she sat down on her usual chair.

'I hate to have to say this, Edith, but it's been noticed that you are having your breakfast brought up to your room. You may find they have added it to your account. Room service wasn't in the original agreement, was it?'

'Oh dear!' Edith pressed a hand to her chest, wide-eyed. 'How frightfully silly of me! No, it wasn't agreed. But Maggie didn't mind when I asked her. I gave her a signed photograph. In its original frame. She's often admired it.' She sighed. 'I hoped no one would notice. I won't do it again, Alice. I can't afford to pay any more than I do. Did Maggie tell you?'

'I'm afraid it was Chef who mentioned it to me. He noticed her with the trays.'

Edith put guilty fingers to her mouth. 'Oh I do *hope* poor Maggie didn't get into any trouble.'

'No. Chef spoke to me and I said I'd deal with it. I just thought I'd better warn you.'

Edith shrugged. 'It serves me right. I'm getting lazy. Can't find the energy to get up in the mornings and come down to the dining room.'

Alice said, 'The couple in thirty-seven

have three or four magazines. If they leave them behind I'll save them for you.'

'Oh Alice, you are a dear!' Suddenly she narrowed her eyes. 'You seem a bit distant, Alice. Is there something else?'

'No, no! I ... I had a restless night, that's all. Have you heard from your niece this week?'

'Not yet but she'll write, bless her. She always does. Eunice loves me like a daughter, you see ... What was all that commotion in the foyer this morning? Mr Warner looked none too pleased and little Miss Maine was in a real spin.'

Alice explained about 'Dr' Stewart and Edith's eyes widened.

'Left without paying? Dr Stewart. Oh my dear! There must be some mistake. Such a dear, *dear* man! Not that it's unknown in the theatre. Especially the actor managers. They'd nip off with the takings without a backward glance. So the cast was never paid at the end of a run.' She shook her head despairingly. 'But not Dr Stewart.' A smile touched her lips. Lowering her eyes she said, 'If it's true, then ... Well, dear heart, I wasn't going to mention it just yet but I may have had a lucky escape. He was definitely making a play for me, you know.'

'Oh Edith! No!'

Edith smiled, her head on one side. 'Oh Edith *yes*! Of course, I pretended not to

35

notice but he *was* interested.' She sighed deeply. 'I have always attracted the wrong type of man, Alice.' She leaned forward to fuss with the folds of her skirt. 'But at least I do attract men whereas you...' She looked at Alice enquiringly. 'Any news from your beloved Sebastian?'

Alice saw what was coming and said, 'No, he hasn't written. Maybe the army changed its mind. They do that at will.'

She had told Edith years ago how she felt about Sebastian, hinting that a betrothal was simply a matter of time, but as time passed she suspected that Edith was sceptical. Alice, mortified by recent events, had never shared the details of her disastrous meeting with Sebastian nor the even more disastrous outcome. In view of her talk with Hester Lightfoot she was doubly grateful that she had kept the problem to herself. She had not the slightest intention of taking part in the deception that Hester had dreamed up and would never speak of it to anyone.

Edith, wrapped up in her own affairs, had already forgotten about Sebastian.

'How terrible if Dr Stewart had swept me off my feet! I'm so easily swayed and he *was* so good-looking. That little moustache of his!' She sighed. 'I do love a neat man and he was a great charmer, you know. He knew how to make a woman feel desirable and not all men can do that.'

Alice realized that they were on a dangerous subject and knew that Edith could talk for hours about her love life prior to the 'awful Gordon'.

Alice stood up. 'I'm afraid I must get on.'

'Oh darling! Wait. I have something for you. Look.' From her sewing bag Edith produced a small lavender bag made of sprigged cotton and tied with white ribbon. 'For your underwear drawer,' she told Alice. 'My mother was always most insistent about lavender for intimate garments.'

'That's very sweet of you, Edith. Thank you. Now I must love you and leave you. I have to check the bedrooms. I'll pop in later if I can.'

That afternoon Henry Lightfoot stood at his drawing-room window, which overlooked the small rear garden, and stared out unseeingly. Around him were the signs of a comfortable life – elegant furniture, quality carpets, windows framed with well-designed curtains. There were also a number of expensive ornaments and a valuable grandfather clock that was a family heirloom. Henry, with his back to all of it, was not a happy man. He had been unhappy since the death of his wife but this grief was different. This was not loss but loneliness.

He stared down into the garden with a

furrowed brow and sighed heavily. The problem was a very unsettling talk he had had with the vicar after the church committee's morning meeting. It had thoroughly unsettled him and he was tempted to confide in his sister, which meant a short journey down the stairs – since he did not entirely trust the newfangled lift – to Hester's large, well-appointed room.

Henry lived in a separate apartment at the top of the building behind a door marked PRIVATE – STAFF ONLY. In fact none of the staff were to be found beyond the notice. Most of them had quarters in the attic rooms well away from the proprietor's apartment. Most of the women shared – two or three to a room. The men had a dormitory which slept eight and the manager had a room to himself. A few staff members lived out and came in daily. These included the woman who did the heavy cleaning, the chef, who lived in the next street with his mother, and the part-time gardener who attended to the window boxes and the small rear garden, which consisted of shrubs in pots and a trellis covered with ancient roses.

Now Henry regarded the plants with a jaundiced eye. The conversation with the vicar had reminded him of his dead wife and the memories were disturbing. He still woke each morning with the promise of a long day ahead devoid of warmth and companionship. The hotel seemed to thrive under Cecil Warner's stewardship and his assistant, Mrs Meredith, and he felt increasingly useless. The vicar had obviously been concerned for him; had no doubt seen him as a pathetic old man. The idea hurt Henry's pride.

Coming to a decision, he made his way along the corridor and down the stairs to his sister's room, where he knocked and was invited inside.

Hester looked from her favourite chair and laid her book aside. 'Henry! Rather early for a visit, isn't it?'

'Suppose it is rather.' He stood awkwardly, his hands fumbling with his watch chain. 'Something odd...' he began. 'A bit of a shock, in fact.'

'Sit down and tell me about it.' She pointed to a nearby chair.

For a moment he hesitated. As usual he was awed by his sister's confident manner. As her younger brother he had found her a dominating presence and had never felt entirely at ease with her. Now, however, since his wife's death, he had no one else even remotely close to him. Not that he had ever felt close to a woman, not even to Marion, but that was a fault of his character.

'It's the vicar,' he said. 'The Reverend Tanner.' He lowered himself on to the chair,

39

breathing heavily. 'Very odd chap. Very intense.'

'Intense? That little tub of a man?'

Henry nodded. 'Kept poking me in the arm ... to make a point.'

'What a cheek.' She frowned. 'Point about what exactly? If he's still asking for a reduction in the—'

'No no! Nothing like that.' He took out his handkerchief and wiped his face. 'Thinks I should get married again. Impudent wretch. Never did like the fellow.'

To his surprise Hester appeared silenced by this information. Never backward in coming forward. An opinion on everything – that was Hester.

He sighed, 'He just *happens* to have a sister.'

At last she said, 'A widowed sister. How very convenient. I suppose he—'

'Spinster.' Henry tried to imagine her and failed.

Hester tutted. 'The cheek of the man! I hope you told him you were not interested.' She was watching him closely.

'He said I looked unhappy.'

'What utter nonsense!'

'He said a man needs a wife ... I said I've had a good wife. I've been most fortunate. Poor Marion.'

Hester shrugged. 'He's trying to get rid of her, no doubt. The sister, I mean. The poor woman is probably a great burden to him but that doesn't mean that he should foist her on to someone else. How old is she?'

'About my age.'

'Ah!' Her expression changed. 'Much too old for you. If you were to remarry, Henry, it should be to someone younger who'd look after you. If you marry an elderly spinster she'll probably fall ill and you'll end up caring for *her*. Not to mention paying all her doctor's bills and the like.'

Henry wasn't listening. He was thinking wistfully about his dead wife. Marion had been such a timid little thing. So helpless. So dependent on him. She had made him feel twice the man he was. If only ... He sighed. 'Like a little bird,' he murmured.

'What's that? A bird?'

'Nothing, Hester. I was thinking aloud.'

She said, 'Do stop fiddling with that watch chain, Henry. You know how it annoys me.'

'Sorry.' He pushed his hands into his pockets and immediately took them out again. 'He wanted me to go to lunch at the vicarage next Sunday. To meet her. You too, of course.'

'And you said what?' Her tone had sharpened.

'That I thought we probably would. What else could I say?'

'You could have said no, Henry. You never did know how to refuse gracefully. I don't

41

want to waste my Sunday meeting his horrid sister and I'm sure you don't.'

'She may not be horrid. Her name's Elspeth.'

'I hate the name. Elderly spinster indeed! You'll have to send her a note to say I'm not well and we won't be going.'

'It seems churlish to—'

'It's churlish to try and palm an elderly relative on a harmless old man! Better still, I'll say you have had one of your turns and are indisposed. That might frighten her off. Sunday lunch indeed! I suppose this old biddy was going to cook it for you!'

'Oh no! I don't think...'

'Buttering you up. Poor old thing. You can't blame them for trying.'

Hester stood up and Henry watched her cross to her writing desk and riffle through some papers – a trick she had when she was trying to buy time.

He said, 'So you don't think I should marry again, Hester?' He felt vaguely depressed. It was rather pleasant to be thought a 'catch' by someone even if it was only a relation of the Reverend Tanner.

'I haven't said that.' She didn't look up from her papers. 'I've said you shouldn't marry this – this elderly spinster.'

He regarded her quizzically. 'Aren't you an elderly spinster?'

'That's quite different. I am not a *needy*

elderly spinster sitting in the middle of my web waiting for a fly to stumble along! Not that I'm calling you a fly!'

'Should hope not!' He shrugged. So that was it. Elspeth was no longer a prospect. He said, 'She's been a nanny for most of her life.'

'Very creditable, I'm sure.' Hester rolled her eyes. 'Marry again, by all means, Henry, if you find someone younger whom you really like who is suitable.'

'Bit of a tall order, isn't it?'

'That's your problem, Henry. All I'm saying is I shan't live forever and in the meantime a new sister-in-law would be rather jolly.' She smiled.

Henry felt a rush of unfamiliar affection for her. She was all he had left in the world. The only person alive who remembered him as he was in his youth. A smart man with a keen mind. Not a bad bowler, either ... and pretty handy with a pair of oars on the river. He had a sudden vision of the young Henry in a boat on the Dee, with Marion leaning back against the cushions at the far end trailing her hand in the water. Henry smiled at the memory.

'You should smile more often, Henry,' Hester told him. 'It makes you look younger.'

Two

After a restless night with very little sleep, Alice felt totally unprepared for her delayed visit to Hester, but when Hester Lightfoot's deadline had expired, Alice had still been undecided so there had been no point in attending. In a fit of defiance she had decided that if it was *that* urgent, Hester could come and knock on *her* door. She had definitely decided against the idea of proposing to Henry Lightfoot, even though she knew that her refusal to co-operate was going to ruin her unborn child's prospects. But it had to be. Before Hester had spoken to her Alice had been making plans for their future, whatever that might be, and she would now start again along that path.

Promptly at eight thirty she knocked on Hester's door and waited. There was no reply. She knocked again and called, 'Miss Lightfoot!'

Perhaps she was ill. Hester Lightfoot was always up and about early. She was about to enter the room when Maggie appeared in the corridor with a breakfast tray.

'I'll take it in to her,' Alice reached for the tray.

But Maggie shook her head. 'This isn't for Her Majesty. It's for number twenty,' she told her. 'Miss Lightfoot cancelled her breakfast last night. She's meeting a friend in the town. The taxi came ten minutes ago. Excuse me but I'm running late this morning.'

Alice stared after Maggie's retreating back. Meeting a friend? At this hour of the morning? She stood irresolute outside the door as a suspicion took shape in her mind.

After her non-appearance last night, the old lady had probably expected her to make an early morning call to explain why she was turning down her proposal. This was Hester Lightfoot's way of making that impossible.

'Very cunning!' Alice muttered but she was aware of a sneaking admiration. Well, two could play at that game! She would *not* go anywhere near Henry Lightfoot and would never refer to the matter again. Hester Lightfoot would not manipulate her so easily.

With a toss of her head Alice turned and made her way downstairs to reception to make her routine check on any guests who might have arrived late the previous night. These would have been booked in by the night porter, Michael Davies.

'Good morning, Miss Maine.'

'Good morning, Mrs Meredith.' Miss Maine turned the visitors book round so that Alice could read the latest entries.

Alice scanned the page. 'Mmm ... Two in number twelve and a Mrs Branner whose name has been crossed out. Why was that?'

'Mick – I mean the night porter...' Miss Maine blushed. 'He changed his mind. She came in alone in a bit of a state. Very pale, he said, and not very tidy. Agitated. He booked her in anyway but then she said she had a child with her and fetched in a little boy...'

'A little boy? How old was he?'

'She didn't say but Mick thought about five or six. He looked very ill. Burning with fever, Mick said. Might have been something catching. He said we can't have all the guests getting ill so...'

She broke off to hand a newspaper to an elderly gentleman who nodded politely towards Alice and then headed for the breakfast room. Miss Maine glanced back at Alice and blinked. 'He did right, didn't he?'

'You mean he sent them away?' Alice was horrified.

'Well, yes. He thought he should get rid of them and...'

Alice's throat tightened and her voice rose. 'Get rid of them? The child was *ill* and he sent them away late at night? Since when has it been our policy to deny...'

46

Miss Maine was looking anxious. 'But when he said maybe and asked for the money in advance she burst into tears and broke down. Poor Mr Davies. It turned out she wasn't Mrs at all because she had no husband and no money either. He thought her an undesirable and...' Seeing the look on Alice's face her words faltered. 'He didn't mean to do anything wrong, Mrs Meredith. Mr Warner had told him not to admit undesirables or – or what Mick calls "the dodgy ones".'

Alice felt a coldness in the pit of her stomach. So a woman with a sick child but no husband was "dodgy and undesirable".

She swallowed. 'Where did they go?'

The young woman shrugged. Alice bit back a stinging remark. Miss Maine was not to blame for the night porter's decision. But somewhere a mother was wandering the streets of Chester with a sick child. Where had they slept? Had they found somewhere more charitable than the Merc Hotel? She fervently hoped so. It was summer but a sick child needed a bed and the attentions of a doctor.

Alice breathed deeply. With a shock she realized she was perspiring and put a trembling hand to her head. Miss Maine's description of the woman and child had created unwanted comparisons. She recalled the defiant speech she had prepared for Hester

47

Lightfoot and it suddenly sounded a little too forceful. *Would* she be able to bring up a child on her own? No doubt Miss Branner had thought so – or perhaps she had had no choice. Perhaps no one had offered her a way out of her troubles. Soon Alice would be an unwanted mother with a child, to be scorned by people like Michael Davies. Alice's lips tightened at the thought of the night porter. He was hardly in a position to criticize, she thought angrily. He had a sly manner and was arrogant with it. Alice had never liked him but now she felt an irrational dislike that bordered on hatred.

'I'll have a word with Mr Davies when he comes on duty tonight,' she said, ignoring Miss Maine's aggrieved expression.

And you can pull yourself together, Alice told herself. The Branner woman is long gone and you cannot help her or the child. She turned to go but abruptly turned back.

'And please remember you are not supposed to refer to the night porter by his Christian name.'

Miss Maine lowered her head. 'It won't happen again, Mrs Meredith. It's just that we're ... we're more than friends and I forget.'

Alice resisted the urge to warn the girl against becoming too friendly with Michael Davies. Instead she said tersely, 'You know the rules, Miss Maine. Please make an effort in future.'

Alice decided to mention the matter to Mr Warner. Romances between the staff were strongly discouraged as they always led to skimped work and a lack of concentration.

'Yes, Mrs Meredith.'

As Miss Maine retired to the office Alice clutched the edge of the reception desk as an unfamiliar faintness swept over her. It also occurred to her that Miss Maine had called her *Mrs* Meredith. The irony was not lost on Alice.

Half an hour later Alice was sick for the first time since she had discovered she was pregnant. She had hoped to escape morning sickness, some women did, but it now seemed she was not going to be among the lucky ones. Alice pulled the chain, emerged from the lavatory and cupped her hand under the tap. After a few mouthfuls of cold water she splashed her face. A glance in the mirror showed a fine sheen of perspiration on a face from which all the colour had vanished. Her defeated expression startled her.

'This is your fault, Sebastian,' she murmured. To the child she added, 'I don't blame you.'

Weak and shaken, Alice longed to return to her room and throw herself on to the bed. A sleep would be ideal but that was out of the question. She had to continue with her work, allowing no one to know of her predicament – which meant she would receive no sympathy or help. This was to be her lot, then, for the next few months. Day after unrelenting day. Steadying herself against the wall, waiting for the worst to pass, Alice recalled the time of the baby's conception and was mortified. She couldn't even pretend that it had been romantic. A frantic coupling which shocked her followed by a deep feeling of disillusionment. Sebastian, a little the worse for drink, had shown her very little consideration and she was glad the child knew nothing of the unhappy event.

'And you never will!'

She would think of a story that cast Sebastian in a more favourable light and – but that wouldn't work. She shook her head. If she married Henry Lightfoot she would have to pretend that Sebastian had never existed.

'Back to work, Alice!' she muttered and straightened up. Her legs felt as if they would scarcely support her and she was lost momentarily in a tide of self-pity. At that moment her resolve began once more to waver.

She was drying her face and hands when Maggie came in search of her.

'Mrs Meredith, Mr Warner's looking for you. You have to pay the window cleaner and the man has come from the upholsterers.' Maggie frowned. 'Are you all right? You look like a ghost.'

'I'm quite well, thank you. Just a little warm.' She straightened and smiled with an effort. 'The upholsterers?' Her mind was a blank.

Maggie nodded. 'Mr Symons. You remember.'

'Do I?'

'Weaselly little man. Eyes very close together. Some of the armchairs in the smoking room have to be re-covered. Mr Warner's busy and he said you could deal with them. The police sergeant's here and he says that Dr Stewart bought a train ticket for London so they'll probably never catch him. He'll just disappear.'

Alice was finding it hard to concentrate. So the wretched man had eluded the police. It hardly mattered. With all her personal problems a bogus doctor was hardly a priority but she saw that Maggie was expecting a little more reaction to the news and said, 'That's a pity.'

'A pity? It's a blooming shame, if you ask me! He shouldn't be allowed to get away with it. Swindling innocent people and telling a pack of lies. Even I fell for it. Still, they might catch him, though I shouldn't bank on it. They never did catch Jack the Ripper. If they did, though, we'd have to give evidence, wouldn't we?'

'I suppose so. You'd better get on, Maggie. I'll be down in a moment.'

Alone once more, she tidied her face and took a few deep breaths. The upholsterers. What a time to choose. She made her way downstairs and found the window cleaner and paid him and thanked him with a few brisk words.

Mr Symons, waiting for her in the foyer, eyed her anxiously.

'You all right, Mrs Meredith? I could come back tomorrow if it suits you better. The girl said you were a bit under the weather.'

'I'm fine.'

Feeling that she might never be fine again, Alice led the way to the smoking room and chose the four shabbiest chairs. Two of them had frayed fabric, one had loose braid and the wooden arms of the fourth were badly scratched. A fifth caught her eye. Something had been spilt on the seat and had left a dark stain.

'Take these five,' she told him. 'We can't afford to lose too many at once, because we have no replacements. We'll need them back by next week, though.'

'Ah yes! The races. You'll be busy then.'

'Very busy,' she agreed with a sinking heart. The hotel was already booked solid and race days were always hectic. Hopefully she would feel better by then.

'Have a flutter, do you?' Mr Symons grinned at her. 'My missus doesn't like me to gamble but I do have a bet now and then. Just don't tell her when I lose. No point in upsetting her. That's the way I look at it.' He grinned and tapped the side of his nose. 'Nice little win last year, though. Won a couple of guineas! Course, I had to tell her. She'd have wondered otherwise. Still, it paid off a couple of debts, bought the missus a new parasol and a bit of baccy for my pipe. A frilly parasol. Sort she'd always fancied. She's a rare one for frills and flounces, my missus.'

Alice smiled, trying to ignore the headache which was developing. If only he would stop his chatter. She followed him out to his van, where the horse snuffled happily in his nosebag. A lad jumped dutifully down and Alice watched as between them they carried the selected chairs down the hotel steps and lifted them into the back of the van.

'Be sure and get them back to us on time,' she reminded Mr Symons as he rolled down the flap and secured it.

'Don't you fret about that,' he told her and raised his hand to his forehead in a mock salute.

Alice saw him off with a nod of her head which she immediately regretted.

She turned back and glanced up at the

hotel. Somewhere within its walls Henry Lightfoot was reading his morning paper and minding his own business. She was about to shatter his peace of mind.

'Mrs Meredith?' Henry Lightfoot looked at her in surprise. 'Do come in.' He opened the door and Alice stepped inside. With a shock she realized that if Henry Lightfoot was persuaded by her arguments, this rather lavish apartment would become her home. There was a large patterned carpet covering most of the floor and the deep windows were draped in dark green velvet. The various tables were highly polished, the walls were adorned with sombre pictures and the furniture was heavy with leather and buttons. In other words, she felt immediately out of place. How could she ever feel at home here? For a moment her courage failed.

'Please sit down.' He smiled, politely trying to hide his curiosity.

Alice sat on the chair he had indicated. She folded her hands in her lap and placed her feet and knees together. She looked at her employer and tried to think of him as Henry but it was impossible. The idea of sudden flight entered her mind but was quickly abandoned. Somehow she had come to a decision although she couldn't remember when it had happened. She was following Hester Lightfoot's advice. Now it was up to him. Even now Alice didn't know whether she hoped he would say yes or no. If he said no she could face her child with a clear conscience but with any luck he would do just that and she could tell his sister she had tried.

He sat down at one end of a sofa and regarded her expectantly. 'Mrs Meredith, how can I help you?' he prompted.

She said, 'I'm expecting a child.' The words seemed to come out of nowhere and Alice was taken by surprise. She had intended to lead up to the subject in some way.

'Oh my dear!' He was genuinely surprised. 'My sister and I believed you were a widow. So congratulations are in order.'

Too late to withdraw the admission, Alice rushed on. 'I'm afraid not. The truth is the baby is ... will be ... a love child.'

Henry Lightfoot was obviously struggling with this information. 'You mean ... there is no father?'

'The father is married to another woman although I...' She faltered.

He held up a hand. 'Please, Mrs Meredith. You have no need to tell me the details.' He sounded hurt, as if she had betrayed his trust in some way. 'Bit of a pickle, eh?'

His mild words were so much worse than if he had shouted at her. Seeing the expression on his face, Alice felt that the full extent of her disgrace had been revealed – to her as well as to him. She felt cheapened and saw herself as the rest of society would see her. A foolish, reckless creature, quite beyond the pale. Her hands tightened on the arms of the chair as she struggled through a sudden wave of darkness.

'I might faint,' she whispered. 'I'm sorry...'

'Faint? Oh dear!' He hurried into another room and returned with a glass of water. Alice sipped it gratefully.

'Does this mean, Mrs Meredith, that you are giving in your notice? I should be so sorry to lose you.'

Alice stared at him over the rim of the glass while she tried to regain control of herself. 'It means that I am in very deep trouble, Mr Lightfoot. In my position what I need most is a husband.'

The blue eyes regarded her without wavering. 'I can see that.'

She forced herself to meet his eyes. 'I have come to you with a ... proposition to put to you, if you will hear me out.'

He nodded, puzzled but still courteous.

'A rather ... An unseemly proposition, perhaps.'

He raised his eyebrows. 'Unseemly, eh? This is intriguing.'

Intriguing is hardly the word, thought Alice with growing desperation. Preposterous would be a better word. While she searched for a way to start she was eyeing him surreptitiously. His eyes were a nice blue and his mouth was still firm. If they married she assumed she would be expected to kiss him from time to time...

She said, 'Are you ever lonely, Mr Lightfoot?'

'Is that any of your business, Mrs Meredith? I don't mean to be rude but that is hardly relevant to what we are discussing.'

'I'm sorry. I'm not doing this very well.'

Alice tried to imagine sitting opposite him at breakfast. How did he eat his food? Did he wear a table napkin tucked into his collar? She remembered her grandfather at Sunday lunch, munching noisily, and saw the familiar trickle of gravy at the corner of his mouth. She closed her eyes.

'Mrs Meredith, are you unwell?'

She snapped them open again. Concentrate, she told herself. 'No, sir, I'm well enough.'

'Then please ... ?' He waved a hand to encourage her.

Alice said, 'I understand you have no children, Mr Lightfoot. No one to inherit when you pass on. I wonder ... That is, I'm suggesting that...' She stopped. It was impossible.

He was looking at her intently and his

expression was not hostile. 'Do go on,' he urged.

'My child may be a boy. Maybe not. It seemed...'

He rolled his eyes. 'I'm a patient man but...' He began to fiddle with his watch chain. Alice couldn't go on. The situation was becoming bizarre and she suddenly saw just how foolish she had been to listen to Hester Lightfoot.

'I'm so sorry,' she muttered. 'This is pointless. A mistake. I have no right to ask anything of you. If you'll excuse me.' She made as if to rise but he shook his head.

She watched his expression slowly change from curiosity to the dawn of understanding. 'Wait! Wait!' he cried. 'I think I see...' After a moment he said, 'You are suggesting that I might adopt your child. Is that it?'

His astonishment and disbelief were obvious. His tone of voice suggested that she had proposed a trip to the moon!

Alice took a deep breath. 'Not exactly. At least that is ... I'm suggesting that the child comes with a mother in tow ... Me.'

Involuntarily he drew back from her and one hand went up to cover his mouth. The blue eyes blinked in amazement.

Alice straightened her back and forced herself to look him straight in the eyes. 'I'm suggesting that you marry me, Mr Lightfoot. If we hurried, no one would know that the child isn't yours. To all intents and purposes he would be yours. Yours and mine, that is.' Her throat was dry and she tried to swallow. This is ridiculous, she told herself as panic set in. You have made a terrible mistake. But having come so far there is no way out.

'I'm sure you are lonely without your wife and I know you were happy together – that is you seemed happy – but maybe she would understand if you married again. I would do my very best to be a good wife – and a good mother to our child. I think, sir, that you would be an excellent and loving father.'

He fell back against the sofa, staring at her. 'Marry you? *Marry you?* Good Lord! Are you quite...' He bit back the word 'mad' and said, 'Do you realize what you're asking?'

'I'm sorry!' Alice cried, immediately crushed. 'I shouldn't have ... that is, I would never have done this but for...' She choked on Hester's name. Whatever happened she must not allow him to suspect a plot.

'You're proposing to me!'

'Yes – I mean no,' she stammered as most of her courage disappeared. 'Please let's pretend I haven't said that. I'll go.' Her voice shook. She wanted to rise with dignity and flee from the room but her legs failed to obey her and they stared at each other, equally shocked.

Henry took out his watch and stared at it as if suddenly the time was somehow important. He said, 'Ah yes!' returned it to his pocket and stood up. Crossing silently to the window he stared out. Alice put a hand to her head, which was thumping painfully. He turned abruptly.

'Does anyone else know about your predicament? About the child?'

This was the difficult bit, thought Alice. The lie. 'Only my doctor. The child is due in seven months' time. In February.'

Henry Lightfoot ran a trembling hand through his hair. 'We both longed for a child ... Poor Marion. It was the only thing that marred our marriage.' He came back to her and sat down. 'I always regretted having no family but it was God's will. You are an extraordinary woman, Mrs Meredith.'

'Yes. I'm sorry.'

'No need to apologize but ... Coming out of the blue like this ... You'll have to give me some time to think ... No one has ever proposed to me before. Bit of a shock, to tell you the truth.'

Alice's heart leapt. So he hadn't totally rejected the idea. 'We don't have much time,' she reminded him. 'We would have to have a quiet wedding – a secret wedding, maybe. Otherwise, the staff might think that we had been ... that we had *known* each other that way before the wedding.'

'Would they really?' The thought obviously appealed to him. 'Do you think so? I daresay they would. Well I'm blowed!'

Alice thought she saw a faint smile on his face but it didn't last.

He said, 'Hmm. That would set the cat among the pigeons! Hah! How would you feel if thcy thought such a thing?'

Alice hesitated. 'It would be a price worth paying. I think once we were man and wife they would soon forget.'

After a long silence he said, 'A child would be fun. Liven the place up a bit. But we'd have to keep it from Hester – I mean the fact that it was your idea. That is, if we did ... get together. I'm not saying we will, you understand. And I would have to say it was my idea. If Hester knew the truth she would never lct me live it down. She's a dear soul but rather strait-laced, you know. Wonder how she'd take to the idea of being an aunt.' He laughed.

Alice said daringly, 'It would changc all our lives.'

'Yes it would.' He regarded her intently. 'You really are a remarkable woman, Mrs Meredith. Quite remarkable. You do realize that I am almost seventy, shall we say. Much much older than you. Old enough to be your father, in fact. You might not like me as a husband. We might— We would probably be more like sister and brother. You're a young woman. A woman in your prime, in fact. You might be unhappy.' He lowered his gaze and began to fuss with his watch chain. 'Unfulfilled,' he muttered. 'Have you thought of that?'

'Yes I have, sir,' Alice told him eagerly. In fact it would be a relief, she thought, to know that it would be a platonic relationship. 'It makes no difference. I have to make a future for my child, Mr Lightfoot. I'm willing to take any risk. I mean I'm not in any position to ... make demands. It's not as though I've been used to it.' She hoped she wasn't blushing.

He smiled suddenly and his eyes were kind. 'Poor Mrs Meredith. This isn't easy, is it, for either of us?'

'No, sir.'

'Suppose you were to regret it later.'

Slowly Alice shook her head. 'I should be eternally grateful. Forever in your debt. Between us we would make you happy, Mr Lightfoot.'

Instinctively she knew that she had said all that could matter to him. She would leave him alone to think it over. She stood up. 'I must get back to work now. If you'll excuse me.'

He accompanied her to the door without another word. As she stepped into the corridor he said, 'I shall let you know shortly what I decide.'

'Thank you, sir.'

As she walked away she waited for the sound of the door closing. It was a long time coming. So he had been watching her. Alice closed her eyes. For heaven's sake! He was going to say yes.

Somehow Alice survived the rest of the day without making any serious mistakes but she was in a state of perpetual confusion, unable to keep her mind on the business in hand. At lunch time she overbooked the tables in the restaurant and in the evening she apologized to the wrong guest for a problem with a bedside light. The hotel, proud of its newly installed electric lighting, still occasionally ran into problems and, when it did, the staff inevitably bemoaned the demise of the soft gas light.

By six o'clock Alice felt exhausted and longed to shut herself away in her room. Her mind was full of contradictions which she was unable to deal with. At one moment she was full of hope that Henry Lightfoot would agree to Hester's plan but as soon as she had convinced herself that he might do so, the prospect of actually marrying him overwhelmed her and she found herself praying that he would refuse. Time and again she imagined a scene in which she was a happy wife and mother only to be tormented by a moment of pure panic when she saw herself trapped in a union of convenience with no chance of ever experiencing the heady excitement of being in love.

'But it's for little Sebastian,' she repeated. 'Stop thinking only of yourself, Alice Meredith! It's too late for that. You sinned with Sebastian and this will be your punishment. At least it will be better for your child.'

Tea time for the staff was taken at different times. The restaurant staff ate between five and six so they were then available for setting tables and waiting on the dinner guests. The housemaids and their supervisors ate between six and seven and were then free to turn down the guests' beds and refill the water jugs while the guests were in the restaurant. As assistant manageress, Alice was expected to attend promptly at six and on this occasion she did so unwillingly, but the moment she entered the staff dining room she realized that her appetite was unaffected. She took her place with the others, eager for whatever the chef had seen fit to provide.

The staff dining room was next to the kitchens – a large semi-basement room at the side of the building with a deep window which overlooked a small area and stone steps which led up to ground level. Outside the window an oleander withered in its stone pot and snails clung to the wall. Alice, with a dislike of all slimy creatures, made a point never to glance that way. The room always smelled of stale cooking and condensation frequently formed on the bare walls but once it was filled with people all that was overlooked.

Maggie was already seated and, ignoring the clatter from the kitchens, she smiled across the table at Alice. 'You look a bit perkier. Real down in the dumps you were when I passed you on the stairs. Never even saw me, did you?' She grinned. 'Hullo, I says, and not a word from you.'

'I'm sorry, Maggie. I was miles away.'

There were a few male members of staff waiting for their tea. The new bootboy, two of the porters and Mr Parkin, who kept a stern eye on the menfolk.

Alice shrugged and quickly changed the subject but she wondered how people like Maggie would react if she, Alice, suddenly went up in the world. How would they treat her when they knew she was marrying their employer – a man so much older? They would count up the months when they eventually saw her condition and they would no doubt snigger behind her back.

A large teapot appeared and cups were filled. There was a large meat pasty, cut into squares, a bowl of pickles, plates of thickly cut bread and butter, home-made goose-berry jam and biscuits. On alternate days, when they didn't have a pasty, there was always a fruitcake.

The bootboy cried, 'Pasty!' and rubbed his hands together.

His outburst provoked a look of disapproval from Mr Parkin. 'Another word out of you, Smith, and you will leave the table and go hungry!'

Alice looked at the young lad. Dan Smith, known as Smiffy to most people, was barely twelve years old with bright ginger hair and a snub nose. She wondered who her child would take after – her or Sebastian. Hopefully Seb, because his soft blond hair curled delightfully and he was tall and slim. For a moment her thoughts were paralysed by a sudden longing for him. She tried to imagine him under a hot Indian sun, going about his duties in his grey uniform. He had never given her a photograph but she had one of him taken with her brother, the two men leaning against a piece of artillery, broad grins on their faces. She sighed. How happy she and Seb would have been. How *could* he have imagined he would be happy with someone else? Damn him!

Maggie said, 'Penny for them, Alice! You're looking grim.'

'Nothing,' Alice told her. To distract her thoughts she watched Smiffy tucking into his pasty as though he hadn't eaten for a week. He had helped himself to a mound of pickles which he was scooping up with his fork. Alice tried to imagine him as a baby, staring up from the depths of a perambulator with an ivory rattle in his hand. No doubt his mother had found him adorable. She tried to see herself and Henry Lightfoot watching their son take his first faltering steps ... or his first spoonful of custard.

'Alice!' Maggie was watching her expression. 'You're miles away.'

'It's nothing!'

Maggie rolled her eyes. 'Be like that!'

Five minutes later, Alice, spreading jam on her bread, tried to calm her thoughts but there had been no word from her employer. Had he consulted his sister, she wondered. Surely he would do so unless he had decided against the plan, in which case he would probably never mention it to Hester. Unless vanity played a part. She chewed thoughtfully, unaware of the whispered conversations taking place around her. Talking at the staff table was not encouraged but Mr Parkin was more than a little deaf.

They were halfway through the meal when there was a knock at the door and Miss Maine entered.

'Please, Mrs Meredith, you're wanted in thirty-five. Mr Lester and his daughter.'

Alice frowned. Father and daughter came

every year to spend a week and visit his elderly mother who lived alone in a small flat on the far side of the town. Arthur Lester was a kindly man with dark eyes and thick brown hair which seemed to resist the attentions of his barber. When he first came to the Mere he and his wife were together as newly-weds. Two years later they brought their first child, a daughter by the name of Perdita. Once a cheerful man, he had later been devastated by his wife's untimely death during the birth of their second child. Neither mother nor baby had survived. Since then he and Perdita had continued to visit Chester but the sparkle had gone from his eyes.

'Is it Mr Lester's mother? I understand she's in the hospital,' said Alice. 'Maybe she's taken a turn for the worse?'

'No. It's Perdita. He says the girl's getting hysterical.'

'Hysterical? How strange. Don't worry, Miss Maine. I'll see to it.'

Glad to have something to take her mind off her own problems, Alice excused herself from the table and made her way upstairs.

She knocked on the door and it was opened immediately by Mr Lester. 'Oh Mrs Meredith! Come in, please. It's so kind of you ... Thank you for coming. It's so unlike Perdita to get herself in such a state but...' He turned towards the smaller of the beds on the far side of the room, where the child was curled up on top of the eiderdown. 'Perdita, here's Mrs Meredith to talk to you. I want you to sit up now and behave yourself.'

The small dark-haired girl peered up at Alice through a tangle of lank curls. Her face was flushed and her eyes red-rimmed. Sorrowful brown eyes met Alice's gaze and fresh tears threatened.

Alice sat beside her on the bed. She reached out and tucked back a few strands of damp hair. 'Hullo, Perdita. Your Papa tells me you're rather sad and we can't have that. At the Mere Hotel we like everyone to be happy.' She smiled. 'Do you want to tell me what's wrong?'

A motherless child, thought Alice. Was that worse than being fatherless? And how on earth did a man bring up a child on his own – unless he employed a nanny? She had never thought to ask.

Perdita looked from Alice to her father and back to Alice.

Alice said, 'I might be able to cheer you up if you tell me what's troubling you.'

Mr Lester said, 'Answer Mrs Meredith, Perdita. Where are your manners?' He turned to Alice. 'This is so unlike her. She's a most biddable child normally. I can't understand it. She says she wants her birthday party tomorrow but her birthday's not until next week. Her aunt has already made her a cake and has invited a few of her school-friends.'

Alice looked at Perdita who appeared quite unmoved by these details. Her small mouth quivered. 'I'll be seven,' she whispered.

'Seven! Goodness gracious you *are* growing up!' cried Alice. 'And your aunt has made you a lovely cake.'

'I don't want a party next week. I want it tomorrow ... *Tomorrow!*' She stared desperately at Alice and two fat tears trickled down her cheeks. Alice took out her handkerchief, leaned forward and wiped the tears away.

Arthur Lester said, 'I've told you, darling, that nobody has two birthday parties. They just don't, do they, Mrs Meredith?'

Alice, staring into the soulful brown eyes, thought that a girl would be nice. A girl like Perdita, perhaps ... But would Henry Lightfoot want a daughter? She had tried to offer him a son and heir, someone to inherit, someone to carry on his 'little empire' and thwart the obnoxious nephew.

Perdita, waiting for Alice's answer, began to cry again and the tears jerked Alice's thoughts back to the present.

She looked at Arthur Lester. 'Two birthdays are out of the question,' she said. 'But what about one real birthday next week and a pretend birthday tomorrow?' She dabbed two further tears from the child's face. 'A pretend party tomorrow? Is that a good idea?'

She glanced at the child's father as he began to stammer his thanks. Perdita had brightened.

'Tomorrow?' she echoed. 'Do you promise?'

Alice nodded. 'It won't be such a special party without your friends but I'll ask Chef to bake you a small birthday cake and make a nice red wobbly jelly. There might even be a small present. How would that be?'

Perdita smiled. 'Thank you.' Her woes forgotten, she gave her father a radiant smile.

Mr Lester said, 'It's really so kind of you, Mrs Meredith. I don't know what to say or how to thank you. I was at a loss. She's never so intractable. I can't understand it. Still, a pretend party sounds wonderful.'

Alice smiled. 'It's no trouble.' She turned to Perdita. 'I have a very nice teddy bear who loves going to parties. Could he come, do you think?'

Perdita was now all eagerness. 'I've got a rag dolly. She could come and they could be friends. Her name's Moppet.'

'Then it's settled. A sponge cake with icing and a cherry on the top, a present and some wobbly jellies!'

Mr Lester looked relieved as his daughter slid from the bed and hurried to find the doll and show her to Alice.

Mr Lester pushed his unruly dark hair from his forehead and said, 'You're what my mother calls "a gem", Mrs Meredith.'

'A gem?' Alice laughed. 'I like that. I'm glad we could help.'

'You're very good with children. Do you have any of your own?'

'No!' Startled, she stared at him. 'That is, I ... Not yet.' She hoped she didn't look as guilty as she felt. All this deceit.

He was looking at her with surprise. 'I'm sorry. I understood that you're a widow and I just thought ... How stupid of me. It's none of my business.'

Alice struggled to recover her composure. 'Not at all. It's ... I hope some day...' Unnerved by the innocent question, Alice was stammering. She also felt the unexpected pressure of tears, blinked frantically and half turned from him.

To her surprise, he took hold of her hand. 'Do please forgive me, Mrs Meredith. I've said something tactless. What an idiot I am! My mother always told me to think before I speak.'

Recovering, Alice forced a smile. 'Don't give it another thought. Now I must have a word with Chef and then get back to my tea. If you'll excuse me.'

Somehow she stopped herself from breaking into a run. Outside, with the door shut behind her, she took a few deep breaths to calm herself. He meant no harm, she reminded herself. He was simply taking an interest – and he thinks I'm good with children. That's nice. She took a deep breath. Poor man has probably decided that I need to work because I've been widowed. Why did I ever call myself Mrs?

Moving towards the stairs she muttered, 'Forget all about it!' At least she was satisfied that Perdita's small crisis was over. Puzzled by the child's distress but amused by her persistence, Alice was still smiling when she returned to the staff dining room to finish her tea.

As soon as she came off duty Alice hurried to Edith's room and was soon ensconced in one of her chairs and recounting the story of Perdita and her birthday. She had almost finished when Edie cried, 'Wait!' She crossed to the chest at the end of the bed and, throwing back the lid, drew out an exquisite straw hat decorated with a large rose made of red silk.

'You need a present for Perdita's birthday and here's the very thing!' she exclaimed. She pulled the hat on to her head and peered at her reflection in the nearby mirror.

'You look lovely,' Alice told her.

'Do I? Still?' The compliment pleased her. 'Well perhaps I do, Alice. I always have thought that actresses age very well. It's partly the fact that we learn to move gracefully. A graceful walk can do wonders for a woman.'

Having admired the hat from all angles, Edith removed it. Twirling it on one finger she gently touched each ribbon and stroked every feather. Suddenly she replaced it on her head, struck a pose, adopted a haughty expression and said, 'Please get up, Oliver. You look quite ridiculous on your knees!'

Alice applauded.

Edith said, 'Lady Larksmith!' Her eyes sparkled at the memory. 'One of my best roles. I had a wonderful parasol in that scene. We were supposed to be on the promenade at Brighton.' Sighing, she removed the hat for the second time. 'If it weren't for Gordon I'd still be acting. Character roles, of course, but some of them are such fun.' She sighed. 'Oh well. All little girls love to dress up. You must tell Perdita to look after the rose so that she can wear it on her first grown-up hat!'

Ignoring Alice's protests she fetched scissors and neatly removed the rose from the straw confection that called itself a hat.

'Lady Larksmith in *Pandora's Revenge* at the Royalty,' she told Alice. 'We played to packed houses, you know, but then Chester always has supported its theatres. The people appreciate drama. I have to tell you I looked wonderful in that play. I can't be modest. I looked absolutely divine. The gown I wore with it was cream lace with red ribbon trim at the collar and cuffs – to match the rose in the hat. It was the first night and Gordon was there in the first row of the stalls. That's when we first met.' She gave the rose a shake and blew on it gently to remove years of dust.

'But your beautiful hat!' Alice protested but Edith wasn't listening. Humming cheerfully, she was delving further into the chest in search of tissue paper. She wrapped the rose carefully and then found some red ribbons in her glove drawer and fashioned an elegant bow to complete the present.

'Give it to her with love from Edith!'

Impulsively Alice put her arms round the thin shoulders and gave her a hug. 'You are so generous,' she said. 'Perdita will be delighted.' She stood up to leave but Edith put out a restraining hand.

'Something has happened, Alice.' she said. 'I don't know if I should tell you or not.'

'Is it about your niece? She's coming to—'

'No ... but she will one day. No, it's about a letter I received this afternoon. By hand.'

Alice was intrigued. 'Good news or bad?'

'I don't know. I'll read it to you but you mustn't interrupt.' She pulled an envelope from beneath the cushion and drew out a sheet of paper. ' "My dear Mrs Brightling, forgive me for my sudden departure. I was, of course, wrongly accused but am unable to furnish proof of my innocence. I have therefore been forced to leave the Mere Hotel but there was no time to make proper—" '

Alice cried, 'Oh no! This is not from Dr Stewart, I hope!'

Edith gave her a baleful glance and went on.

' "—to make proper farewells. I am desolate that we have been parted this way and wonder if you will be gracious enough to—" '

'Edith! He's a rogue!' Alice could see at once where this was leading.

' "—to meet with me at the—" ' Edith stopped. 'I shan't read the next bit to you, Alice, in case you tell the police. He signed it "Your desperate friend, Bertie." ' Edith looked at Alice and her expression was defiant. 'I know you'll tell me not to go but ... I truly did take to the man, Alice, and if he's been wrongly accused...'

'Edith, he's a con man. A trickster. He probably sees you as a wealthy widow and sees a chance to—'

'Oh really, Alice!' With an extravagant gesture, Edith crumpled the letter and pressed it to her chest. 'I should never have trusted you. I should have known you would adopt this attitude.' She closed her eyes and breathed rapidly. 'You'll have to forget everything I've told you. I needed to confide in someone but ... The poor man! Poor Bertie!'

'Edith! You've never called him Bertie before. Don't you see? He's playing on your sympathies.'

'He trusts me, Alice. What am I to do?'

Dismayed, Alice attempted to calm her. 'You don't have to do anything,' she told Edith. 'You can ignore the whole thing.'

'But after all we've been to each other...'

'You weren't anything to each other. He just flattered you and you found him—'

'It wasn't like that!'

'Just ignore the letter, Edith. Maybe he'll think you didn't receive it.'

'But he obviously *needs* me.' Edith opened her eyes. 'If only this hadn't happened – this terrible accusation. I *knew* he was attracted to me. I told you, didn't I? A woman can tell these things. Oh poor Dr Stewart! Bertie, I mean. What will he do if I turn my back on him?'

Alice regarded her friend with a growing sense of helplessness. 'But Edie, if he is a – a liar as it appears, it won't be good for you to get mixed up with him. Can't you see that?'

Edith covered her face with her hands. 'It's so hard for a woman in love to betray—'

'You aren't in love with him, Edith. Don't exaggerate. You hardly know the man.'

'But that's where you're wrong!' Edith's eyes flashed. 'I always felt drawn towards him. I felt that he was lonely. Some men can't survive without the love of a good woman. They go ... to the bad. Well, not exactly to the bad but they go astray. I might be the right woman for him, Alice. I might be able to change him.'

Alice was losing patience with her. 'You've got a kind heart and you're sorry for him. That's all it is.'

Edith stared at her. 'How would you know, Alice? You are hardly an expert on love and romance. I've kept my feelings for him hidden until today but – but now that he has thrown himself on my mercy...'

Alice found it hard to tell if Edith's acting talent was coming to the fore or whether she was truly distressed. She hesitated. 'All I can say is please take care,' she said at last. 'Only you know how genuine your feelings are but, at the risk of hurting them, if I were in your shoes I'd step very carefully.' She stood up, unwilling to prolong the discussion and aware that she, too, was being drawn unwillingly into the situation. 'I must go. And thank you for the rose. Perdita will be thrilled with it.'

Edith followed her to the door. 'You won't tell that dreadful sergeant, will you? I don't want Dr Stewart arrested because of me. You must promise to say nothing, Alice.'

Alice groaned inwardly. 'I'll forget we ever had this conversation,' she said opening the door.

'That's no good. You must *promise*!' Edith was once more the tragic heroine, clutching the letter while her voice trembled.

'I promise. There. I've said it.'

Alice stepped out into the corridor and closed the door before Edith could exact any other promises. As she made her way towards the kitchen to arrange Perdita's party, she tried to ignore the uneasiness she felt. Edith seemed determined to think the best of the wretched man and Alice could see that the letter had excited her and that she was flattered by his attention. As long as Edith decided not to meet him perhaps no harm would come of it. Alice frowned. She had given her word that she would not inform the police, although that was obviously what she ought to do. Now she thought she might live to regret her rash promise.

Three

As Alice made her way downstairs the following morning, she was feeling frail and on edge. She had spent a restless night and had been sick on rising. Unable to face the staff dining room, she now felt empty and a little light-headed. There had been no word from Henry Lightfoot or his sister and she was resigned to the fact that he was going to reject her suggestion. It was no more than she had expected. Her proposal was outrageous and if she were in his shoes she, too, would refuse. But at least he should have told her – even a note pushed under her door would be sufficient if he didn't want to face her again.

In the dining room she saw Mr Lester and Perdita and hurried across to assure them that the party would take place as planned at four thirty with cakes and jellies.

'And crackers to pull!' she told Perdita. 'So you'll have some party hats to wear.'

Chef, entering into the spirit of the little party, had found a few crackers left over from Christmas.

The child looked a little wan, thought Alice, with dark rings under her eyes. Perhaps she hadn't slept well either. Alice's own childhood came back to her suddenly and she saw herself as a tousle-haired nine-year-old, wide awake still as the church clock struck midnight and unable to believe that the night would ever pass to allow the birthday to become a reality.

'Is your teddy bear really coming?' Perdita whispered.

Alice nodded. 'He was very excited when I told him and he is going to wear his best bow.'

'What's his name?'

'Teddy Cuddles – because he's squashy and cuddly.'

Perdita's smile was slow in coming.

Mr Lester said, 'Are you all right, Mrs Meredith? You look a little weary. A little what my wife used to call "moithered"!' He smiled. 'It was one of her favourite words.'

Moithered? That was the understatement of the year, thought Alice. She wished he wouldn't look at her with such kindly concern. She wasn't used to it and it undermined her. It was taking all her efforts to appear brisk and in control and all she could do was shake her head. She was very afraid that if she spoke to him at all she would break down and cry on his shoulder.

'Well,' he said with some reluctance. 'We

81

mustn't keep you, Mrs Meredith. We know how busy you are.'

At that moment Maggie arrived at the table with the Lesters' breakfast tray of tea and toast and Alice made her escape.

She glanced across the room to where Edith sat in solitary splendour at her small corner table. Edith pretended not to see her and busied herself with a pair of kippers, poking them suspiciously with her knife and delicately extracting a few bones. Remembering their last conversation, Alice wondered whether she should make a last attempt to dissuade her friend from any meetings with the doctor but reluctantly decided against it. Edith Brightling was a grown woman and could make her own decisions.

Mr Warner appeared beside Alice. He was stroking his moustache, a sure sign that he was annoyed. He said, 'Miss Lightfoot would like to see you in her room as soon as it's convenient. I'll have to cover for you here until you get back.'

'*Miss* Lightfoot?' Alice's heart began to beat faster. Ah! She could see it all, she decided bitterly. Henry Lightfoot had told his sister and was leaving her to break the bad news to Alice. Typically cowardly, she thought, trying to whip up some resentment. Anything to mask her deep disappointment and humiliation.

'Yes, *Miss* Lightfoot.' He frowned. 'Why do you ask? Were you expecting a summons from—'

'No, no! It's ... I thought...'

He looked at her suspiciously. 'Is something wrong? You look a bit upset.'

Alice tried to look indignant. 'Of course I'm not upset.'

'Nothing I should know about then?' He obviously didn't believe her.

'No!' Her voice shook slightly and she prayed he would let the matter drop.

He tutted irritably. 'Go now, then, and get it over with. Come straight back as soon as you can. I've got letters to write and I want to catch the post.'

Alice hurried thankfully from the room but once outside she came to a standstill, unable to muster enough courage to learn her fate. Now that the summons had come she was frozen with fear. Whatever decision he had made, she would be shocked by it. To marry him would be a lifetime's penance but *not* to marry him would be marginally worse.

'Please hurry, Mrs Meredith!' Mr Warner was glaring at her from the dining room door. 'You're wasting time.'

'I'm sorry! Yes, of course. I'll go up. Now.' She glanced round dazedly. 'Yes. Thank you.'

She was babbling. Stop it, Alice. Pull

yourself together at once, she urged. Somehow she left the dining room and climbed the stairs. By the time she reached Hester Lightfoot's room she felt extraordinarily weary and her heart was racing with anxiety.

'Come in!'

Pushing open the door, Alice was confronted by both brother and sister, who stood together by the window. They had been laughing together and Alice forced her stiff lips into an apology for a smile.

Hester stepped forward, her hand outstretched in welcome but there was a subtle lack of warmth in her manner. 'Mrs Meredith. Henry has told me your exciting news.'

Alice swallowed hard, tried to speak but found herself tongue-tied. She looked at Henry who came forward and took her hand in his. 'I hope you didn't mind, Alice. I couldn't wait a moment later to share the news with my sister.'

'No. Not at all.' He had said yes. She stared at him, overwhelmed. His eyes were shining with excitement and she found herself smiling in return. He wanted to marry her!

Hester indicated three chairs grouped together and they all sat down.

Hester glanced from her brother to Alice. 'I admit I was very surprised. It's rather sudden. Quite unexpected.'

She certainly *looked* surprised, thought

84

Alice, surprised in her turn. Hester's expression was not entirely enthusiastic. In fact she conveyed the impression that she had been mortified by the news, which, considering it had been her own idea, suggested considerable acting talent.

Hester continued. 'Let's say I had never imagined Henry would decide to wed again at his age but, since he has done so, I hope he has made a wise choice. I have offered him my congratulations.'

Alice risked another glance at Henry who reminded her of a naughty schoolboy who has just been forgiven for a prank. He smiled at her shyly but said nothing and Alice realized what an effort it must have been for him to face up to his older sister and risk her disapproval.

Alice said, 'I'm so glad you approve, Miss Lightfoot.'

Hester said, 'My brother was always very secretive. I recall when I was about eleven that he kept disappearing and refused to tell me where—'

'Oh Hester!' he protested. 'Not that old rabbit story! We've got better things to talk about.'

Undeterred, Hester went on. 'A neighbour had given him a baby rabbit but we were not allowed to have pets and—'

'Mrs Meredith – I mean Alice – doesn't want to hear all that.' He smiled at her. 'We have more important things to talk about. I have asked Chef to send up a bottle of champagne in five minutes exactly. Then we shall celebrate our betrothal. Would you like that ... dear?'

Alice nodded, her throat dry. So it was going to happen. She had saved her child but had pledged herself to a marriage of convenience. Alice had to admit, though, that her husband-to-be was carrying off their deception with unexpected panache. Certainly with more than she herself could immediately summon.

'Champagne? How wonderful.'

If only she could relax and accept what would generally be seen as her good fortune. Plucked from her position among the staff to be the future wife of the owner. It came to her that now she would be able to confide in both Maggie and Edith Brightling. How would they react to her sudden elevation, she wondered?

At that moment the door opened and Maggie came in with a tray, champagne and three glasses. She flashed a glance at Alice in which shock was clearly visible and Alice guessed immediately that she had been listening at the door before coming in. Now there would be no need to tell the staff, she thought wryly.

'Thank you,' Henry wrestled the cork from the bottle with a satisfying plop and

Alice watched as he filled the glasses. Feeling that she ought to show a little more enthusiasm, she smiled at Hester.

'Miss Lightfoot, I—'

'Call me Hester, please.'

'Oh yes! Thank you, Hester ... I'm so pleased that you welcome the idea.'

'As I've already told you, I'm a little surprised by Henry's *urgency* but he says he wants to put an end to his loneliness as soon as possible and I accept that. He has already spoken to the Reverend Tanner and the banns will be called this coming Sunday for the first time. Thank you, Henry!' She accepted her glass of champagne.

As Alice took hers from Henry she noticed the slight tremor in his hand. So he *was* nervous too. It made her feel marginally better.

As they touched their glasses and took the first sip it dawned on Alice that this celebration signalled the end of her life as she knew it. She would be a married woman with a home to look after, a man to care for and a baby to prepare for.

'To your future happiness!' Hester smiled at them both. She looked at Alice. 'I'll be honest and admit that I do hope your union will be fruitful.'

Henry said, 'Hester! What a thing to say to the poor woman.'

Hester ignored him. 'Poor Marion was

never able to give Henry a child but it has always been his heart's desire. Now, with a new young wife, God may yet smile on him at last.'

Alice felt her face burn but to her surprise Henry put a hand lightly on her shoulder. It was warm and firm and not unpleasant but it brought back memories of Sebastian which Alice knew she must force from her mind. Sebastian had betrayed her and he now belonged to another. And so did she.

'I'll drink to that,' Henry said and managed a conspiratorial wink which Hester missed.

Hester said, 'You'll move in with Henry, of course, after the wedding, and I will be on hand. I'm sure a husband is a great comfort but sometimes a woman needs to talk to another woman. And we must have a new gown made for you, for the wedding. We're going to be very busy in the next few weeks.'

Henry removed his hand from Alice's shoulder. 'When shall we tell the staff? I thought as soon as possible.'

Alice felt a wave of panic. 'Oh not too soon, ma'am! I mean, maybe...' She fell silent. What she meant was that once the betrothal was official everyone would change towards her. 'That is, I'd like to carry on for a few more weeks or months.'

'Months?' Henry frowned. 'We shall be married within the month, my dear. I'm sorry to rush you but I've never been a patient man.'

Hester gave Alice a meaningful look. 'As soon as possible, Alice.'

'Yes, ma'am.'

Henry laughed. 'And stop calling her ma'am. We must be Hester and Henry from now on – in private. And you will be Alice, naturally. No more Mrs Meredith.'

Hester said, 'You might like your own maid, Alice. You could choose one of the housemaids and we could train her.'

'Oh no!' Alice clapped a hand to her mouth. It sounded so ungrateful but the idea appalled her. Someone to help her dress? She certainly wasn't ready for that. She valued her privacy too much. The Lightfoots mustn't take her over body and soul.

'I'll think about it,' she promised hastily, seeing Hester's disappointment.

Henry smiled at her. 'Don't take any notice of us, Alice. We're just two old fogeys and we're excited. It's all going to be very different for you and we understand that. Lots of changes but nothing to be afraid of and you mustn't let us pressure you in any way. Just whisper in my ear if anything troubles you and we'll sort it out together.'

Surprised, she looked at him gratefully. He had understood her feelings exactly.

At that moment the clock struck ten and

89

Alice jumped. 'Poor Mr Warner! He was standing in for me in the dining room! I said I wouldn't be long. He'll be furious.'

Hester laughed. 'Then you run along. If he's angry with you blame it onto us. Say you couldn't get away.'

Alice excused herself and hurried downstairs. *Say you couldn't get away*. Hester's innocent words echoed ominously in her mind. *Couldn't get away*. Her heart thumped uncomfortably and she could hardly breathe. Everything had happened so quickly, she was left bewildered and full of apprehension. She was committed and, once married, she wouldn't be able to get away. If she had made a mistake she had only herself to blame.

At the foot of the stairs she paused, clinging to the banister. 'What have I done?' she whispered. Closing her eyes she tried desperately to see Sebastian's face but his image refused to appear. Even Sebastian was lost to her and with him her past life. The Lightfoots' honeyed trap had been sprung.

Promptly at four thirty Perdita appeared with her father in the dining room and Alice hurried to meet them.

'Happy birthday!' she cried and bent to give the little girl a quick hug. Perdita, pale but excited, was wearing a pale blue dress with a smocked bodice and a frilled collar. She was carrying the rag doll, which was dressed in red and white spotted cotton with a bow in her woolly hair.

Perdita said, 'Papa and I have been walking along the big high walls. We could see the river and the racecourse but there weren't any horses, were there, Papa? And we saw the very special clock and Grandmama was asleep so we came home.'

Mr Lester nodded. 'It's difficult to know how to pass the time,' he told Alice. 'I think the walk was a little too much for her but when we went to the hospital my mother was sleeping. The sister said she had had a bad night so we didn't wake her.'

'Poor Grandmama! She's very poorly.'

Alice led them to a small table which had been decorated especially for her with a posy of flowers and a lace tablecloth. In one of the seats Teddy Cuddles waited, resplendent in his blue bow. 'This is Teddy Cuddles,' said Alice. 'He says he would like to sit next to you and maybe Moppet could sit on your other side.'

It was quickly agreed and Perdita and her father also sat down.

'Mrs Brightling has sent you a present,' Alice told Perdita.

'Oh Papa! May I open it now?'

'Of course, darling.'

The little girl was delighted with the red

rose and her father promised that when she was older he would buy her a hat to pin it on.

'Please thank Mrs Brightling. It was so generous.'

The Chef brought in a plate of tiny sandwiches, a cake with candles and a tray of jellies topped with cream. Alice accepted one of the sandwiches and promised to return in time for a slice of birthday cake. As she left them a sandwich was being placed on the plates in front of the bear and the doll and Perdita was beaming.

Half an hour later, as Alice made her away along the corridor on the first floor, an arm reached out and pulled her into the shadows. It was Maggie.

'Tell me it's not true!' she demanded. 'You're not going to wed that miserable old devil! You *can't*!'

'He's not a miserable old devil!' Alice hissed. 'And you shouldn't eavesdrop, Maggie.'

'But why? *Why*, Alice?' Maggie stared at her.

Alice glanced round nervously. 'I can't talk about it,' she protested. 'I'll tell you sometime but—'

'Tell me *now*!'

'There isn't time. I've got things to do.'

'Well, just say it isn't true.'

Alice hesitated and Maggie gave a shriek of horror. 'It *is* true! Oh Lordy, Alice, are you out of your mind? That dry old stick? Oh you can't mean it! You're not that desperate surely? What about Sebastian? I thought you and he were—'

Alice pulled her arm from Maggie's grasp. 'Sebastian's married. That's why.' She longed to explain about the baby but that was out of the question.

Maggie's jaw dropped. *'Married?* Oh he can't be. That's terrible. What happened? Did you quarrel? Oh Alice, you poor thing!'

'I can't talk now but I promise I'll tell you – as long as you don't go telling all the others.'

She clapped a hand to her mouth. 'I'm sorry, Alice. I did just mention it...'

Alice groaned. 'I knew you would!'

'When I saw you in that room with them and the champagne and everything ... But your Sebastian *married*! I can't believe it of him. The sneaky wretch!'

Fortunately for Alice a guest appeared at that moment to complain that the water in her wash jug was tepid and Alice grasped the chance to end her conversation with Maggie. She scurried downstairs to order a new jug to be taken up to room fifteen. Having done that she determined to keep out of Maggie's way but almost at once was waylaid by the manager.

'Mrs Meredith, can you spare a moment in my office?'

As Alice followed him she was rehearsing what she should say about her forthcoming marriage but it seemed Mr Warner had not heard the rumours.

'About this wretched doctor,' he began. 'I've heard from the police in the past ten minutes that he's been spotted locally. At least they think it's him but he's tried to disguise himself. Dyed his hair and he's shaved his moustache.' He shook his head with a disparaging gesture. 'Seems he has a thoroughly murky past. Aliases. Bouncing cheques. Petty theft. Once involved in an affray but he was not the instigator. Apart from that, you name it – our doctor has done it! The police are asking everyone to keep an eye out for him so if you hear anything let me know and I'll pass it on to Sergeant Flint.'

Alice hoped she didn't look as guilty as she felt. 'You don't think he'd dare to return to the Mere, do you?'

Mr Warner shrugged. 'I wouldn't put anything past the blighter. Chap like that has no scruples. No sense of decency. Wouldn't have thought he'd even return to Chester knowing that he's been rumbled but there you are. Cheek of the devil, these people.' He smiled suddenly. 'I see there's a birthday party going on. Nice little thing, isn't she.

Patricia, is it?'

'Perdita, sir.'

'Ah yes. Her father had some very nice things to say about you, Mrs Meredith. Well done. A satisfied guest. That's what it's all about.'

'Thank you, Mr Warner.'

Alice was dreading staff tea time. She had no idea how many of the staff would have heard about her forthcoming marriage nor how they would have received the news. She returned as promised to Perdita's birthday party and enjoyed a slice of Chef's best iced sponge but she noticed that Perdita was running out of energy and was troubled by a nasty-sounding cough. Her face was flushed and her eyes had lost their sparkle.

Alice lowered her voice. 'Would you like the doctor to call?'

'I think it may be croup. I'll give it until the morning.'

'Early night maybe?'

'Definitely. I don't think I shall be very late myself,' he confessed. 'Tomorrow I think an easy day is indicated. No more sightseeing for little feet! A quick visit to the shops for a colouring book and a box of paints, maybe.'

Alice nodded. 'I'm sure we keep a few storybooks somewhere. I'll find them and send them up to your room.'

She moved on around the dining room

with a smile or a few words for each guest. Alice was trying to decide whether or not to tell Edith what she now knew about Dr Stewart. She knew the news would be unwelcome but surely the poor woman was entitled to know the truth. Not telling her might be the worst option. She waited until the dining room had emptied and then, coming to a sudden decision, knocked on Edith's door. There was no answer. Alice looked in the reading room but was again unlucky. Downstairs at reception she asked Miss Maine if she had seen Edith.

'She went out to post a letter about an hour ago...'

'But the postbox is only five minutes away.'

'Maybe she's gone for a walk or met someone she knows. You know how Mrs Brightling loves to talk.'

Alice frowned, already having doubts. Was she really entitled to meddle?

'Never mind,' she said. 'I'll speak to her later. Do you know where the children's storybooks are kept?'

'There are a few in the big sideboard in the dining room. A bit worse for wear I'm afraid.'

Alice found them and they certainly were in a bad state. She tutted at the faded covers and frayed spines of the books. *The Adventures of Mr Fish* and *English Fairy Tales* were in the best condition so she pushed the rest to the back of the cupboard and decided the hotel should have some new books for children. And maybe some games.

'A toy cupboard!' she cried, delighted with the idea. A chest somewhere full of books and toys to satisfy children of all ages. Mentally she made a list – snakes and ladders and ludo, jigsaw puzzles, nothing noisy that might offend other guests. Maybe a doll's house for the girls and some tin soldiers for the boys. She smiled remembering her brother at eight, sprawled in front of the fire with his soldiers. Probably when his desire to be a soldier was born. 'First battalion, the Cheshires!' she muttered and sighed. It was beginning to dawn on her that she would probably never see Sebastian again and she tried to recall her last glimpse of him as she saw him off from the station platform. He was leaning out of the window *and smiling*. No doubt with relief, she thought with a surge of bitterness, but this was overtaken by sadness as she realized that he would never see his child. Would never even know that he *had* a child by Alice Meredith. He would have other children by his wife but Alice's child would remain on the shadowy fringes of his life. Suppose the baby was a boy and grew up to look just like Sebastian. Would Eddie guess the truth? If so, all she could do was deny it. For everyone's sake.

She forced herself back to the present. Tin soldiers and maybe a set of wooden farm animals or a Noah's Ark. Suddenly she realized that if she waited a few weeks there would be no need to ask anyone for permission to provide a toy chest. She would be Mrs Henry Lightfoot and no one would deny her. She was astonished by the idea and cautiously pleased. Being married to Henry Lightfoot would have its compensations.

Later that afternoon Henry sent for her and she presented herself as requested. She was soon seated at one end of the large brown Chesterfield with her husband-to-be ensconced in a matching armchair on the other side of a small table on which a tray of tea and biscuits had been set. For a long moment neither spoke. Henry was regarding Alice with undisguised pleasure and she hoped her own expression was not too apprehensive.

'Almond biscuits,' he said at last. 'My favourites. Mother used to make them for Sunday tea. It was such a treat to be allowed to share a meal with our parents. Nanny was very kind but tea in the nursery was rather dull. Hester has the recipe somewhere if you want it. Will you pour?'

Alice found it difficult to imagine that he had ever been a small boy and instinctively glanced round the room in search of a family photograph.

'Hester has all the family photographs,' he told her. 'She's always been interested in the family history and hated the idea that our strand of the family was coming to an abrupt end. Unfortunately she said as much to poor Marion in an unguarded moment and was never forgiven. We do have a nephew, Donald. My brother's son but...' He shrugged as he took his teacup from Alice. 'We don't see eye to eye. That's a kind way of putting it. My brother assumed that because we were childless we would automatically take Donald into the hotel but we didn't want to. Marion didn't like him. She never really trusted him. A sly little boy. Once I recall he hid a valuable candlestick and the maid was blamed. Just before she was sacked the candlestick was found in Donald's bedroom.'

Alice was appalled. 'What did he have to say for himself?'

'He tried to lie his way out of it. A nasty child. Such a shame. My brother deserved better.' He sipped his tea thoughtfully. 'He was arrogant, too. Donald, I mean. The truth is Hester hated him and she is now a junior partner in the Mere. A sleeping partner, if you know the term.'

Alice didn't know it but she murmured something inaudible and made a mental note to find out.

Henry helped himself to a biscuit and ate it thoughtfully. Alice took another look round the room. The only bright spot was a bowl of cream roses. There was nothing that made it personal; nothing that said it was Henry's home, except, perhaps, the bookshelves that lined one wall.

Henry went on. 'Donald was spoilt as a boy – you have to blame the parents for that but he was their only child. They lavished love and attention on him and he threw it all back at them. Went off to the wilds of Australia and not a word from him in six years. Worried his parents half to death as you can imagine. Then turned up like a bad penny expecting them to pay off his debts.' He shook his head sadly.

Alice was beginning to relax a little. Smiling, she helped herself to a biscuit.

Henry beamed. 'That's it, my dear. I want you to feel at home here. He watched her for a moment then began to fiddle with his watch chain.

'I'm sorry I didn't warn you earlier – about telling Hester. It was thoughtless of me. I was so excited once I'd decided I approved of your idea. I couldn't wait to make it all happen and I simply rushed down to Hester's room to break it to her. I thought that if I didn't tell someone it might all disappear.' He laughed. 'I thought about it all night. I daresay you did, also.'

'I thought you'd decided against it.'

'Hester was wonderful. Really. It was a shock, naturally, but she quickly rallied. She said she wants whatever makes me happy. That's so like her. I'm sure the two of you will get along splendidly.' He reached forward suddenly and took hold of her hand. Then he kissed it, released her and sat back. 'You don't mind?'

Alice was disarmed by his honesty and charmed by his excitement. 'Of course not.'

'We have to learn to love each other or Hester will suspect something. She's very sharp.'

Alice felt that some show of affection on her part was called for and searched her mind for something suitable to say. 'I don't think it will be difficult to love you, Henry.'

'Oh my dear girl!' His eyes filled with sudden tears but he quickly blinked them away. 'Mrs Meredi— I mean Alice. Oh! I *must* remember. Let me confess now that your proposal did shock me. It seemed very audacious.'

'It *was*!' Alice agreed.

'But over the years I have come to admire you. I like your spirit and you are good with people. But I never would have thought of anything happening between us. Now that it has, I'm delighted and so is Hester.'

Alice was beginning to like him. She felt

badly about having deceived him and was sorely tempted to tell him the truth. But that would ruin everything. If she wanted to make him happy she knew she must keep him in ignorance.

He leaned back in his chair. 'How is your health? I believe there is something called morning sickness.'

Briefly Alice explained.

'How perfectly beastly!' he said. 'You must leave your own doctor and transfer to mine. Hester and I are with Dr Barnes in Vicarage Road. He's the family doctor. Took over from his father, Cecil Barnes.' He smiled suddenly. 'He'll be astounded when we tell him about the child!' He tapped the side of his nose. 'We must never disillusion him!'

Henry's enthusiasm was infectious and Alice grinned. 'We shall have to think of some names. My father was Arnold, my uncle was William and an uncle that died young was Victor – after Queen Victoria.'

'Our family rather goes in for Nevilles and Henrys. Not very enlightened, are we?' His eyes widened. 'It might be a girl.'

'My mother is Clarice.'

'Ours was Adeline.' His grin was suddenly boyish. 'This is awfully good fun, isn't it – Alice?'

'Yes it is.' In a way, that was true, Alice reflected. Before this betrothal all her thoughts about the child had been full of dread. Now she could begin to enjoy the prospect of motherhood.

'I'm looking forward to telling Hester about the child,' he admitted. 'She'll be an aunt. Not that she isn't Donald's aunt, but an aunt to *my* child.' He glanced at her quickly. 'I may refer to the child as mine?'

'But of course, Henry!' Impulsively she gave him a quick kiss on the cheek. 'Your child. My child. Our child!'

They both laughed.

He said, 'We could tell Hester a month after the wedding? What do you think?'

'I agree.'

'The sooner the better so that we can talk about it freely. I hate having secrets from her. She was a rather bossy elder sister but if anyone threatened me in any way she would always defend me. I remember once that a local boy started to bully me. he had a dog on a lead and he threatened to set it on me. I expect it was as docile as a kitten but I was terrified of them both. Hester found me crying one day and weedled the truth out of me. I was about eight then and she was sixteen. She found out where he lived, knocked on the door and told his mother what he was up to.'

'Well done, Hester!' Alice was intrigued by this insight. 'Did the bullying stop?'

'Yes it did. He always called me cissy after- wards but I didn't mind that. Hester told me to poke my tongue out at him and I did.' Abruptly he stood up. 'Come and see the spare bedroom. We could make it into a nursery.'

Alice followed him across the room to a door which led into a large gloomy bedroom. Alice resisted a shudder as she compared it to her own little den below the roof. They crossed the room to a smaller one which was similarly gloomy.

'Poor Marion used to sleep here quite a lot,' Henry told her. 'She was often in poor health and had sleepless nights. She hated to think she was disturbing me. What do you think, Alice?'

The single bed boasted an ornate brass bedhead and in the far corner Alice spotted a commode. There was a stale smell of sickness and a hint of antiseptics.

Ghastly, thought Alice, but she gave an appreciative murmur. 'We could make some changes,' she suggested. 'Perhaps a lighter wallpaper. A few pretty pictures on the walls.' Throw open the windows, she thought, and let in some fresh air.

'Anything you like, my dear. Money no object. A vulgar phrase, I know, but true. We'll plan it together – but not a word just yet. The last thing Hester will expect is a child.'

Ten minutes later the little interview came to an end and Alice escaped to her own room. She threw herself on to the bed and pressed her face into the teddy bear. Thoroughly confused, she didn't know whether she was happy or sad but she did know there was no going back.

'Sebastian, I hate you!' she whispered into the teddy's fur. 'This is all your fault!'

But it wasn't entirely his fault – and Alice knew it.

Four

At six o'clock the staff assembled in the dining room, Alice among them. She had braced herself for some teasing and was determined to keep her temper but she need not have worried. It seemed Henry had also foreseen what might happen. Before grace was said he entered the room, his step springy, his expression one of cheerful anticipation. All eyes were turned his way for it was rare for the owner of the hotel to put in an appearance. Maggie kicked Alice under the table and rolled her eyes.

He said, 'I hope you'll forgive this intrusion. I won't keep you long from your meal but I believe you would like to be among the first to know my news. Alice Meredith has kindly agreed to become my wife and we hope you will all continue to support us as you have done in the past. Mrs Meredith will continue to work among you for another two weeks.'

He smiled at Alice who immediately found all eyes upon her as she half stood, gave a small embarrassed nod and sat down again.

Smiffy cried, 'Hear hear!' and began to clap his hands and one by one the others joined in.

Excited by his small success the bootboy then sang the first line of 'For He's A Jolly Good Fellow' but Mr Parkin said, 'That will do, Smith!' and gave him a look that spoke volumes.

Undeterred, Henry went on remorselessly. 'We shall marry at one o'clock on the thirtieth of July. Those of you who are free of your duties are welcome to attend the service but there will be a staff party for all of you in the evening.'

One of the men cheered and Maggie cried, 'Thank you, sir, and God bless you both!'

Mr Parkin rose to his feet. With barely a smile he said, 'On behalf of the entire staff I would like to offer congratulations to you both. We shall all, I know, continue to serve you and the Mere to the best of our capabilities.'

'Thank you, Mr Parkin.' With another smile Henry was gone, leaving Alice the focus of attention. For a moment the room was silent as they looked at Alice and each other in astonishment.

Someone whispered, 'So, it's true!'

Miss Maine said, 'Isn't this exciting!' She looked at Alice. 'How did it happen? When did you know?'

Smiffy cried, 'A party! A bloomin' *party!*'

There was a roar of laughter which eased the moment and allowed Alice to look up and smile shakily. A clamour broke out as everyone began talking at once.

'You sly old thing! You kept that quiet!'

'Marrying *him*? You'll be in clover, all right!'

'And you never said anything. Not a word!'

'What's been going on then?'

'Done all right for yourself, you have!'

Alice answered as best she could but inevitably the mood of shocked excitement gave way to a new wariness as it dawned on each of them that Alice would no longer be 'one of them' but 'the enemy'. Some fell silent, hoping that any adverse comments and disparaging references they had ever made in the past about their elderly employer might not be held against them. As their expressions changed Alice could bear it no longer. As soon as grace had been said she took her plate of bread and cheese, mumbled an excuse and left them to it. Returning to her room she sat on the bed and finished her food but it tasted like sawdust in her mouth. She washed it down with a glass of water and tried to stop the trembling which filled her body.

The teddy bear in its blue bow stared ahead from its button eyes and Alice wondered how Perdita was. She picked up the bear and hugged it, comforted by its familiar feel.

'Stop being ridiculous, Alice,' she whispered. 'You've got what you wanted. Now you must learn to deal with it. The good and the bad. Go and break the news to Edith.' It would never do for her friend to hear the news from one of the staff. Alice took a few deep breaths and hauled herself from the bed.

'Nobody said it would be easy!' She replaced the bear at the top of the bed and set off downstairs.

As she reached reception Mr Warner gave her a forced smile and said, 'Wonderful news, Mrs Meredith. I've just heard. I wish you all the best but we shall be sorry to lose you.'

'Thank you, Mr Warner. It's rather sudden and I'm still trying to get used to the idea.'

'We all are, Mrs Meredith.'

While Alice was wondering how she should interpret that remark, Miss Maine reappeared carrying her teacup. She set it down and reached under the reception desk.

'This letter came for you this morning, Mrs Meredith, but somehow it was put with the guests' letters. It was handed back to me an hour ago ... Did you know the little Lester girl was poorly?'

'No I didn't.' Alice took the letter and recognized her brother's handwriting. She would have to tell Eddie, of course, about her marriage, and Eddie would tell Sebastian. 'What's wrong with Perdita? Did Mr Lester call in the doctor?'

'Yes, he did. They think it's whooping cough and the doctor looked very grim and they've taken her into the hospital.'

'Good heavens!' Alice stared at her, the letter forgotten. 'That poor man. His mother is already in the hospital with a broken arm!'

Miss Maine said, 'My grandmother had whooping cough and nearly died but the old lady next door knew this old, old remedy. You find a woman whose married name is the same as her maiden name and she makes a currant cake. The sick person eats some of the cake and is cured but it has to be the same name, you see, or else—'

Mr Warner said, 'Did she survive? Your grandmother?'

'Yes, she did. I don't know how it works but—'

'Luck of the draw,' he said dismissively. 'Not everyone dies from it. Fifty fifty, probably.'

Alice said, 'Let's hope it's croup.'

Mr Warner laughed. 'Our neighbour swore by the breath of a piebald horse!' He laughed again. 'First catch your horse, I told her!

110

It's nonsense.'

Miss Maine said, 'Who cares as long as it works!'

Distracted by the bad news Alice ignored them. Should she go upstairs and read her brother's letter, go to the hospital for news of Perdita or visit Edith to tell her about the wedding? Before she could make up her mind, Miss Maine said, 'Mrs Brightling isn't back yet. It's not like her. She's missed lunch as well as tea and you know how she is.'

Alice nodded. Edith, as a permanent resident, paid for full board on a discounted rate but begrudged every penny of it. Determined to extract every scrap of value from the arrangement, she rarely missed a meal.

'I think she was meeting a friend,' she told them. 'But let me know if she also misses dinner.'

Alice thought about Mr Lester. It was possible that if he was on his way back to the Mere she might miss him if she went to the hospital. She decided to go upstairs and read her letter.

It was short and to the point.

Dear Alice,
All well with me hope your the same.
Good news. Yours truly is being made
up to Lance Corporal. My first stripe.

111

Probably my last to. Cant hardly believe it. Seb's wife is in the family way. Bit quick off the mark, I told him. Only joking. How's Chester? Remember me to the barmaid at the Pied Bull. Your loving brother Eddie.

Alice read the letter again but the words blurred on the page. She thrust it back into the envelope and pushed it under her pillow. '*Seb's wife is in the family way. Bit quick off the mark...*' So whose child would arrive first, she wondered. Nellie Callard's child or the one born to Mrs Henry Lightfoot? Closing her eyes, she tried to drive away the bitterness. Forget him. He's not worth it. *Not worth it!* What had Hester said? *The man's a cad. You've had a lucky escape.* It was the truth. Now she had a decent man. A man who was prepared to take her into his life and bring up another man's child. She tossed her head.

'And Eddie's got a stripe. He'll be thrilled.'

She would write to Eddie with congratulations and would tell him at length about her own approaching marriage to a very rich man – but not mentioning Henry's age! And not forgetting to assure Eddie at length that she was deliriously happy and – and *so* lucky that all the other girls envied her and just hinting that Sebastian had done her a favour by marrying Nellie!

She smiled. Eddie would be sure to tell Seb and Seb would realize what a terrible mistake he had made.

'Would he?' she whispered.

Would he care? She swallowed. Probably not. Alice imagined him holding his first child aloft and laughing. A proud father. She snatched up the bear and hugged it fiercely, the way she herself needed to be hugged at that moment. The way Sebastian had hugged her all those years ago when she was the brightest star in his sky.

Later that night Alice lay in bed longing for sleep but wide awake. It had been a long tiring day, full of surprises, and Alice's mind stubbornly returned to these. Mr Lester had returned from the hospital in the depths of despair. His daughter's croup had been diagnosed as whooping cough and was approaching the most difficult stage of the disease. Ironically, his mother's condition had improved slightly, for which he was hugely grateful. Her bruises were fading and her arm was less painful. Why had fate singled Mr Lester out for such trials and tribulations, she wondered, when the odious Dr Stewart behaved so badly yet seemed to live a charmed existence.

Which brought her to Edith Brightling who hadn't returned to the hotel by the time Alice had come up to bed. Which was ten thirty-five. So where was she? Mr Warner had talked about notifying the police but had decided against the idea because of the unfortunate publicity that might follow. Alice had decided against telling what she knew about Edith's letter in the hope that she would return to the hotel safe and sound. Now that she gave it more thought she began to doubt that she had made the right decision. Suppose something terrible had happened to Edith ... Tormented by doubts Alice lit her bedside candle and looked at the clock. Twenty past twelve. She reached for her dressing gown and put on her slippers. She would go down and speak to Mick Davies, the night porter. He would know whether or not Edith had returned.

Alice moved swiftly through the dimly lit corridors and down the stairs until she came in sight of reception. To her surprise Mick Davies was leaning across the desk in conversation with a woman whose appearance at once rang alarm bells in Alice's mind. The woman, who appeared to be in her twenties, was dressed in a flamboyant yellow and black dress which had seen better days and over this she wore a short fur-trimmed jacket. Beneath a straw hat adorned with feathers, her curls were an unnatural red. The woman and the night porter swung round at Alice's arrival and stared at her in dismay.

'Mrs Meredith!' Mick's thin face was a study.

Alice realized with a jolt that his expression could best be described as furtive. His tone, too, had held a certain deference that would not have been there had it not been for Alice's forthcoming marriage. Now, suddenly, she was a force to be reckoned with. The idea pleased her.

She said, 'Good evening. I came down to see if Mrs Brightling has returned.'

'Yes, Mrs Meredith.' He ran anxious fingers through dark wavy hair. 'But only just. She turned up about half an hour ago, bold as brass.'

'Well, that's a relief. Was she alone?'

'Yes she was, except that she arrived in a taxi. There could have been someone else...'

Alice, relieved, was nonetheless still curious. 'Did she appear indisposed in any way?'

'Not as I could see.'

While they had been talking the young woman had turned away and was pretending to leaf through one of the hotel's brochures. Alice thought quickly. If Miss Maine was 'walking out' with Mick Davies this woman could hardly be his ladyfriend. She said, 'And how can we help this young lady? Miss ... ?'

Mick said, 'Gaydon. Marie Gaydon. She

was just leaving.'

Marie Gaydon turned to face Alice. 'Yes. At least ... I ...' She turned helplessly to Mick Davies.

'*Mrs* Gaydon was just asking directions,' Mick said smoothly.

A little too smoothly, thought Alice, her suspicions growing.

Mick went on. 'She and her husband are looking for another hotel – Blossoms, wasn't it?' He looked meaningfully at the young woman, who quickly nodded. 'She got a bit lost.'

Alice glanced down in search of a wedding ring but the woman was wearing white lace gloves and the ring, if there was one, was not visible.

Mick said, 'Her husband's outside in the taxi.'

Marie Gaydon said, 'That's right. He is.'

Alice looked at her coldly, aware now that she was hearing nothing but lies. She said slowly, 'And your husband sent *you* in to ask for directions? Isn't that rather un-usual?'

After a short silence Mick said quickly, 'He's got a gammy leg.'

At that moment Alice noticed a small pile of shillings on the counter. At the same moment, Mick's hand slid over them.

'And the money?' She held out her hand. 'What is that for?'

Mick's confidence wavered. As he hesitated, with the money still clutched in his hand, a portly man appeared at the foot of the stairs. He wore a long bathrobe and his feet were bare. He looked the worse for drink and he clung grimly to the banisters as he stared blearily in their direction.

'Wha's your game, Davies?' he demanded. 'I've been waiting the bes' part of an hour! Did you get one or didn't you? Tha's all I want to know.' He let go of the banisters and took a few stumbling steps in their direction.

Alice looked at the three of them and suddenly saw the neat set-up. This portly man wanted a woman and Mick Davies was prepared to provide one for a fee. Surprised and deeply shocked she saw that Mick had once more laid the money on the counter and was pushing it towards the woman.

Mick made a last desperate effort. Ignoring the portly man, he turned to the woman. 'Well, Mrs Gaydon, I think you'll be able to find it now. The hotel. Blossoms.' With a jerk of his head he indicated the door.

'But ... I see. Yes.' She began to back away but then stopped and looked at the money.

Alice said, 'Is that money yours?'

She said, 'It's Mick's cut but I haven't—'

Mick groaned but the portly man had now reached the edge of the reception counter and was leaning heavily against it. He surveyed both women, blinked several times and turned to Mick. 'I didn' wan' two of 'em.'

Alice's jaw tightened. She said, 'Good, because you're not getting either of them. The Mere Hotel does not supply women. You'd best go back to bed.'

'Back to ... Whaddya mean?' He peered more closely at Alice. 'It always did. Why the hell...' He swayed and almost fell.

Alice was becoming hot and bothered. The situation was becoming more bizarre by the minute.

Mick glanced at the woman and said quietly, 'Hop it!'

'Not without some money!' She glared at him. 'If it's not on, then I want it back. I can't waste time here.' She glared at Alice. 'You're messing me about, the pair of you!'

Alice looked at Mick. 'Give her the money.' To the young woman she said, 'Take it and don't come back. If you ever show your face here again I'll call a constable.'

Marie Gaydon snatched up the shillings and slipped them into her pocket. She glanced at Alice and said, 'Miserable cow!' then disappeared through the front door and was swallowed up by the darkness.

Alice, her heart thumping, turned to Mick Davies. 'Help this gentleman back to his room, Mr Davies. And don't think you have got away with it. I shall report this to Mr

Warner in the morning.'

For a moment he regarded her insolently. 'I shan't be here in the morning, Mrs High-And-Mighty Meredith!' he told her. 'Nor any other time. I just quit. Got it?'

She looked at him furiously. 'But this gentleman—'

'Take him back yourself. I'm all done here.'

'If you leave now you won't be paid!'

He laughed in her face. 'Don't make me laugh! I've been paid handsomely over the last nine months – but not by the Mere!'

'We'll report this to the police!'

But she knew at once, and so did he, that they would do nothing of the sort. The resulting publicity would be bad for the hotel. Mick Davies would get off scot-free and there was nothing they could do about it.

Mick Davies picked up his jacket, lifted the desk flap and allowed it to crash down again. Strolling with studied nonchalance towards the door he opened it and followed Marie Gaydon outside. Fuming but helpless, Alice watched them go. Nine months! She closed her eyes in despair. She would have to speak to Mr Warner. Surely he knew nothing about the nightly deceptions.

Without warning, the portly man lurched towards her and clutched her arm.

'You're very pretty ... but where's the other one?'

Alice regarded him with loathing and silently cursed Mick Davies. Now they had no night porter and she would have to drag this pathetic man back to his room unaided. But to which room?

'Your room number,' she said, trying unsuccessfully to prise her arm from his podgy fingers. 'Do you know it? Can you remember?'

By way of an answer, he released her arm, staggered unsteadily to the nearest armchair and collapsed into it. She found the signing-in book and carried it over to him. 'What's your name?'

'My name? My *name* ... Stanley. Tha's it. Stanley.'

'Stanley what?' She ran her finger down the list of names. 'Stanley Winchester?'

He shook his head.

When had he arrived, she wondered. She studied the previous day's entries and the day before that. 'Stanley Cootes?'

He brightened. 'Cootes! Tha's me.'

She closed the book and returned it to the desk. 'Room fifty-one.' She stood over him with her hands on her hips. 'Up you get, Mr Cootes. It's bedtime. No young women – just sleep for you.' She held out her hands and, grumbling, he grasped them and, with a huge effort on both sides, he was soon on his feet. Unsteadily they made their way towards the stairs and one by one they mounted them. But by the time they reached the fifth, Mr Cootes could go no further and sat down.

'The lift!' Alice exclaimed. 'Why on earth didn't I think of that?'

Ten minutes later they were standing outside his room. The door was unlocked and Alice pushed him inside. 'Get yourself into bed and go to sleep,' she admonished.

Would he recall anything of this encounter in the morning, Alice wondered as she closed the door and hesitated outside. There was no night porter and she was indirectly responsible for that. So should she take his place? It meant staying awake for the rest of the night.

'No!' she muttered. 'I need my sleep. No one is going to criticize me because I'm the new soon-to-be Mrs Lightfoot!' She laughed aloud, trying to get used to her changed status.

She locked the front door and went back to her room. Once back in bed her anger subsided until she could reflect with amusement on the little drama at reception. So Mick Davies had been earning himself a small fortune by allowing street women into the hotel for the pleasure of some of the guests. She would certainly report the matter to Mr Warner, because he would have to find a new night porter. He might not want it to go any higher, though, for it would cast a doubt over his own control of the staff under him and he wouldn't wish that. She would have to assure him that she would say nothing of the matter to Henry. Her loyalties were certainly decided on this but what Henry didn't know wouldn't hurt him and they would see that nothing similar happened in the future. They could warn the other hotels not to employ him but that involved admitting that the Mere had been duped for months. We'll take it no further, she decided with a yawn. Put it down to experience. Sleepily she turned over and, with a faint smile on her face, was soon fast asleep.

Next morning Alice forced herself to rise a little earlier than usual and made her report to Mr Warner. To her astonishment he showed less surprise than she had expected.

'Night porters!' he tutted irritably, smoothing his moustache with a touch of irritation. 'They're a race apart. Always up to something. But I know a young lad who might take his place. Came in a few weeks ago in search of work. I'll send the bootboy round with a note asking him to come in and see me.'

He looked a little sheepish, Alice thought. Had Mr Warner been a night porter at some time in the past, before he came to the Mere? Was it common practice and had anyone else been aware of what was going on? Perhaps she was the *last* person to know instead of the first. The possibility annoyed her.

She hurried up the stairs and was soon knocking on the door of Edith's room. A sleepy voice called, 'Come in if you must!'

'I must!' said Alice with a smile. Closing the door behind her she leaned back against it. Edith was lying on the bed fully clothed except for her shoes. Her eye make-up had smudged and her hair was dishevelled. Alice, sharply reminded of her own last encounter with Sebastian, felt her hopes for Edith fading.

'I heard!' Edith told her, before Alice could speak again. She struggled into a sitting position. 'Mick Davies told me when I got back. You're going to marry old Light-foot. You sly creature! Never a word to me, your oldest friend. I—'

'And *I* heard —' Alice interrupted her — 'that you didn't come home until after midnight! Naughty stop-out!'

Edith brushed back a stray curl and smiled enigmatically. 'I had better things to do.' She raised her eyebrows.

'Such as — or shouldn't I ask?'

'You shouldn't. Not unless you want to be shocked. You may see me as an elderly over-the-hill actress but there are others who—'

'Let me guess. You were with Dr Stewart.'

'Was I?' The smile deepened. Edith smoothed back her hair with an affected gesture. 'You didn't confide in me about Mr Lightfoot so I don't think I shall tell you anything.'

Alice felt a great wash of pity for her. There was no way she could allow Edith to remain in ignorance about Stewart's true character. 'What does he look like without his moustache?' she asked, her voice unintentionally harsh.

Edith's eyes widened. 'How did you know that?'

'The police have a new description of him. He was seen in Chester.'

Just how devious could the man be, Alice wondered.

Edith said, 'Was he ... with anybody?'

'Not that I know of – unless he was with you.'

Edith tossed her head. 'I shan't deny it. He's very much in love with me. I told you as much days ago but I don't think you believed me.'

'I hope he behaved as a true gentleman.' I hope he was more of a gentleman than Sebastian, Alice thought ruefully.

Edith smiled. 'A gentleman in love can be forgiven much!' She gave a fake yawn and patted her mouth delicately.

How wonderful it would be to shake her, thought Alice. 'So he's in love with you, is he?'

'Is old Lightfoot in love with you?'

'Don't keep calling him old Lightfoot!'

'But he is old, Alice! Twice your age. Maybe three times. Who knows?' She abandoned her pose and slouched back against the pillows. 'Why on earth did you say yes to him? He's old, old, *old*! You're not going to tell me you love the man.'

'At least he's not a crook.'

'Bertie is *not* a crook. It was all a misunderstanding.'

'So he's coming back to settle his bill, is he?'

Momentarily disconcerted by the question, Edith glanced away then busied herself with a glass of water from the decanter on the bedside table. She sipped it. 'Not exactly, but I'm settling it for him. A loan, that's all. He has to speak to his bank manager.'

'Oh Edith!' Alice moved to sit down uninvited on a nearby chair. She regarded her friend with growing dismay. 'The police have been here again. He's committed other offences. He's been to prison, Edith.'

'I don't believe it! And even if it is true … we all make mistakes. You shouldn't listen to lies, Alice. You know how the police are. They need to solve a crime so they pick on an innocent man. It's a spiteful attempt to blacken his name.' She swung her legs down and stood up, stiff with annoyance, and fussed with her clothes. 'If you can't speak well of him, Alice ... If you won't give him the benefit of the doubt, then we've nothing more to say to each other.'

'I only want to save you from disappointment.'

'I don't need saving, thank you. I'm not a fallen woman.'

Not yet, thought Alice. *I'm* the fallen woman but I've been saved. Who will save Edith? 'I didn't mean to offend you.'

Edith moved to the long oval mirror and took the pins from her hair. Reaching for a brush, she began to pull it gently through her hair. 'He loves my hair,' she said. 'He loves my eyes. He loves everything about me. Can you say that about old – about Mr Lightfoot?'

No, Alice confessed silently. Henry appeared to find her attractive but he was hardly besotted. But then neither was Bertie Stewart. He was obviously trying to wheedle money out of poor Edith – and succeeding.

Edith turned to her. 'I'm going to see him again, Alice. I don't care what you think. I never thought I'd ever find another man I could love.'

Her voice broke – or was she acting? Was

this the role of the devoted woman or was her emotion genuine? Alice couldn't be sure but either way lay heartache. 'As long as you don't live to regret it.' She regarded her friend anxiously.

'I might say the same to you about your beloved!' Edith gave her a sharp look. You could rue the day you said yes if a younger man comes along and you're running around after a sick old man...'

'Henry is perfectly healthy.'

'Now he is. Give it a few more years and who knows. At least Bertie is still young and fit. Face it, Alice, Henry Lightfoot is too old for you!'

'And Dr Stewart is too bad for you! He's a scoundrel!'

A knock on the door interrupted this dangerous exchange and Alice was grateful for the interruption. The last thing she wanted to do was alienate Edith. Maggie put her head round the door. 'Mr Warner's looking for you,' she told Alice. 'It's Mr Lester's daughter. She's critical!'

'Oh no!' cried Alice.

Edith's eyes widened. 'Not that dear little mite!'

'I must talk to him.' Alice turned from Edith as this new crisis took priority. 'He's at the hospital, I suppose.'

With a hurried farewell to Edith, Alice rushed from the room and made her way downstairs to reception.

Mr Warner said, 'He sent a message from the hospital. Says Perdita's asking for you. I think he's hoping you'll join him at the hospital before visiting time ends.'

'Oh dear! May I go?'

'I think you must.' He gave her an odd look.

'What is it?' she asked.

'Well, I'm not likely to refuse you anything now, am I?' Smiling, he handed her a florin. 'Take this. I've sent for a taxi. It sounded urgent.'

Alice hid her embarrassment as well as she could, realizing fully for the first time how awkward the next few weeks would be for the rest of the staff. Knowing she was going to marry their employer, they would be careful how they treated her and more respectful when they spoke to her. It wouldn't be easy for her, either. The simple camaraderie had gone for good. No matter how much an individual might like her, they would be wary now that she had Mr Lightfoot's ear. She sighed. Pausing only to fetch a shawl, she hurried outside to the waiting cab and was whisked through the streets to the City Hospital.

Five

Alice's robust constitution meant that she had never been a patient in the hospital and for that she was thankful. The City Hospital was a largc, sombre building that had once been Chester's workhouse, an institution dreaded by all as a final home for those too poor to keep any other roof over their heads. In appearance it was a forbidding building and inside, despite the alterations, the glazed brick walls robbed it of any feeling of homeliness. Alice had vague memories of visiting her grandmother here many years ago and the mingled smell of sickness and disinfectant was immediately recognizable. Alice felt a small shudder as she entered the gloomy hallway.

'I'm looking for Mr Lester,' she told the woman at the desk. 'Perdita Lester was admitted with whooping cough yesterday.'

The woman riffled through a sheaf of forms. 'Up the stairs, turn left.' She pointed briefly.

Dodging an elderly man being pushed along in a bath chair, Alice followed her directions, her depression deepening. A small queue of dejected people waited at a hatchway, each clutching a small page torn from a doctor's pad. Feet clattered on the floor and echoed around the high ceiling, drowning out the few whispered conversations. She hurried up the bare stairway, passing a middle-aged man with his head heavily bandaged. His white face suggested that he might faint at any moment and Alice moved quickly to her right so that he need not release the handrail to pass her.

The children's ward contained twenty beds, ranged either side of the room, but not all the beds were occupied. Some were screened from view by floral curtains on a rail. In other beds the young patients mostly chatted to their visitors but a few remained prostrate and silent, watched over by an anxious parent.

'Mrs Meredith!'

She saw Mr Lester peering from behind one of the curtains. He rose to his feet, pulled back the curtain and beckoned to her. Alice made her way quickly towards them. On the bed to Perdita's right a boy of about ten watched her with interest and then whispered something to an elderly woman Alice took to be his grandmother. Beyond him, a small girl with a scarred face and tufty red hair sat alone, engrossed with a musical box which played a scratchy rendering of 'Oranges and Lemons'.

Alice was soon inside the small curtained world of the invalid. Perdita lay in the bed, her face red with the exertion of coughing. Her eyes were almost glazed with exhaustion. A nurse on the far side of the bed was trying to spoon some medicine into her mouth.

'Thank you for coming, Mrs Meredith.' Mr Lester took her hand and pressed it warmly. 'I'm sorry to bother you but Perdita keeps asking for you. She's very ill.'

The nurse turned to them and something in her expression chilled Alice. It was a deep compassion.

Alice asked, 'Will it tire her to talk?'

'It won't make any difference, bless her. She can listen.'

Mr Lester sat down heavily and covered his eyes with his hand, too choked to speak. Alice smiled at the little girl, who opened her mouth to speak but was overtaken by a burst of coughing which ended in the familiar whooping sound – a long inhalation as she desperately tried to draw air into her congested lungs. Finally she closed her eyes, panting with the effort and Alice knew that the strain on her small heart must be enormous.

The nurse left them and Alice leaned forward. 'Hello, Perdita. I'm sorry you're not well. I see you've brought Moppet with

131

you.' She smiled.

'Moppet's ... not ... well.' Perdita managed the whispered words with difficulty.

'I'm sure she'll be better soon.'

At that moment the small red-haired girl appeared between the curtains and examined Alice with interest. Mr Lester said quickly, 'I don't think you should be in here, dear.'

'I can!' She tossed her head. She looked at Perdita who smiled faintly. Then she asked, 'Are you going to die?'

Mr Lester drew in a sharp, agonized breath.

Alice cried, 'Of course not! What a thing to say!'

Smiling at Perdita, the girl held out the musical box. 'You can have a go,' she told her. 'Just turn the key.'

Perdita held the toy but made no effort to wind it up. The child turned to the adults. 'I fell in the fire. Ma was asleep and she didn't know and then I screamed and screamed until she woke up and threw some water over me. My hair was burned but now it's growing again. My name's Mary Monohan and I live at number thirty-two.'

Her matter-of-fact tone startled Alice and she exchanged a bemused glance with Mr Lester who was recovering from the shock of her question.

Alice said, 'You'd better go back to your

own bed, Mary.'

As though she hadn't spoken, Mary turned towards Perdita who was now struggling to turn the key of the music box. 'I'll do it for you.'

Perdita relinquished it. 'I'm ... nearly ... seven,' she whispered. 'Had ... a party!' She smiled at the memory.

The girl said, 'I'm nearly eight!'

The little tune began again and at once a nurse popped her head round the curtains. 'Oh there you are! How many times do I have to tell you not to bother people. Back to bed now.' She took hold of the girl's arm as Perdita began another bout of coughing. Her father raised her up to a sitting position and held her until the nurse came back. Alice watched helplessly as the attack intensified, Perdita struggled desperately for breath and the nurse stabbed repeatedly at a bell on the wall which brought the ward sister at a run. On the coverlet the abandoned musical box played on. As it finally fell silent, Perdita's whoop also came to an abrupt end and she fell back against her father's chest. Her eyes rolled in her head and her breathing seemed to have stopped.

The ward sister cried, 'Please! Outside the curtains! We'll do what we can!'

Mr Lester rose unsteadily to his feet and Alice took hold of his arm.

'No!' he cried. 'I can't leave her!' He

133

looked at Alice with horror in his eyes.

'We must let them do whatever they can do. For her sake.'

Unwillingly he allowed himself to be led outside the curtains and there they waited. A white-coated doctor rushed through the ward and in through the curtains and a muffled consultation took place. Mr Lester stared out of the window, his face ashen, his body trembling.

Mr Lester staggered and almost fell and Alice grabbed his arm to steady him. 'She's dying!' he cried. 'I know she is! Oh God!'

'She won't die,' Alice insisted, guiding him on to a chair which another visitor brought for him.

Arthur Lester collapsed on to it, his head in his hands. Suddenly he turned to Alice. 'The birthday party!' he stammered. 'This is why she wanted it so early. She knew she wouldn't be here to...' He clutched her hands. 'But how did she know?'

Alice said, 'Don't think like that. We don't know yet ... They're doing everything they can.'

He was shaking his head. 'Perdita's dying. I'm losing her – and somehow she knew. She *knew!*'

The doctor joined them then and the moment Alice saw his face she was forced to accept the terrible truth. There was defeat in his eyes and regret in the downward tilt of his head.

'Mr Lester, I'm so sorry. We did every-thing humanly possible but the little heart...'

'I'm sure you did.' Mr Lester looked dazed. 'May I sit with her now? I want to hold her for as long as I can.'

'Of course.'

The nurses came out one by one and added their commiserations.

Alice hesitated, unsure whether to stay or go. Did he need her? As if in answer, he turned. 'Will you come with me – just for a few moments.'

Alice nodded. 'I'd like to say goodbye.'

The sister straightened up as they entered. The nurses had tidied the bed and smooth-ed the pillow. Perdita lay peacefully, her arm round the rag doll.

'I'm so sorry,' said the sister, her eyes full of tears. Struggling with her own grief she laid a hand gently on Mr Lester's arm. 'She was a beautiful child. You will have some wonderful memories of her.'

He leaned over to kiss his daughter's face, then sat down beside her to hold her hand. Alice moved to the other side of the bed and kissed the little arm that held the doll.

The sister had slipped away, leaving them together.

Alice watched the tears slide down the bereft father's face. 'She's at peace now,' she said and then she, too, was weeping.

Speechlessly, Mr Lester glanced up at her and held out his hand. She moved round the bed to stand beside him. Not knowing how to comfort him, Alice put an arm round his trembling shoulders and together they watched Perdita, fixing her sweet face in their memories while there was still time.

Alice made her way back to the hotel on foot, her thoughts sombre. Poor Mr Lester. His wife already dead, he had now lost his daughter. Only his elderly mother remained. What on earth would he do, Alice wondered. Move nearer to his mother, perhaps – presumably that would depend on his work. She had no idea what he did for a living. He might be unable to change location.

'I'm back, Mr Warner,' she announced five minutes later as she hurried into reception.

He looked at her face. 'How's the little girl? Not...'

'Yes. Perdita died.' Fresh tears sprang into Alice's eyes but she brushed them away. 'Her father is still at the hospital. He has to break the bad news to his mother, who's in another ward, and there are all the other arrangements to be made for the funeral.'

'He's having her buried in Chester?'

Miss Maine came down the stairs and caught sight of Alice's face.

She said, 'Oh no! Don't say the poor little mite...'

'I'm afraid so.' Alice swallowed hard. 'Mr Lester will be back later. Warn the rest of the staff, please, so that they don't all ask him about his daughter.' She turned back to the manager. 'Perhaps he will move to Chester if he can, to keep an eye on his mother.'

'So we'll lose one of our regulars.'

'I suppose he wants Perdita's grave to be nearby.' She glanced at the hall clock. Nearly eleven. Guilt filled her for the time she had been absent from her job but there had been no way she could let Mr Lester down at such a time. She tried to imagine him breaking the sad news to his mother and wished she could have done more to help him.

Miss Maine said, 'I think he's some kind of writer. Mr Lester, I mean. Books on military history. That sort of thing. He talked about it one day last summer. Showed me his latest book.'

Maggie appeared from the stairway trailing a mop and some cleaning cloths. 'Room fifty-one. Can't get in. His do-not-disturb notice is still on the handle.'

Alice sighed. 'Mr Stanley Cootes. Probably sleeping off all the drink he had last night. Give him another hour...'

'But I've finished up there!' Maggie looked aggrieved.

'Well, you'll have to start again, won't you? Bang on the door. If he doesn't answer get the pass key and let yourself in.'

'Ah, Mrs Meredith! You're back!' They all turned to see Hester Lightfoot.

Before anyone could inform her of the tragedy she went on. 'Please come up to my room, Mrs Meredith. I need to speak with you. I'm sure Mr Warner can spare you for ten minutes.'

As she walked away in the direction of the lift Maggie giggled. 'Summons from on high!'

Mr Warner rolled his eyes. 'Go on then – but remember, the auditors will be here at twelve thirty and they will expect to see you.'

Alice frowned. 'They never come on Saturdays.'

'They do this week. Mr Hamlin's been off sick and is trying to catch up. There's not likely to be a discrepancy, is there?'

'Not to my knowledge.'

The books for kitchen expenses were checked every month by Hamlin & Sons. Costings were done each week, anticipating the sums required for the chosen menus. The once-monthly check by Hamlin's was intended to keep the kitchen staff aware of the need for careful management. If there was ever a suspicion that anyone was creaming off money, the auditors would be called in for an extra scrutiny of the books. Fortunately it rarely happened.

Now Alice frowned. The day was running away with her. And now she had to see Hester.

'I'll be down by twelve thirty,' she promised the manager and almost ran up the stairs before anyone could present her with another problem.

Hester was waiting with a bolt of heavy cream lace and a book of paper patterns. 'I didn't think you would have time to think about your gown,' she told Alice, her eyes sparkling with excitement. 'I hope you don't mind but I've decided that this will be my wedding gift to you. My own dressmaker, Delia Pagett, will run it up for you as soon as you have chosen the design.'

Hester was right, thought Alice guiltily. She had given no thought at all to what she would wear. 'It's most kind of you, Miss – I mean Hester, but I really don't feel like—'

'I want you to look truly wonderful. I'm looking forward to seeing Henry's face when you walk down the aisle. Now come and sit with me for a few minutes and choose the pattern. I thought cream lace because then you can wear it afterwards for the theatre or, if you keep it simple, a dinner engagement.'

Dutifully, Alice moved to sit beside her on the long sofa.

'And tomorrow, Alice, we will all three attend the service to hear the first banns called.' Hester opened the book and laid it on the small table so that they could both see it. At last, seeing Alice's lack of enthusiasm, she asked, 'Something has happened. What is it?'

'Mr Lester's daughter died this morning.'

'Oh my dear! That sweet child!' Hester's sorrow was genuine. 'We must send a wreath to the funeral.' She sighed. 'How is he taking it?'

'He's broken-hearted, as you'd expect.' Alice tried unsuccessfully to hide her impatience.

Hester tutted. 'But isn't that God all over! One child dies and another is on the way. I keep seeing these patterns in life and I wonder how anyone can fail to see the hand of the Almighty at work in this world of ours. I hope you are a believer, Alice.'

Was she a believer? Alice wasn't sure but she said, 'I am, yes,' because it was the simplest answer. But in her heart she failed to see how her own coming child could compensate Arthur Lester for the loss of Perdita. This was not the time, however, for a religious discussion. She must pick one of the designs as quickly as possible so that she could go back downstairs and get on with her work.

Hester smoothed the lace admiringly and

then turned to the pattern book. 'If you see one you like but it needs a few changes, my little woman can easily do it. She's an absolute wonder. Now let's see...'

The pages turned but Alice found it hard to concentrate. Instead of the designs, all she could see was Perdita's face and her shocked father clinging desperately to her hand.

'Now this is rather pretty but possibly a little young for a woman of your age, wouldn't you say ... Or this one ... Ah! Now, I can see you in this – the neat neckline would flatter you...' She looked hopefully at Alice, waiting for some sign of enjoyment, willing her to share the excitement. With a sigh she went on through the book. 'Definitely not that one! The low neckline is quite unsuitable for a wedding. Not decorous at all...'

Alice made an effort. This dress was going to be Hester's wedding gift and Alice felt required to show more pleasure in the decision-making. The various sketches were beginning to blur when at last they came to one she liked. Straight, with a high collar and bishop sleeves. As she pointed to it, Hester beamed.

'Alice! You have chosen my own favourite! Isn't that extraordinary. I studied them all earlier and I knew I preferred that one but I was determined not to influence you. This one it shall be – and not a word to Henry. Bad luck to see the gown before the day.' Happily she marked the page and closed the book. 'I haven't had a chance to tell you, Alice, how thrilled Henry is about everything. He looks years younger and is half in love with you already. What did I tell you?' Before Alice could answer she went on, 'I've told him to take you out somewhere – for a stroll along the Groves, perhaps – so that you can get to know each other away from the Mere – and to be seen together. It's not natural for a couple on the verge of marriage to see so little of each other. Or you could go for a gentle walk along the city walls – the exercise will do Henry good. Of course, he used to be a useful rower and often took Marion on the river but I think that's possibly beyond him now.'

At last she had run out of breath. Alice said, 'I really have to keep up with my work, Hester.'

'Of course, dear, but I must just tell you. When Henry broke the news to me – about *his* proposal to *you* – I pretended to be a little cross. Being kept in the dark, you see. He told me he had been fond of you for some months but had only recently "sounded you out", as he put it.' She laughed. 'He said you were agreeably surprised and said yes almost immediately. He didn't mention the child, of course. It's given him a new lease of life, Alice! It's a long time since I've seen him so animated. He's such a—'

Alice broke in. 'I'm sorry but I promised Mr Warner...'

'Ah! That's another thing. I've seen to that, Alice. Your job has been advertized and we shall interview some of the applicants next week so that you will have a chance to train whoever we choose as your replacement. I shall expect you to join me at the interviews. You know better than I do what the position entails.' A bright smile lit up her face. 'Poor Alice. You look so nervous but don't worry. Everything will sort itself out and I shall see that nothing goes wrong. You and Henry will be good for each other, you'll see.'

As the clocks struck seven that evening, Alice found herself strolling self-consciously along the Groves with her arm through that of Henry Lightfoot. The Dee was busy with river traffic of all kinds from rowing boats to pleasure steamers and the air was shrill with the cries of holidaymakers enjoying themselves. Children ran and skipped, ignoring the shouts of their watchful parents who, dressed in their starched best, meandered along the river bank, intent on seeing and being seen. A man with a stall sold toffee apples and a swarthy gipsy woman in a bright skirt and shawl wandered among the people, offering sprigs of lucky lavender.

Alice had worn her best blue dress and a straw hat and Henry was resplendent in a darkly striped blazer and a pale trilby. Alice tried to look at ease but she felt she couldn't resist the feeling that she was playing a part. Beside Henry, she felt her clothes looked shabby and her best buttoned boots felt cheap – which they were. How, she wondered, would she ever look the part of Mr Lightfoot's wife? Was he going to make her an allowance for clothes? She also wondered whether Hester's generous gift was in fact a way of ensuring that Henry's wife was suitably dressed for the occasion of the wedding.

'So is your mother coming to the wedding, Alice?' Henry asked.

'I don't know, sir – Mr – Henry.' She looked up in confusion to see him smiling down at her.

'Dear Alice, it will take time,' he said. 'Don't let it worry you. I want you to be happy. I want you to be the happiest woman in the world!'

Alice squeezed his arm. 'You're very good to me.'

'Not at all. *You* are very good to me. You accepted my proposal!' He gave her a large wink.

He really is quite nice, she thought with

relief. Suppose he *had* proposed to her. Would she have accepted? She wanted to say yes to that but she was unsure how she would have felt about him if she had not been nudged into it by circumstances.

They paused to watch the passengers disembark from one of the steamboats and Henry glanced at her.

'Shall *we* do that one day, dearest? Go up river on the steamboat?'

He said 'dearest' in the most natural way and Alice envied him. She didn't think she would ever be able to utter an endearment without feeling a complete fraud. Strange, she reflected, how quickly he had stepped into his role, while she still found hers difficult. She must try harder. It was only fair.

He said, 'Would you like a pearl necklace, Alice – as my wedding gift to you. A choker, perhaps?'

She stared at him aghast. A wedding present. Did that mean she should buy one for Henry – and if so, how?

'What's the matter? Don't you like pearls?'

'No ... I mean yes, but no, it's not that. I mean...' She looked at him desperately. 'I have almost no money. Just a few pounds saved up against a rainy day.'

'Ah! Is that all? For a moment I was worried.' He smiled. 'The other matter I wanted to talk to you about was your allowance. Starting from Monday I shall pay a regular sum into your account and—'

'I don't have an account.'

'Oh but you do. I have opened one for you at my bank. From Monday onwards you will have a regular sum to call your own. Does that solve your problem?'

Relieved, Alice stammered her thanks and they walked on in silence.

'I think, Alice, that we are doing rather well in this little game of ours. I'm not a gambling man by nature but I think this particular gamble will pay off. I do believe time will prove us the winners.'

'I do hope so.' Alice relished the word 'game'. It helped to think of it in those terms. If it was a game they played, the two of them against the world, it could be fun.

'But now we must make our way back,' he told her. I mustn't tire you in your delicate condition but it is so pleasant to walk again with a pretty woman on my arm. Quite a tonic for an old fogey like me!'

Alice put a finger to her lips. 'Ssh! That's a secret for the time being.'

'What is? Me being an old fogey?'

'No! The delicate condition.'

He chuckled. 'I can't wait to tell everyone! To see their faces.'

As they retraced their steps Alice was aware that her feelings towards Henry were slowly changing. He might be a great deal older than she was but excitement suited him. She was aware of the change that was taking place. Hester was right. As they turned for home, his eyes shone, his voice was eager and there was a new spring in his step.

As soon as they returned to the hotel they went their separate ways. After changing into her everyday clothes, Alice went to reception to find the manager talking with a youngish man with very pale hair and a thin face. He looks about seventeen, thought Alice, or is it that I am so much older.

'Mrs Meredith, this is Dennis Slate,' the manager informed her. 'He's applying for the job of night porter. His references seem satisfactory but I wanted you to speak with him before we decide. I take it the audit was acceptable.'

'It was, yes. There was a slight overspend but, as Chef reminded me, the family that were expected last Saturday for the wedding breakfast had to cancel because the groom was injured and was taken to the City Hospital.'

'Kicked by a horse. I remember now. He was a jockey, wasn't he?'

Alice nodded. 'Chef managed to use up some of the food by changing the Sunday menus but inevitably some was wasted. Nobody's fault but we are charging them twenty-five per cent of the agreed price.'

Mr Warner nodded and left them and

Alice led Dennis Slate into the office.

Her first question was, 'How old are you, Mr Slate? You look a little young for the job.'

'Twenty, ma'am, last April. I could grow a moustache if that would help. I grown one once but me ma didn't like it.'

'That might help. An air of authority would be helpful. Where else have you been employed?'

'The Grosvenor, ma'am, as a bootboy, but, like Ma says, I'm ambitious. So then I got made up to lift boy. Nice uniform. I done that for two years till I got ill with me chest and got sent down Bognor to a sanny for two and a half years and then—'

'A sanitorium? Was it consumption?' Her tone sharpened.

'Yeah, but I'm cured.'

' "Yes" not "Yeah".'

'What?'

'Try to remember to say "Yes" instead of "Yeah". Our guests will appreciate it.'

'Right.' He looked baffled.

'You have a doctor's certificate, Mr Slate? A clean bill of health?'

'I gave it to Mr Warner.'

'Hmm. What does your father do?'

'He's a driver on the trams. Done that all his life. He missed the horses when they switched to electric trams but he got the hang of it. Never had a day off sick. He's proud of that, is Pa.' He looked at her

148

earnestly. 'I could do the job, ma'am. Night porter, that is, not trams. I'm a hard worker. I've got a young woman and we want to get hitched, like!' When he grinned he looked even younger.

Alice sighed. 'Did Mr Warner mention a probationary period of six weeks?'

'He did, ma'am.'

'Well, we'll see how you get on. Wait here for Mr Warner.' She turned to go and then turned back. 'Do you know him?'

'Yes ma'am. His sister's married to my uncle. In the family, like.'

'So did he tell you why the last man was sacked?'

'Yes ma'am.' He frowned. 'Unbecoming behaviour. That's what he said but he never said what, like.'

'*Very* unbecoming behaviour! Just bear that in mind, Mr Slate. This hotel has a good reputation and we intend to keep it. We shall be watching you.'

Twenty, she thought, as she went upstairs. If only she could turn the clock back eight years and know what she now knew. 'But I can't,' she muttered. 'None of us can. You make your bed and you lie on it.' She wondered briefly what Mick Davies was doing. Probably found himself another job. Maybe a better one. Some people always landed on their feet.

She knocked on Mr Lester's door but

149

there was no answer. Presumably he was busy with the various arrangements that a funeral demanded. She then went to Edith's room and had better luck.

Edith called out, 'Come in!' and glanced up.

Alice saw with some alarm that she was packing.

'Oh it's you, Alice.' Edith's tone was cool. 'You're just in time.' She folded a blouse and laid it in the carpet bag which lay open on the bed. 'I just need a few things. A hold-all is sufficient. And before you ask, I've settled Dr Stewart's bill and I want to hear nothing more on the subject.' She reached for a pair of slippers, wrapped them in a sheet of newspaper and tucked them in beside the blouse.

Alice ventured into the room. 'You're not leaving the Mere, are you? Oh Edith! You can't mean to—'

'It's none of your business what I do or where I go or with whom I go.' Edith tossed her head. 'But since you are a friend I'll set your mind at ease. I am not leaving the Mere. At least, not permanently. Dr Stewart and I are going to spend a few days in Paris. We shall take the train down to London and another to Folkestone and will catch the steam packet to Boulogne.'

'Paris?' Alice's mind was immediately filled with disastrous visions of Edith's past life. 'How can you bear to go back there? That's where Gordon died.'

'Of course it is. You don't need to remind me. I know Paris very well but Bertie's never been. I shall be able to show him the city. A second chance for me.' She paused to smile dreamily for Alice's benefit. 'We shall do all the usual things – the Eiffel Tower, the Louvre, go to the theatre.' She lowered her voice. 'Bertie has a fancy to visit the Folies Bergère!' She gave a trilling laugh that set Alice's teeth on edge. 'Oh Alice! Don't look so priggish! It's not exactly a den of vice. And don't worry. I shan't forget you. I'll bring you back some French perfume! How would you like that?'

'But I thought Dr Stewart was having a problem with his bank.'

'That's only temporary. I'm paying and he'll reimburse me later on. I trust him, Alice. He's been much maligned. All he needs is a good woman and now he's found one.' She picked up a nightdress and began to roll it up. 'He says I'm "an influence for good"! Isn't that sweet?'

This, thought Alice, will be the ruin of her. The bogus doctor would take all her money and then abandon her. But Edith would never be convinced. So what could be done to save her? 'Have you thought carefully about this, Edith?' she asked, still searching for a way to delay Edith's adventure. 'On my honour, I am only asking you to consider for—'

'Don't, Alice!' Edith closed the hold-all and looked up. The bright expression had gone. In its place Alice saw desperation. 'Don't ask me to consider anything. I've thought long and hard and this is what I want,' she said. 'What else have I to look forward to? Do I want to eke out the rest of my days at the Mere, counting every penny? No offence meant but it's hardly the centre of the enlightened world! And if it was I couldn't afford to do more than exist. I can't even afford to have a breakfast tray brought up to my room! I really can't sink much lower.'

'That's nonsense!' Alice protested. 'Thousands of women would envy you your security. A guaranteed roof over your head, three meals a day, friends who—'

'I get the picture, thank you, Alice. Fine for you to talk, with your rich husband-to-be! I live on my memories and some of those are bleak enough, believe you me!'

Alice swallowed, unable to answer. For once Edith was not acting. Her voice held the painful ring of truth. I could notify the police, thought Alice. Anonymously. Stewart could be stopped at Folkestone harbour. He would be arrested and Edith would still have most of her money intact. It was a tempting idea but it might go terribly wrong. Edith might guess who had alerted them and, if so, she would never forgive Alice.

But was she entitled to interfere with Edith's life? Perhaps this was Edith's way of changing her life ... Suppose by some miracle it turned out well. Could Dr Stewart change his ways? It seemed unlikely but if he could put the past behind him ... Edith was taking a risk but so was Alice by marrying Henry. Marrying Henry Lightfoot was a way out of her predicament. How would she react if Edith tried to stop her?

'As long as you're certain, Edith.'

'It's too late now to change my mind.' Edith averted her gaze and gave a quick glance around the little room that had been her home for so many years. 'Wish me luck, Alice.'

'Good luck. Take care of yourself.' She stepped forward and put her arms round Edith in a quick hug. 'You can tell me all about it when you come back.'

'If I do!' Edith rolled her eyes. She was acting out her fantasy again, her eyes bright, her expression arch. 'It depends on Bertie's investments. They are set to mature any day now. We might move on to Switzerland for a week or two. Don't worry if I'm away longer than you expect.'

Alice immediately began to worry afresh. Was this Dr Stewart talking? Covering his tracks, perhaps.

She said, 'But you are coming back?'

'Of course I am. I'm keeping on my room.'

'Did you know about Perdita? She died earlier today. I thought you might like to wait until after the funeral.' Even as she uttered the words, Alice knew in her heart that nothing was going to deter Edith.

'No! The poor child. That poor father!' For a moment or two Edith was distracted from her preparations. 'But I hate funerals.' She thrust a clean handkerchief into her pocket and picked up the hold-all. 'I shall wait downstairs for the taxi,' she told Alice.

Alice went downstairs with her and was grateful that the taxi arrived promptly. As Alice waved her friend off she felt a growing unease but tried to banish the feeling that she should have tried harder to prevent her departure.

'Forget it. It's her life!' she reminded herself. 'I have enough problems of my own.'

The church of St John the Baptist, in Vicars Lane, was filling up rapidly as Hester, Henry and Alice joined the stream of people hurrying inside. Alice was comforted to see that her own best clothes were no worse than many of the other women in the congregation. On the way in they stopped repeatedly so that Henry could introduce her to various friends and business acquaintances.

'This is Alice Meredith who has kindly consented to become my wife.'

For the fifth time in as many minutes, Alice felt curious eyes upon her. News of the marriage had no doubt aroused surprise and some doubt among Henry's friends, although all were quick to wish her well. Hester spoke convincingly of a bond between them growing gradually over the past year and Alice hoped that the truth would never leak out. It would suggest that she and Henry had something to hide – which, of course, they did.

Only Mrs Wolsey smiled thinly. 'How do you do, my dear? I was so surprised to hear the news. When poor Marion passed on we never dreamed that Henry would ever find anyone to match her. Or would even attempt to do so. She was a wonderful woman. We all adored her, didn't we, Sarah?'

Sarah, her sister, nodded vigorously. 'Indeed we did. She was very gracious. Very thoughtful. Very kind. An inspiration to us all.'

Alice caught all the nuances of the little speech. Henry had betrayed his first wife's memory by deciding to remarry. That was her message and it came across loud and clear.

Henry said quickly, 'I like to think Marion

155

would have approved.'

'Oh, do you think so?' Mrs Wolsey looked unconvinced.

Hester said, 'As you say, Marion was so kind. She would hate to think of Henry alone in his final years.'

Henry, raising his hat to another passing friend, tightened his hold on Alice's arm as Hester continued.

'She always hoped that Henry would marry again if she preceded him into a life hereafter.'

Mrs Wolsey showed exaggerated surprise. 'She never expressed such a wish to me.'

Hester smiled. 'You were hardly in her confidence the way I was. Marion always maintained that Henry would die of loneliness without a woman's love and support. And I agree.'

'But he has you, dear.' Mrs Wolsey's smile had faded.

'I am much older than Henry and I won't last forever.'

'But *I* am alone and I survive.'

'What choice do you have?' Hester turned to Alice. 'Poor Mrs Wolsey lost her husband seven years ago. We all secretly hoped she would marry again but we've been disappointed.' She gave Mrs Wolsey a look of deep commiseration and Alice almost laughed. The suggestion, that she was unable to attract another man, was not

156

too carefully veiled.

Sarah understood it, also, but was uncertain how to reply.

Mrs Wolsey pretended to be unaffected by the snub but a tightened mouth and flushed cheeks gave her away. Pretending not to notice this, a smiling Henry led Alice and Hester into church.

'I fear those two will not be receiving an invitation to the wedding!' Hester murmured. 'I shall remove their names from the list. That will infuriate them and serve them right. A thoroughly objectionable pair. I could never see what poor Marion saw in them. Pay her no heed, Alice.'

The service began and as usual Alice took pleasure in the hymns for she had a pleasant voice and enjoyed singing. She stared at the aisle. In three weeks time I will be walking down there, she thought, in the cream lace dress – but without a father to give me away. She had written to ask Eddie if he could get leave from his regiment but she suspected that he wouldn't try very hard. He hated formality and the idea of giving the bride away would fill him with horror.

The service continued. Prayers. A reading. When the banns were finally read they came as something of a shock and Alice was grateful when Henry took her hand in his and squeezed it. Sitting between Henry and Hester Alice felt as though she were being protected. But from what exactly? What *did* people think of her, she wondered. Possibly they saw her as gold-digger or a 'jumped-up little nobody'. After him for his money! She could almost hear the whispers. People like Mrs Wolsey would be merciless. And imagine what would happen when the baby arrived so promptly? Fingers would be counted and months ticked off. That could lead to only one conclusion – that Alice and Henry had been lovers before the marriage actually took place. Then they would assume that he had been forced to marry. She marvelled that Henry was taking all this in his stride. In fact if anything he appeared to be enjoying the attention. Perhaps, after a very sober life, he was enjoying the notion that people would see him in a new guise. A dark horse! She smiled.

During the long and rather dull sermon that followed the notices, Alice allowed her thoughts to drift. She must remember to seek out Mr Lester and see if there was anything she could do for him. And they must order flowers on behalf of the Mere to send to Perdita's funeral. She wondered if Mr Lester's mother would be out of hospital and able to attend the funeral. No doubt she would offer some hospitality afterwards if she were fit enough. Perhaps, if not, Mr Lester would like a small buffet to be served in the smallest function room of the hotel.

Cold meats and salads, perhaps. They could keep the cost down to a minimum for him.

She was awoken from her reverie by a sharp elbow.

Hester whispered, 'Wake up. It's the last hymn.'

Guiltily Alice found the place in her hymnal and they all rose to sing 'Praise, my soul, the king of Heaven'.

Six

Just before ten two days later a taxi pulled up outside an elegant block of flats over-looking the Roodee racecourse. Arthur Lester helped his mother out and paid the driver.

'Thank the Lord it wasn't my ankle,' Agnes told her son as she made her way up the stairs. 'At least I can still get about.' She was pale and her face was etched by her recent sorrow. Her slow movements were not a proof of any physical weakness but a sign of the dreadful lethargy that she and her son both felt.

Fumbling with the key, Agnes unlocked the door and they went inside. The flat was small but bright and had been comfortably furnished.

'Arthur!' Agnes stared at a bowl of mixed flowers which stood in the middle of the polished table. 'How thoughtful you are, dear!'

'To welcome you home, Mother.'

For a moment her eyes filled with tears but she briskly brushed them aside. Arthur knew that she was thinking of her granddaughter who lay in her coffin at the undertaker's nearby. He knew that she was remembering the many occasions when the little girl's laughter had rung through the flat, brightening their lives. Days that would never come again. He put a hand to his own eyes, fighting back his grief. He hadn't wanted his mother's return to her home to be sadder than it need be, although he couldn't pretend that their lives would ever be the same again. The loss of his only child had extinguished a light for both of them forever. Their future had been snatched away and the years stretched ahead without hope.

'You sit down, dear, while I make a pot of tea,' he suggested but Agnes wouldn't hear of it.

'But your arm...' he protested.

'It will give me something to do,' she insisted. 'And I must get used to using it. That's what the doctor said. I mustn't let it stiffen up.'

Sighing, Arthur gave in.

For a moment or two he stared out across the racecourse. Three men were walking the course on their daily tour of inspection. In the stands the cleaners were busy, weaving their way along the rows. A man with a can of paint was working his brush along the rails of the track in readiness for the next big

161

occasion. There was no race meeting today and no hint of the breathless excitement and glamour such a day would eventually bring. He had brought his wife to the races on several occasions, to spend a few elegant hours in the County Stand. Closing his eyes, Arthur conjured up her image. Dressed in a lilac-coloured gown with a white parasol fringed with lilac tassels, she had stood at those same rails, her face radiant, her hair wind-blown as the ground vibrated beneath the thundering hooves that raced along the track. The last occasion had been the year before Perdita was born. Then he had been a proud and happy man. Now both wife and child were gone. He prayed they were together and wondered in his darkest moments how long it would be before he could join them.

In the kitchen Agnes was pouring the tea.

'I have something to tell you, Mother,' he said as he carried the tray into the parlour for her.

'I know what it is, Arthur. It came to me in a dream.'

'Not one of your famous dreams!'

'You shouldn't mock my dreams! I've told you before. They are a glimpse into the future.'

'I've made a decision and I want to hear no arguments, Mother!' Settled in the cheerful parlour he began the speech he had practised the previous night. 'I have decided to move from London to Chester.'

'I knew it!'

'Partly because I shall be haunted by memories if I stay where I am but partly to be near you. We are both going to be lonely and we are both getting older. It makes sense, Mother, don't you think?'

She sipped her tea. 'But where will you live, Arthur? I'd love you to come here but the flat is much too small.'

'I'll find a flat this side of the town. One within walking distance. I can afford it now that my books are making decent sales at last.'

She gave him a long look. 'And you would also be nearer to Mrs Meredith!'

He glanced up in surprise. 'Mrs Meredith?'

'The lady at the Mere. The manageress.'

'What on earth makes you say that?' He was annoyed to discover that he was stammering.

'Oh don't pretend, Arthur.' She patted his knee with her good hand. 'You speak of her so often I cannot help noticing that you are interested in her.'

'Oh dear! Was it so obvious? Now you've embarrassed me.'

'She sounds a very nice person, dear. Very capable. You say she offered to provide some refreshments after the funeral.' Her voice

163

faltered but she controlled her emotions with an effort. 'I think we should accept. I really cannot manage any hospitality here with only one good arm. And I'd like to meet her.'

He sipped his tea self-consciously. 'I'm afraid I raised your hopes unnecessarily, Mother. Mrs Meredith is spoken for.' He had tried to sound brisk and unaffected but failed.

She stared at him. 'But you thought she was married and then you thought she might be a widow because there was no sign of a husband and she lived in at the Mere and – oh dear! I was beginning to hope ... Did you get it wrong?'

'Not exactly, Mother.' Why on earth did she have to bring this up now, he thought miserably. 'I was too slow. She's just become betrothed. One of the housemaids mentioned it. It's been quite a shock for everyone. They'd kept it very quiet apparently. I could kick myself but ... Anyway, that's not to be. Sorry, dear.'

His mother's face fell. 'Oh Arthur! I had such hopes. I had this feeling whenever you spoke of her. And last night I had this strange dream. Why didn't you tell me she was getting married?'

'Because I didn't find out until this morning and, anyway, I didn't know that you had guessed how I felt.'

'Well of course I would know. I'm your mother, aren't I?' She regarded him reproachfully. 'Who is she marrying? Do you know?'

'She's marrying Henry Lightfoot.'

'Do I know him?'

'He owns the Mere, Mother! Of course you know him.'

'Good heavens!'

'Exactly.' He finished his tea. 'Her name's Alice.' He didn't know why he said it.

'Oh darling, how thoughtless of her. Not even to give you a chance! And she was so wonderful with Perdita. When I think of the little party she arranged for her 'pretend' birthday...' Agnes's eyes filled with tears. 'She had to have that party. Sweet little precious. At least that made her happy right at the end of her life.'

Arthur nodded. 'There never would have been a party ... Mrs Meredith made it happen. I shall always be grateful to her.' He sighed.

Agnes narrowed her eyes. 'But isn't Mr Lightfoot very elderly?'

'Mother!' In spite of himself, Arthur laughed briefly. 'You mustn't put the fluence on the poor chap just because I'm in love with—' He stopped, appalled at the slip.

'In love with her?' His mother was staring at him, wide-eyed. 'Oh Arthur! I didn't know you felt that strongly. Oh my dear, can't you do something? Ask her. Explain. Before it's too late. You're closer to her in age. He may be wealthier than you but does he love her the way you do? Does she love him?'

'She would hardly agree to marry the man if she felt nothing for him. No Mother, it's too late and you mustn't fret about it.'

'But you have so many years ahead of you, Arthur.' She clasped her hands. 'You could make each other so happy.'

'I'd like to think so but we don't know that. You mustn't get carried away. I'm trying to be pleased for her. It's a wonderful match. She'll be secure for the rest of her days. I said to her once that she should have a family.'

'Well, there you are then! You did mention it to her. And what did she reply? Does she want a family?'

'It doesn't matter now what she replied, does it? It's too late.'

Agnes went on unperturbed. 'Some women these days choose to remain single although I can't see why. Some women want a career instead of a child. They want to compete with the men.'

'Compete with the men? Of course they don't.'

'They *do*, Arthur! Only the other day a friend told me of her niece who wants to become a *doctor*. She's turned down a very nice man. She wants to be a *doctor*. If that's not competing I don't know what is.'

Arthur wasn't listening. 'I don't think she actually answered me. She looked startled at the very idea.'

'So she didn't say she wanted a family. That's exactly what I've been saying. I blame it on the suffrage movement. All this talk about votes for women ... It has encouraged some headstrong women to decry motherhood and choose a different kind of life.'

'I wonder if she will.'

'Will what, Arthur?'

'Start a family. Mrs Meredith I mean.'

'At his age?' Agnes snorted.

'Mother, Henry Lightfoot isn't in his dotage! He can't be more than sixty-five. Stranger things have happened.'

There was a protracted silence. Then Agnes brightened. 'I shall meet her after the funeral. I shall talk to her. Sound her out.'

Horrified, he cried, 'Please! You must do nothing of the kind. I don't want to have to worry about what you are up to. It's going to take all my courage to get through the funeral.'

There was another long silence while Agnes refilled the cups.

She said at last, 'Perdita brought the two of you together in a way. To me that's an omen, Arthur.'

'To me it's a coincidence.'

She leaned over and kissed him. 'We shall see, Arthur. We shall see.'

On the day of the funeral the mourners were due in the function room at three o'clock and Alice made herself late for the service by her determination that nothing should go wrong. She wanted everything to be perfect. When she reached the church they were singing the first hymn and Alice slipped into a pew towards the back so as not to disturb or distract anyone. She saw Mr Lester with an elderly woman with her left arm in a sling and assumed she was his mother. Hester was there with Henry. There were a few London friends, most of whom had travelled up by train and were booked in at the Mere overnight. She spotted Maggie nearer the front. Perdita's coffin, heartbreakingly small, was raised on a set of trestles and topped with a spray of white lilies. Alice felt a moment's regret that Edith Brightling couldn't be present. Was she really on her way to Paris or was that a red herring to throw the police off their track?

It was a simple service. The vicar spoke of a short and innocent life and a man Alice didn't recognize talked movingly about his young niece. When the service ended they all followed the coffin out to the churchyard, where a grave had already been prepared. Alice found herself standing next to Mrs Lester.

Turning to Alice the woman whispered, 'My son is broken-hearted.'

Alice lowered her voice. 'We are all very sorry about Perdita.'

'You've been very good to her. I just wanted to thank you personally.'

'She was a delightful child,' Alice replied.

When it was finally ended, she had a quick word with Henry and Hester then hurried back through the town as arranged, ahead of the other mourners.

Back at the hotel Alice was pleased to see that the simple cold collation had been set out attractively on a white damask cloth. Cold roast beef and ham, Russian salad and cold new potatoes dressed with oil and lemon. Chairs were grouped around small tables and waiters were on hand to serve people. Young Smith had been smartened up and stood stiffly to one side in case there were any last minute errands to be run or messages to be carried. He caught Alice's eye and smiled nervously. Trays of sherry waited on the sideboard and tea was brewing for those who preferred something non-alcoholic.

For dessert Chef had made two large strawberry tarts which would be served with a cream custard and there was ice cream as an alternative. There had been more people than Alice had expected but then she knew very little about Mr Lester's life in London. As the subdued guests began to drift in Alice made a rough count of twenty-nine people but Chef assured her he had a game pie ready in case it was necessary.

Mrs Lester approached Alice. 'This looks quite splendid,' she said. 'I'm most grateful.' Lowering her voice she added, 'I would like to settle the account before I leave if you can have the bill ready.'

'There's no hurry for it. I could put it in the post for you.'

'Thank you but no. I don't get around too easily and once I'm back at the flat I shall rarely venture out, even to post a letter.'

'Then I'll see to it,' Alice smiled. 'I'm glad you were fit enough to be at the church. Is your wrist still painful?'

'I grin and bear it, as they say. It was a very nice service, wasn't it?'

'Quite perfect, Mrs Lester. Perdita deserved nothing less. It's a terrible tragedy.' She glanced at the trays of sherry to see that they had been replenished. People were beginning to gather in groups, speaking in low tones, recalling the child they had lost.

'But now poor Arthur is alone.' Mrs Lester seemed reluctant to join them. Alice was too polite to interrupt her but she wanted to check the serviettes.

'How terrible,' she murmured.

'First his wife – she died in childbirth, you know...'

'In childbirth!' Alice felt a sudden chill and prayed silently that she would survive to bring up her child.

'And now his only child is taken from him. God certainly moves in a mysterious way. It is enough to test anyone's faith.'

Alice regarded her helplessly. 'Perdita is at peace,' she said, immediately aware how trite that sounded.

Mrs Lester said, 'She's with our Lord – but what about the living, Mrs Meredith? What about Arthur?' Her voice shook. 'My son has every right to feel bitter. But he isn't. He has somehow retained his beliefs. That's the sort of man he is.'

'I think I would be, in his shoes.' Alice confessed.

The chef was trying to catch her eye. 'If you'll excuse me...' Alice began but Mrs Lester refused to take the hint.

'My son tells me that you are to be married shortly. He was rather surprised. It all seemed very sudden. He had noticed you, you know.'

'Excuse me a moment.' Alice moved away to speak to Chef. A few more people had come into the room and she agreed that the game pie was going to be necessary. She also

171

slipped away and returned with more serviettes and signalled to Smith to find help and bring in another table.

To her surprise she once again found Mrs Lester beside her. The older woman smiled. 'So was it a sudden decision – your betrothal?'

'It *was* sudden. Yes. I ... Neither of us was quite sure ... It's a big step but Henry was determined we would make it work.' Alice hated lying but she thought probably Henry would like that version. She said, 'The banns were called last Sunday for the first time.'

'I hope you'll be very happy. Mr Lightfoot is a very fortunate man ... He speaks very highly of you, you know.'

Startled, Alice blinked. 'You know Mr Lightfoot?'

'Not Mr Lightfoot! My son, Arthur. He very much admires you.'

'We consider him a valued guest.'

'So you should, Mrs Meredith. He's been very faithful to the Mere. Eight or nine years he's been coming here. More than that, probably. He wouldn't dream of staying anywhere else. Mrs Meredith looks after us, he says.' She gave a little laugh.

At that moment Mr Lester himself joined them.

'Mother! Do come and sit with me.'

'I was just saying to—'

'Mrs Meredith is very busy, dear.' He took her arm. 'The Clarksons are here. We're sitting together.'

'But I—'

'They've come all the way from Romford, Mother!' He gave Alice an apologetic look and she smiled her thanks.

She saw that the new table was being set up and sent Smith to the kitchen for the second batch of bread rolls. All around people were beginning to relax a little and a more hopeful note filled the air. There were a few smiles and less tears and Alice knew that the food and drink was starting to take the edge from the grief. She moved quietly and efficiently through the room and, engrossed in her work, jumped a little as someone grasped her elbow.

'Henry! You startled me!' She smiled.

'I was wondering if you were feeling up to all this, Alice.' He leaned a little closer and whispered, 'I don't want you to overtire yourself.'

Alice noticed several of the waiters exchanging looks at this small intimacy but told herself that was natural enough. She was now an object of curiosity to the rest of the staff and must get used to the idea.

Alice whispered, 'We're both fine, Henry!' and he laughed with pleasure.

'Hester will be down later if she feels up to it. She was a little upset so I insisted that she lie down and rest. Funerals always depress her. Just a fluttery heart but she worries about it. Mother lived with it for years but Grandmother died early. It's a family thing.' He looked round the room. 'Everyone happy? With the arrangements, I mean.'

Alice assured him that they were.

'Is there anything I can do?' he asked.

'You might help yourself to food and join that elderly man there.' She pointed discreetly. 'He's all alone and rather unhappy.'

'Good idea, Alice. And if Hester comes down send her to join us.'

As he made his way across the room Alice was surprised to realize that he no longer seemed such a remote figure and, for an elderly man, he looked very presentable. Quite attractive in a way. She smiled at the idea. Perhaps their walk together by the river really had brought them closer. We do need time to get to know each other, she reflected.

Chef was serving the game pie and Alice went to the kitchen for a fresh bowl of salad. So, the appetites were not impaired, she thought with satisfaction. Her mother had always maintained that plenty of food after a funeral helped to foster a sense of reassurance and well-being among the bereaved.

Henry caught her eye and she hurried to him. He excused himself for a moment from his companion and stood up. 'I almost forgot,' he said. 'My mind's like a sieve these days! Hester asked me to tell you she needs you for a fitting tomorrow morning at eleven. And it will be you and me interviewing this afternoon for your replacement.'

'Oh but I thought Mr Warner—'

'It is all arranged. I've spoken to Mr Warner. And I've seen the new night porter. He seems rather young but I understand we needed to replace Davies at short notice.' He remembered his companion and smiled at him. 'This is Mrs Meredith who will soon be my wife.'

Hiding his obvious surprise, the man rose to his feet and shook Alice's hand.

'My very good wishes to you both!' He was almost as tall as Henry, much younger but pebbled glasses hinted at very poor eyesight.

Henry said, 'Mr Bourke is a neighbour of Mr Lester in London.'

Mr Bourke smiled at Alice. 'So, soon all this will no longer be your responsibility. Are you looking forward to that?'

A minor panic seized Alice. Was she looking forward to giving up her work? 'I haven't ... Yes. I suppose I am ... At least, I haven't had much time to think about it.' She had never been a lady of leisure and suddenly wondered how she would fill her days. Then she remembered the baby. Of course. A child would take up much of her time.

Henry was smiling at her. Now he put a hand on her arm. 'After a few months your present life here will be nothing but a half-remembered dream.'

'I shall miss my friends, I daresay.'

'You will have new friends.' He leaned closer. 'With a husband and a baby you will have your hands full!'

Alice returned the smile and made her excuses.

An hour or so later she was back in the office working out the Lesters' bill. She was feeling very tired, and her back ached and suddenly she thought it probably *would* be nice to be 'retired'.

Miss Maine put her head round the door. 'Sergeant Flint to see you.'

Before Alice could reply he had entered the room without waiting for an invitation. Alice saw a burly man with a weatherbeaten complexion and steely grey eyes. He shook Alice's hand briefly, took off his helmet and looked pointedly at a chair.

'Do sit down, Sergeant,' Alice said, doing likewise. She was desperately hoping that he had not found out about the information she had witheld earlier. Miss Maine was lingering in the doorway but Alice signalled her to leave them. If she was going to be reprimanded by the sergeant she had no wish for Miss Maine to be a witness.

The sergeant cleared his throat. 'It has come to our notice, Mrs Meredith, that a guest from this hotel has recently been seen with a man we believe to be Albert Stewart, alias Dr Stewart, who is wanted for questioning in relation to several frauds.' He subjected Alice to a long hard look. 'Can you tell me anything you know about this? I have to remind you that refusing to co-operate with the police can have serious consequences. Withholding information is not wise. Not wise at all.'

Alice stared at her hands, frozen with indecision. Should she or should she not tell what she knew of Edith's romance? She was already fearful for Edith's future. Perhaps this was her last chance to save her friend from a disastrous relationship. And if she *did* pretend ignorance and was later discovered in the lie, whatever would Henry think?

'Mrs Meredith?' Sergeant Flint prompted.

'Who is this guest?' she asked, playing for time.

'A Mrs Edith Brightling. A resident. I understand she is a friend of yours. A close friend.' He raised his eyebrows.

'She is a friend, yes ... but at the moment she is away from the hotel.'

'Alone?'

'I think she was meeting a friend.'

He leaned forward and his grim

expression had become a scowl. 'Mrs Meredith, your manager has told me that if anyone knows what is going on it is you. May we please stop playing games? Where is Mrs Brightling?'

So Mr Warner had given the information. Alice could hardly blame him. He had no reason to protect Edith and every reason to protect the hotel and himself from any whiff of scandal. She decided she would have to tell what she knew. In a few brief sentences she explained the background, adding that Edith had gone to Paris with Albert Stewart.

'I tried to dissuade her,' she told him, 'but she wouldn't listen. She has ... has formed an attachment to the man and refuses to believe any ill of him. I've been very anxious for her but I had given my word not to betray her.'

His expression said it all. 'Women!' he said disparagingly. 'Your mistaken loyalty has done your friend a great disservice.'

In spite of her feelings of guilt, Alice bridled at his attitude. 'I don't see why you condemn us for being loyal. Men are praised for it, I believe.'

He gave her a withering look. 'It may interest you to know, Mrs Meredith, that a customs officer at Folkestone reports seeing a man and woman boarding the Boulogne ferry in the early hours of this morning. The

178

man fits the description of Albert Stewart.'

'And – the woman?'

'Unfortunately we were not interested in the woman so no note was taken of her appearance at that time. However, they were talking with some animation and were obviously together.'

'But what has Edith done that is so wrong?' Alice asked. 'She's fallen for a cad but that's not a crime. It's sad but it's not—'

'Have I said she's done anything wrong?' He sighed. 'Mind you, associating with a known criminal is hardly the action of an upright citizen ... but no. Edith Brightling has committed no crime.'

Alice was becoming impatient. She had a lot to do and she didn't like Sergeant Flint. 'So why are you here?' she asked. 'Why are you looking for her if you don't accuse her of anything?'

He almost smiled and that unnerved her.

'The fact is, Mrs Meredith, we're alarmed for her safety. Our police sent word to the French authorities at Boulogne to arrest the man and to interview the woman. When the time came for the passengers to disembark, Albert Stewart was alone. Furthermore he swore that he had boarded alone, that he had simply met his companion in the queue and that he had not spoken to her since.'

Alice's irritation vanished and fear took its place. 'But that's ... isn't that impossible? If she boarded then she must have...' She frowned. 'What about her luggage? She took some clothes with her. I saw her pack a bag. An old carpet bag. Didn't anybody find her luggage?'

He shrugged. 'They searched the ship. No trace was found of her. You do see, Mrs Meredith, why we fear for your friend's safety? If only you had spoken up earlier.'

She could see satisfaction in his expression and cursed her stupidity. Why on earth hadn't she done the sensible thing? She sat back in her chair, dazed by the news, all the fight knocked out of her. 'I'm so sorry,' she stammered. 'At the time I thought it was for the best. With hindsight, of course...' Her voice trailed off as her mind grappled with the awful possibilities. With an effort she asked, 'What do you think has happened to her?'

He straightened up. 'We are not in the habit of making wild guesses, Mrs Meredith, but let me just say it is not unknown for a passenger to go overboard.'

Alice gasped. 'Oh no! Not Edith!'

He went on. 'Sometimes it is an accident. Sometimes it is suicide. Occasionally it is murder.'

'*Murder?* Oh no!' Deeply shocked, Alice thought desperately. 'What about him?

What does he say? Have they questioned him?'

'I've told you. He refuses to admit that he even knew her name. Oh don't worry, Mrs Meredith. The French have him in custody and we will extradite him very quickly. But will he tell us anything? I doubt it. Not if it's going to incriminate him.' Abruptly he stood up. 'I would be grateful if you would let us know immediately if Mrs Brightling gets in touch with you again – which I very much doubt. For the moment we are treating her as a missing person.'

Alice struggled to her feet on leaden legs. She felt badly shaken as the fear grew. Edith was in danger – or dead – and it was partly her fault. 'I...' She swallowed but her mouth was dry.

At that moment Mr Lester put his head round the door. 'If my mother's bill is ready I'll take it to her.'

'Come in,' she said shakily. 'I was just preparing...'

He said, 'Are you all right, Mrs Meredith?'

Miss Maine followed him in. 'Excuse me but there's a Mrs Dymott at reception. She's come about your job.'

'My job?' Alice stared at her in total confusion. Suddenly she was at the point of panic. The room seemed to press in on her.

'The interview, Mrs Meredith, with you and Mr Lightfoot.'

181

'Oh...' Alice's sight blurred and she shook her head to clear it. 'I feel ... Please...'

Someone said, 'She's very pale!'

Miss Maine said, 'She's going to faint!'

Everyone seemed to be talking at once but Alice's voice failed her.

'Look out! She's going!'

'Here's Mr Lightfoot!'

She felt someone clutch at her arm but then she was falling and everything went dark...

When she regained consciousness and opened her eyes, she saw that she was lying on the sofa in Hester's sitting room. She and Henry were staring down at her with anxious expressions.

'My dear!' said Henry. 'You gave me such a fright.' He took hold of her hand.

Alice struggled to sit up but Hester said, 'Don't, Alice. Just rest for a few more minutes. You fainted. Luckily Henry was there for the interview. He carried you up here.' She held out a glass of water. 'Have a few sips, Alice, and put us out of our misery. Are you ill? Is there something you haven't told us? I wanted to send for the doctor but Henry wouldn't allow it. He is being very obstinate for some reason.'

Dutifully Alice sipped the water while she tried to understand exactly what Hester was trying to say. She felt very cold and clammy but the cold water had a bracing effect. She returned the glass and struggled to a sitting position. 'No, I'm not ill,' she said. 'There was just too much going on at once. And I had been talking with Sergeant Flint and he told me that Edith is missing and it was such a shock.'

Henry said, 'Poor Mr Lester was quite alarmed. He blames himself for bothering you at such a busy time.'

Hester still stared at Alice. 'And you're certain you're not ill, Alice? You would tell us, wouldn't you? We would see to it that you got the very best medical care.'

What, thought, Alice, is she trying to tell me? She looked at Henry who stared back at her. They were thinking the same thing but the decision was his. Suddenly he said, 'We do have something to tell you, Hester, but it's nothing bad. The reason for Alice's faint is ... The fact is, Hester, Alice and I have been...' Words failed him. A bright spot of colour had appeared in his cheeks.

Hester said, 'You are not making any sense.' She looked at Alice.

Alice took a deep breath, although she was about to tell Hester something she already knew. It seemed ridiculous but she had promised.

'Henry and I are expecting a child,' she announced.

Hester looked astonished. Really, thought

Alice admiringly, she was a great actress.

'A child? But that's impossible! Henry – I mean, we've always thought...'

Alice said, 'Well, it happened.'

Hester shook her head. 'After all these years!' She clapped a hand to her mouth. 'But the wedding isn't until...' Her eyes widened. 'Everyone will know you've been ... more than friends...' She turned to Henry. 'You took advantage of Mrs Meredith? I can't believe that of you. I won't believe it.'

Alice said, 'He didn't ... It was nothing like that. I was...' She broke off. She wanted to say that they had been so much in love it was inevitable but that meant more lies. That was going too far. 'I ... I was a willing partner, Hester. No one is to blame.' She smiled reassuringly at Henry.

There was a long silence. Henry's expression was a confused mixture of guilt and pride. Alice wondered what was going through his mind.

Hester said sharply, 'Love apparently addles the brain! I'm surprised at you, Henry. Heaven knows what Mother would have said. She'll be turning in her grave, no doubt. And now there's to be a child! No wonder you go round fainting, Alice! No wonder you are both in a hurry to be wed...'

By this time, however, Henry had recovered. 'No one is more surprised than I am.' He leaned down and kissed Alice and managed to wink at her at the same time. 'It was the last thing I expected to happen.'

Alice looked from one to the other. 'Are we forgiven, Hester? We meant no harm. You will be an aunt again and Henry will be a father at last.'

For a long moment Hester hesitated then allowed a smile to creep across her face. 'I do believe I have forgiven you already! If it's a boy, that is. No wonder you fainted. You must give up your job at once.'

Henry said, 'I say, Hester, you really are a brick to take it like this.'

Alice stood up. 'I feel much better. We have an applicant waiting downstairs for my job and there's Mr Lester's bill...'

Henry put his hands on her shoulders and gently pushed her back into her chair. 'You sit down, Alice. I am perfectly capable of interviewing Mrs Dymott on my own and I'm sure Mr Warner will have seen to the bill. You rest here with Hester and I will be back as soon as I can.'

When he had gone, Alice and Hester regarded each other soberly.

'I feel unkind,' Alice confessed. 'Deceiving him like this.'

'Maybe you do but it is too late to think about unburdening yourself. We must live with our consciences. He would never feel the same about you and he would certainly resent my interference. His pride is at stake, Alice. Men are like that. I know him.'

'Are you sure?' she said unhappily. 'Isn't honesty always the best policy?'

'Of course it isn't! If a man is unfaithful to his wife but truly loves her and wants to preserve her from pain, he should suffer his guilt in silence. If it troubles him, so much the better. That is his punishment. If he tells her and asks forgiveness, she may give it but then maybe she can never forget. The precious trust is lost and he has punished her as well.'

Alice stared at her. 'You sound very certain.'

Hester shrugged. 'My closest friend was betrayed by her husband and he chose to tell her the truth. She was dead a month later. Gassed herself. I never spoke to him again.'

'How terribly sad!' Alice was chastened.

'So you see? Henry feels in control. You asked him but the decision was his. He'll be humbled if he learns that it was my idea and that we conspired together to trick him.'

'Trick him? Oh dear. That makes me feel worse!'

'A bad conscience is the price you have to pay, Alice, to save him from pain. Now, enough said. Are you really feeling better?'

Alice nodded.

'Then tell me what has happened to Edith Brightling. You say she is missing?'

Quickly Alice repeated what Sergeant Flint had told her, concluding, 'He didn't seem to hold out much hope for Edith's safety.'

'You mean he might have killed her?' Shocked, Hester pressed a hand to her heart. 'Surely not! He's a con man, not a murderer.'

'If he's talked her out of all her money he might have no use for her. He may simply have pushed her over the side.'

'But then all he had to do was call for help and say it was an accident. No one could have blamed him. They might have suspected him but they would have no proof.'

'Her luggage is also missing. He must have thrown it after her.' Alice was afraid to hope. 'Stewart may not have known the police were watching for him. He wouldn't have expected anyone to notice that they arrived together. He pretended not to know her, remember. Oh poor Edith! I can't bear to think how she must have felt if she *was* pushed over the side. Falling all that way and knowing...' She swallowed hard. 'Especially because she trusted him. Not only was she being killed she was being betrayed and she would have known that.'

'We mustn't look on the black side, Alice.'

They looked at each other fearfully. Alice could see that, in spite of her words, Hester was worried.

Alice put a hand to her head. 'I blame myself. I should have told the police that she was in contact with him. This would never have happened if I'd been sensible.' She looked at Hester with anguished eyes. 'I keep imagining her thrashing about in the water while the ship sailed on.'

'Well don't! You'll make yourself ill and there's the child to think about.' Hester frowned. 'I just can't see Stewart as a cold-blooded murderer. There has to be another explanation. Could she have disguised herself? She was an actress once.'

'But why should she if everything was all right?'

'I don't know.' Her expression changed. 'It might have been suicide.'

'Suicide? Oh no! Not Edith!'

'Maybe they had a quarrel,' Hester suggested, 'and she discovered that he only wanted her for her money and threw herself over the rail in a fit of despair.' She shook her head. 'We have to face the fact that we may never know the truth. Unless her body is washed up somewhere – and even then we won't know *how* she ended up in the sea. Oh the foolish woman! How could she have trusted him?' She shrugged. 'At least the doctor is in police custody. No doubt he will be interrogated and might confess. Not that it will do any good. There will be no chance of finding her alive but at least we may know what happened. Try not to dwell on it, Alice. All we can do is wait and pray.'

Seven

The following morning Alice rose as usual and was soon back at work. Mrs Dymott had passed her interview and was expected around nine so that Alice could begin to explain the way the hotel worked, introduce her to staff members and generally prepare her to take over Alice's position.

As Alice checked the dining room, making sure that all the tables were laid correctly, the thought of Arthur Lester lingered at the back of her mind. Poor man – and his poor mother, waking to the remembrance of their dreadful loss. She stared at the familiar table setting and tried to concentrate. Cutlery, crockery, butter dish, china bowl full of sugar lumps and another with brown sugar for the porridge, milk jug, china honeypot in the shape of a beehive, glass marmalade dish, salt and pepper for the eggs and bacon, toast rack. Her eyes narrowed. Something was missing but what? She looked at the adjoining table. Ah! The table napkins. She fetched them from the large sideboard and, as she did so, caught sight of the few children's books half-hidden in the corner. It reminded her of Perdita and of her decision to provide a proper toy box full of attractive toys and books. Or maybe it could be a children's corner. Perhaps they could call it Perdita's Corner in memory of Arthur Lester's little girl. He would like that. She sighed.

One by one the guests drifted into the room and took their places at the tables reserved for them. The waitresses bustled about taking orders and soon the room was full of the soft hum of people enjoying breakfast. With a little satisfied nod, Alice left the room and went in search of Mrs Dymott.

Mary Dymott was middle-aged, small and plump with a mass of frizzy dark hair which she wore piled on top of her head. Her dark brown eyes suggested an Italian ancestry and in answer to Alice's question she replied vaguely that she thought her great-great-grandmother might have come from Italy. Her two daughters were both recently married and her husband's health was un-reliable so that she had become the bread-winner.

'It's an interesting job,' Alice assured her as they toured the bedrooms. 'Fairly routine to some extent. You'll be mainly responsible for the behaviour and work of the women on the staff. They bring up the hot-water jugs, empty the chamber pots where appropriate, see to the bedrooms while the guests are at breakfast, which involves making up the beds and tidying the rooms. Changing the beds when the guests check out, of course.'

She ran a finger along the marble top of the washstand and nodded. 'This has been cleaned properly.' She checked underneath. 'The jug has been refilled with cold water and –' she bent to check below the stand. 'The pail has been emptied and wiped clean. That's Ethel. This is one of her rooms. She's very reliable. You'll get to know which ones you must keep an eye on. We've also got dining room staff. The women serve the breakfasts and the lunch but we have men in the evening to serve dinner. Mr Parkin also keeps an eye on them.'

They moved on.

'How much experience have you had?' Alice asked.

'I was a senior maid at my last hotel. In Brighton. I took over when my superior was off sick or on holiday. My husband has just lost his job again. We have a small top flat near the hospital. So I'll be coming in daily instead of living in like you. Mr Lightfoot thought seven o'clock was probably the right time but I was to check with you.'

Alice smiled. 'I'm afraid he was an hour out. I start at six. Sometimes earlier but that's because I live in and can manage it. Six will mean you are one step ahead of the rest of the staff!'

They both laughed.

Downstairs again, Alice explained the kitchen side of the work. You'll have to work with Chef over the menus and help Mr Warner keep a check on dining room expenditure. We call it a costing sheet. You'll soon get the hang of it. The meals, for instance. We allow thirty-five per cent for the actual cost of the meal and the rest is overheads and profit. The auditors take a look once a month.'

Mrs Dymott nodded. 'Mr Lightfoot said I was to come in every day until you leave and help you. To help lighten your load! If I'm here you can take a few hours off here and there. Like today. You've got the dressmaker coming for your wedding dress. Exciting, isn't it?'

Alice nodded but in fact she had forgotten and was secretly glad of the reminder. She didn't want to offend Hester. The wedding gown was, after all, Hester's wedding present to her.

Mrs Dymott said, 'What about the bar?'

'Mr Warner mostly deals with that. He keeps an eye open for any suspicious discrepancies but they're harder to spot. He watches the cellarman and the drayman to see that they aren't up to any of the usual tricks. A slow turnover is hard to prove but you needn't worry about that. Concentrate on the rooms and the dining room. And I'll still be around! I'm not going far after the wedding! We'll still live upstairs.' She laughed and she fancied Mrs Dymott appeared relieved. 'Perhaps you'd like to spend some time in the dining room now. Get to know the staff and see how the clearing-up is done plus the preparation for lunch time. Just watch, smile and nod. You'll soon get the feel of it.'

Leaving Mrs Dymott to her initiation, Alice glanced at the clock. Still plenty of time to check on something that had been bothering her. Mr Stanley Cootes. Had he booked out or was he still installed in room fifty-one? She hurried upstairs and along the passage and tapped on the door. There was a do-not-disturb notice on the handle but Alice ignored it. She knocked loudly.

'Mr Cootes. This is Mrs Meredith. I'd like a word, if you please.'

Still receiving no answer Alice gently turned the door handle and found it locked so used her pass key. Stanley Cootes was sitting up in bed still in his nightshirt, a cigar in one hand and a glass of whisky in the other. He seemed unaware of her presence and she could see that he was very drunk. The room was a total mess with clothes scattered across the floor and several trays of half-eaten meals stacked beside the bed. Alice tightened her lips. Someone should have reported this. There was a smell of stale cigar smoke overlaid by something worse. Had he been sick? Or had he used the chamber pot several days in a row? The clean towels had not been used so he hadn't washed.

'You disgusting wretch!' she muttered angrily.

He had stayed in his room, sending down for room service. Presumably none of the domestics had been able to gain entry to clean the room. Alice stepped closer to the bed and at last he turned his head and squinted at her through a haze of cigar smoke. Henry must never see this, she thought frantically. No one should be allowed to get into such a state, she thought guiltily. There had been a breakdown of organization somewhere along the line.

'Mr Cootes,' she said loudly. 'I would like a word with you. The cleaners have obviously—'

He glared at her. 'Get out! I don't need anything.'

'I will not get out! I'm Mrs Meredith, the manageress.' Ignoring a discarded shirt and some socks, she took a few steps closer. 'Listen to me, Mr Cootes. This can't go on. I want you to get up, wash and dress yourself. Do you hear me?'

'You can sod off!' he muttered, his expression truculent.

Alice bit back harsh words. No matter how obnoxious he was, the man was a guest. 'Then you must go for a long walk. Go anywhere you like but while you are out the cleaner will come in and deal with your room. It's in a terrible state. It smells disgusting!'

'Disgustin'? I don' know wha' you mean.'

Alice raised her voice. 'Get up, Mr Cootes, and clean yourself up!'

He winced at her tone. Draining the last of the whisky in one gulp he pressed the glass to his forehead. 'Can't you see my head aches?'

Alice longed to throttle him. 'I can have you thrown out of this hotel and I will if you don't do as I say.' She retreated to the door. 'Do you hear me? Get up, Mr Cootes.' She went out slamming the door behind her.

He's got to go, she told herself furiously. And the sooner the better. I shall speak to Mr Warner about him. She blamed herself for forgetting about him after the business with the night porter.

Downstairs she found Lena, one of the domestics, and told her to take a jug of hot water up to room fifty-one. 'And don't stay with him on any account,' she told her. 'He's drunk and he's in a foul mood. I wouldn't trust him further than I could throw him! Just tell him Mrs Meredith says he's to sort himself out. The room's like a pigsty.'

Nasty little man, she fumed. He was not the sort of guest they wanted at the Mere. She marched across to reception and asked Miss Maine for the hotel register. Finding the entry, she was dismayed to discover that he was booked in for two weeks.

'I think not!' she muttered. He had a home address but there was no telephone number. Did he have a wife, she wondered. Or an indulgent mother, perhaps.

Miss Maine was helping one of the guests with a road map of the town but when she had finished Alice asked, 'Do we know anything about this man Cootes in fifty-one?'

Miss Maine nodded. 'He was having a moan with the barman one night. Seems his wife has thrown him out. He says he "went off the rails a bit" a few months ago and then he lost his job. They had a row and he was sent packing.'

'She threw *him* out? She must have been the owner of the house, then. Maybe he married a rich woman.' Alice shook her head. 'Rich or not, I pity her.'

Miss Maine frowned. 'But if he has nowhere to go we can hardly turn him out. I mean, poor chap.'

Alice took a series of deep breaths until she was marginally calmer then said, 'Then he can find himself another hotel. I don't want him here.' Aware of Miss Maine's expression she tapped her fingers indecisively on the desk. Perhaps she was being a bit harsh. 'Maybe we'll give him one more chance. Twenty-four hours to pull himself together. If there is no improvement he'll have to go.'

'Couldn't you write to his wife? Ask her to take him—'

'Write to his wife? Are you out of your senses?' Alice felt her calm deserting her once more. 'What is he to us? *He's* the one who should be writing to his wife, not me. Going off the rails could mean anything!'

Seeing that she had gone too far, Miss Maine hurriedly changed the subject by asking after Edith. 'It was all in today's local paper, about her going off with him and disappearing and everything.'

'No news at all,' Alice told her. 'I don't want to think the worst but I'm terribly worried. It doesn't look good, does it? Oh, here's Mr Lester with his cases.'

He looks so tired and drawn, she thought sadly, and her heart went out to him. No doubt he found it impossible to sleep. How would he ever find happiness again?

He came up to her and took her hand briefly. 'I just wanted to thank you for everything. You've been a tower of strength. Mother and I are so grateful.'

'It was a pleasure, Mr Lester. Don't give it another thought.'

'And such splendid food. We think you handled it very well. I'm sorry I added to your problems when I came for the bill. I had no idea you were under such a strain. Are you quite recovered?'

'Quite. It was just a faint. Nothing serious.'

'I'm here to settle up. I'm going to sleep on Mother's sofa for a day or two until she is over the worst of the shock and then I shall go back to London. I have to sell my flat. I'm moving to Chester. And may I ask the date of your wedding? Mother loves a wedding and I would like to be there too.'

'I shall send you two invitations, then.'

'Oh no! I meant we'd like to—'

'No arguments, Mr Lester. You will both be our guests on the day. Henry will be delighted.'

'He's a very lucky man. Are your parents coming?'

'I doubt if my mother will make the journey. Since she was widowed she lives in Ireland with her sister and brother in-law. I know she will hate the thought of the journey. She's terrified of the sea crossing. It can be horribly rough.'

'So who will give you away?'

'My brother, if he can get leave from his regiment. He's with the Cheshires. Ah! Here's Miss Maine with your bill.'

He wrote out the cheque and Miss Maine said, 'Your taxi has arrived.'

Alice walked with him to the door to see him off. When she returned she found a middle-aged woman waiting at the desk. 'Can I help you?'

The woman was tall and thin, dressed in a fashion that was slightly too young for her. 'I'm Miss Pagett, Miss Lightfoot's dress-maker. She's expecting me.'

Alice said, 'Is it eleven already?' and stepped forward. 'I'm Mrs Meredith.' They shook hands.

'Of course I recognize you,' said Miss Pagett. 'Our paths have crossed once or twice.' Her expression changed. 'I was reading about Mrs Brightling in this morning's paper. Such a tragedy. I used to see her, years ago, when she was Edith Ellway. Her stage name. I was a regular theatre-goer when I was younger. My mother used to say I almost lived at the Royalty! She was so lovely – Edith Ellway, I mean. Those eyes!'

Alice said, 'We're all praying for her.'

'I saw her in *The Tempest*, once, and in *Summer's Shadow*. She could play any part but she was best at romantic characters. She took the lead once or twice.' She sighed.

'How could she have been so trusting? Poor, *poor* creature!'

Alice could only nod as all her fears for her friend resurfaced.

'But listen to me! I'm chattering on and we have so much to do. This dress is going to be wonderful! Absolutely *wonderful*! I was so thrilled to be asked to make it. I was rather worried that you hadn't been consulted in case you preferred your own dressmaker but Miss Lightfoot assured me you'd be delighted.' She studied Alice for a moment with narrowed eyes. 'With your skin tones the cream lace will look perfect.'

Alice smiled. 'I may as well come upstairs with you now.'

As they moved towards the stairs Lena scuttled past with a jug of hot water and clean towels for Mr Cootes.

Miss Pagett whispered, 'At this time of the morning!'

'A late riser!' Alice rolled her eyes and resisted the urge to make further comment.

Alice endured the fitting in a daze of disbelief. Who would have thought, a few months earlier, that she would be standing in Hester's drawing room being draped in expensive cream lace and fussed over by an excited dressmaker. Who would have believed that she was soon to marry a wealthy man, retire from work and give birth to a child. *Henry's* child. She had made a vow never to think of Sebastian again. From now on the child was hers and Henry's. That was the only fair thing to do. Nursing secret thoughts about her sweetheart would be a deceit and Henry deserved better than that.

Admiring herself in the mirror, Alice was surprised to see an attractive flush in her cheeks and began to think about how she would look walking up the aisle on her brother's arm.

'Hester, will you come with me to choose the shoes and the flowers?' she asked.

'Try and stop me!' laughed Hester. 'I think a small posy. We don't want to hide the gown.'

Miss Pagett said, 'A cream headband can look very striking. Maybe a few white flowers on it and a wisp of something flimsy to soften it.'

'And you must have something borrowed,' Hester reminded Alice. 'I have a beautiful embroidered garter which Mother wore at her wedding ... And something blue?' She frowned.

'Some tiny pale-blue flowers could be incorporated in the headband,' Miss Pagett suggested.

'Wonderful!' cried Alice. 'And I rather fancy buttoned shoes. Satin, perhaps?'

'White kid,' Hester suggested. 'They will

last so much longer.' She smiled suddenly. 'I do believe, Alice, that you are becoming caught up in the excitement at last. Henry was beginning to worry. He thinks your energies are still devoted to your work and not to your future.'

Alice smiled. 'I am still employed by the Mere,' she pointed out. 'Until I actually give up, I shall do my best for the hotel.'

A knock at the door brought a shriek from Hester. 'I hope that's not Henry! He mustn't see you in your wedding gown. It's very bad luck!' She rushed to the door and leaned against it. 'Who is it?'

'It's me, dear. Henry. I've—'

'Go away, Henry. I told you not to—'

'Oh! The fitting! I'm sorry. I brought up the post for you and Alice.'

Hester opened the door a few inches and thrust out her hand. 'Let me have the letters.' She took them, taking care not to allow him even the smallest glimpse of his bride-to-be.

The dressmaker put away her pins and tape measure and gave a satisfied nod.

'That's all for today,' she told them, carefully removing the lace and folding it between layers of tissue paper. 'I shall need another fitting in two to three days time.'

'Let us know,' Hester told her, 'and we'll arrange a time. And thank you for all your help and advice. I knew Alice would be in good hands.'

Alice, struggling back into her clothes, also thanked her and said she'd be looking forward to the next visit. As soon as they were alone again, Hester handed over a letter and Alice cried, 'It's from Eddie!'

'Open it, my dear. I hope it's more interesting than mine.' She waved the sheet of paper. 'My lending library tells me my annual fee is due again. Where does the time go? We shall have to enrol you, Alice, as soon as you have more time on your hands. Do you like to read?'

She waited in vain for an answer. Alice was staring at the contents of her envelope. 'He can't come,' she stammered. 'Eddie ... He was caught out of bounds and is confined to barracks for six weeks. He says...' She swallowed hard. 'He says his best friend has offered to come in his place!'

Hester stiffened. 'His best friend? I thought his best friend was what's-his-name!'

'Sebastian. Yes, he is.' She read out the scrawled letter.

Dear Allie,
What an idiot I am. Sorry old girl but I've been a nauty boy. Stayed out late without a pass and Im confined to baracks for the next six weeks. Lucky not to lose my stripe so wont be at the

wedding. Seb says he will stand in for me but I don't think youll like that idea so told him no thanks.

God bless

Eddie xx

Hester sat down heavily and the two women regarded each other soberly.

Hester said cautiously, 'Does that mean he definitely won't be coming?'

Alice sat down heavily. 'It should mean that. It *must*!'

'You'd better write to the man and make it clear. We can't have him turning up. He'll ruin everything.' Hester clasped her hands in obvious agitation. 'I can't imagine what Henry would say if he heard about this. Your Sebastian must have a skin like a rhinoceros to even think of attending your wedding.'

'It must have been a joke!' Alice was trying hard to believe that.

'A joke! Then it was a joke in the worst possible taste!' Hester said sharply. 'You must write at once.'

'I'll write to Eddie tonight,' Alice promised. 'I'll tell him I've asked someone else who has accepted. They don't know about the child, of course, and Sebastian is married to Nellie. He couldn't mean any harm but I still don't want him anywhere near Chester – now or at any time!'

'I should hope not! That sort of man

wouldn't let something like a wife deter him from causing a scene. Oh dear!' She put a hand to her heart. 'This has really upset me, Alice. Promise me you will write at once and forbid him to set foot in Chester on the day of your wedding.'

Privately Alice thought that forbidding Seb to do anything was asking for trouble but she agreed. She would write a carefully worded letter to her brother, begging him to dissuade Sebastian from doing anything stupid. To her surprise the thought of seeing him again did not immediately set her heart a-flutter as it would once have done. He had a wife, and a child was on the way. He was nothing to her. Nothing.

Hester regarded her with a worried frown. 'We'll find someone to give you away,' she said. 'I'll talk to Henry. He must know someone ... unless!' She brightened. 'What about Mr Lester? You tell me he is invited. Perhaps he would step into the role. I'm sure he'd be only too pleased to help out.'

'He might. Yes.' Alice thought about it.

'Then we must contact him as well.' Recovering from her fright, Hester smiled again. 'What a lot of decisions we are making, Alice. I really think we make a good team.' She looked at the clock. 'Now it is past midday and poor Mrs Dymott may be feeling a little lost. Perhaps you should find her and see how she is getting on. And don't miss your own meal. We can't have you fainting again.'

Mrs Dymott was in reception talking to Mr Warner about the bookings for the following weeks.

'We do try,' he told her, 'to avoid single-night stays if possible once the summer season is in full swing. A booking for, say, Wednesday night means that we may lose a whole week's booking for that room. Single-night bookings are a recipe for financial disaster in July and August – and on race days, of course. We have to be diplomatic, of course, and frequently tell people that we have no vacancies. On race days we take a minimum two-night stay. People under-stand.'

Alice apologized for interrupting them and asked if anyone had seen Mr Cootes. They hadn't.

'I'd better see what's happening,' Alice told the manager.

Her knock on the door of room fifty-one produced no answer. The door was locked and she was immediately worried. Was he in there in a drunken stupor or had he gone out? Downstairs she established that he was not in the dining room or the lounge and that his key had not been handed in. Which meant he was in his room. Mr Warner had explained the problem to Mrs Dymott and the three of them conferred. It was decided that Alice should let herself in with the pass key and she hurried upstairs again, crossing her fingers that no harm had come to him. She now blamed herself for not calling in a doctor earlier. There was such a thing as alcohol poisoning, she knew. Was he perhaps ill?

Letting herself in she found him slumped in the bed, his mouth open, snoring loudly. The room had been tidied and the window was pushed up to allow some fresh air in. She turned back to the bed. A smell of burning alerted her to a smouldering patch on the bedside rug where a cigar stub had burned itself out. He had obviously washed and shaved and Alice watched him for a moment with relief.

'At least you're still alive, Mr Cootes,' she muttered. But could there be more to it?

She left him to his sleep. A half-empty whisky bottle on the bedside table told its story and she took it downstairs with her to prevent further complications.

Mr Warner listened to her report.

Alice said, 'If he isn't up and about by this evening and able to eat something, we might have to call the doctor.'

Mrs Dymott raised her eyebrows. 'The doctor?'

'He might be unconscious or in a coma for all we know.'

Mr Warner looked doubtful. 'Who is going to pay the bill?'

'Maybe we could contact his wife.'

'From all accounts she doesn't want him back,' he reminded her. 'You're too soft-hearted. We'll catch him when he's sobered up, see that he gets nothing more to drink then give him something to eat and present him with the bill.'

'And if he won't go?' Alice could foresee difficulties.

'We'll call him a taxi and bundle him into it. If he protests we'll threaten him with the police.'

Having overheard the conversation, Miss Maine joined them. 'A woman came in around nine this morning, asking if we had a Mr Wittingstall staying here. Rather posh. She seemed disturbed and ... anxious. You don't think...'

They all turned to her.

Mr Warner said, 'Wrong name.'

'She seemed a bit odd. She described him. Said she was supposed to meet him but had forgotten the name of the hotel. I thought it was a bit odd at the time but we were busy and—'

Alice asked, 'Did the description fit our Mr Cootes?'

Miss Maine's face fell. 'It could have been Mr Cootes. I didn't give it a thought at the time.'

Alice said, 'His wife's come in search of him! It could be.' They all looked at Mr Warner.

Miss Maine said, 'She might come back...'

Mr Warner tutted. 'And she might not. I think we may have missed our chance.'

'I'm sorry, Mr Warner, but how was I to know?'

Alice said, 'No one's blaming you. But *if* she should come back...'

But Miss Maine was staring past her. 'There she *is*!' she cried, pointing to a woman who was coming in through the door. 'That's *her*!'

A slim middle-aged woman hesitated inside the doorway. She was fashionably dressed in dark green and carried a furled parasol which matched the silk of her jacket and skirt. Her hair was expertly styled and her complexion was perfect.

Mr Warner backed away. Lowering his voice he said, 'You deal with her, Mrs Meredith. This needs a woman's touch. I've got more important things to worry about.'

Miss Maine, looking deeply relieved, went back to her desk and Mr Warner retired to the office.

Alice approached the woman, who was hesitating inside the door as though wondering whether to stay or go.

'Mrs Wittingstall?'

The woman jumped. 'Yes, but how...' She

stared at Alice.

'I'm Mrs Meredith, the manageress. May we talk for a few moments? Perhaps a pot of tea?' She indicated the lounge, which was conveniently deserted. 'I think I can help you.'

Mrs Wittingstall followed her to a coffee table surrounded by three chairs and sank down into one of them with a look of utter exhaustion. Alice ordered the tea then joined her.

'We have a Mr Cootes staying here,' she said. 'He fits the description that you gave to our receptionist this morning.'

'Oh thank God! Cootes was it? I wondered if he'd use his own name. That was his mother's name! Martha Cootes. It must be Stanley.' She sat up. 'I must go to him. I've been so worried.' She made to stand up but Alice told her he was sleeping and suggested a few more minutes wouldn't make much difference.

The tea tray arrived and she busied herself pouring milk and tea. 'Help yourself to sugar,' she said. 'There's no hurry. Your husband is quite safe.'

The woman's hand trembled as she added two spoonfuls of sugar to her tea.

Alice went on in a calm tone of voice. 'Mr Coo— I mean Wittingstall, has been rather distressed but I'm sure he'll be pleased to see you.'

'Distressed? Oh no! Does that mean what I think it means? He does drink too much on occasions. It's one of his weaknesses. What exactly has he told you?'

'He told the barman you'd thrown him out.' Smiling to soften the words Alice continued, 'He was feeling rather sorry for himself. Went off the rails. That was how he described it.'

Mrs Wittingstall sipped her tea for a few moments until the need to unburden herself became too strong for her to hold back. 'That's an understatement. He was unfaithful. I found out. Yes, I did tell him to go ... It wasn't the first time, you see. I gave him chance after chance. He's an accountant in my father's firm so...' she shrugged. 'He married into the firm and it's been ... too easy for him.' Her mouth trembled suddenly and she fumbled in her purse for a handkerchief.

Alice decided then that she would not mention Marie Gaydon. Husband and wife obviously had enough problems without her adding to them.

She said, 'Marriage isn't easy, is it? I'm sorry you've had ... all these difficulties but it might be worth saving. That's for you to decide.'

For a moment they sat in silence while Mrs Wittingstall regained her composure. She set down her cup and saucer. 'I haven't come to take him back – although I will temporarily. I came to satisfy myself he didn't do anything stupid. I told myself I was glad to see the back of him but then I wondered ... I know how weak he is. I didn't want him to throw himself off the pier or under a train. I don't want that on my conscience.'

Alice wondered whether he had tried to drink himself to death but said nothing.

Mrs Wittingstall stared down at her hands. 'My parents don't want me to try for a divorce but I'm determined, with or without their help. I know it won't be easy but I believe I have grounds...' She sighed. 'My father thinks it will damage the firm. He didn't want me to wed Stanley and I opposed him. I think Father feels I should now suffer the consequences of my actions ... But we can't go on ... We shall see.' She glanced up. 'I mustn't bore you with my troubles, Mrs Meredith. If you would tell me his room number ... ?'

Alice jumped to her feet, grateful that the room was tidy and that Stanley looked reasonably presentable.

Mrs Wittingstall rose also. 'Has he ... ? I mean, is there any damage? Stanley can be very careless when he's drinking.'

'A small burn in the carpet, a crack in the bathroom mirror. The Mere has occasionally suffered much worse. It comes with the territory I'm afraid.'

Mrs Wittingstall fumbled in her handbag and drew out a ten-pound note. 'Will this cover the damage?' she asked, thrusting it into Alice's hand.

'It's much too much!' Alice tried to return it. 'Three or four pounds. I'll add it to the bill.'

'Please do – but won't you take this just to please me? To salve my conscience. You keep it.'

Alice looked down at the money and an idea came to her. 'I'm planning to set up a play box for guests' children, to help them through rainy days. If I did accept this I would use it to buy books and equipment.'

'By all means! That's a splendid idea.' She stood up. 'Now I must brave Stanley in his den. When he's sober enough we'll come down.'

'Will you need a taxi to the station?'

'No. Our car is in your car park. The chauffeur is used to waiting.'

'I'll send a cup of tea out to him.' Alice hesitated. 'Would you like me to come upstairs with you or...'

'No thank you. I'd rather deal with it alone.'

'Room fifty-one. Good luck. Let me know if I can help in any way.'

Alice watched her walk towards the lift and shook her head. It seemed to her sometimes that everyone in the world had problems. Mrs Wittingstall was obviously rich, undeniably beautiful and appeared in excellent health but still her life was far from perfect.

'Be thankful for small mercies, Alice!' she told herself and began to think how she would spend the money for Perdita's Box.

Eight

Alice awoke very early the next morning after a restless night. She hurriedly washed and dressed. She had intended to write to Eddie the previous evening but had found various excuses to delay until it was too late. Now, as she forced herself to sit at her small desk and put pen to paper, she changed her mind. She would write direct to Sebastian and would be firm but fair. Dipping the pen into the inkwell she decided she would be gracious about his offer but make it clear that the idea was not acceptable. She would pretend her husband-to-be had forbidden it. The letter must be brief and to the point – and above all dignified. Not a word of regret, not a hint of the hurt he had caused her, not a word of blame.

Dear Sebastian,
   My brother has told me of your kind offer to take his place at my forth-coming wedding. However, Henry, my fiancé, does not care for the idea and

has chosen one of his friends to walk
me up the aisle. But thank you for the
offer...

Now she was strongly tempted to add a little
– but was that wise? No doubt his wife
would see the letter and she might read it.
Did Nellie know about Sebastian's earlier
relationship with Alice, she wondered.

I expect Eddie has told you that I am to
wed Mr Lightfoot who owns the Mere
hotel. He is older than I am but we are
very fond of each other and I look
forward to my new life...

That didn't sound too boastful but would
let him know that she was making a good
marriage.

'With no thanks to you!' she muttered
with a wry smile.

She longed to tell him that she was
expecting their child but it was out of the
question. Much as she longed for him to
know the truth, Alice knew she must write
nothing that might provoke him into
coming to the wedding.

Trust that brother of mine to mess
things up. Now he cannot attend but
my mother plans to make the trip from
Ireland so I will be well represented...

In fact Alice's mother was making no such plans and the family would be notable only by their absence. She had expected Edith to be there but now that was unlikely. Poor Edith was not going to be anywhere. She was probably dead.

Alice brushed aside tears. She mustn't make her eyes red, because Henry was taking her out to dinner at the Grosvenor Hotel. Just the two of them. Hester had insisted that he and Alice must spend more time together and had declined the invitation. Later in the day Alice was going shopping for a new suit. There was no way she was going to appear with Henry in her usual clothes but was determined to live up to her new position in society. She was looking forward to it but also dreading the time when she might make a mistake and let Henry down. It wasn't going to be easy but she really did feel that he was more than a little fond of her and hopefully he would be patient and helpful.

I hear that you have married and are expecting a baby. My best wishes to you both.
Your friend Alice Meredith...

Before she could change her mind about any of the wording, Alice blotted the page, folded it and slipped it into the envelope. She would leave it on the desk with the guests' outgoing mail and Miss Maine would hand it to the postman when he arrived.

As soon as she was dressed she set off along the corridor but was surprised to hear a click behind her. She turned and saw the bootboy outside room thirty-one. He was standing with his hands behind his back, staring at her with wide innocent eyes.

'Smiffy? What are you up to?'

'Nothink.'

'You've just come out of that room!'

'I never!'

'I heard the door click. Tell me the truth.' She closed the distance between them until she was towering over him. The innocent expression was wavering. 'What were you doing?' she repeated.

'Nothink. Honest!' He glanced round as though expecting help to arrive at any moment. 'I was looking for Mr Robbins' boots, that's all. He forgot to put them outside last night.'

His face had turned a bright pink but still Alice was undecided. She had no wish to accuse him unjustly.

'So you went in to collect the boots and you've just come out.'

He nodded eagerly.

'So where are the boots?'

'What?'

'Mr Robbins' boots? Where are they?'

His mouth fell open. 'I didn't ... That is, I couldn't find them.'

'So Mr Robbins is still asleep in his room.'

He nodded.

'How did you know the door would be unlocked?'

'I didn't. I just tried it. One of the other lads was saying that folk don't always lock their doors cos they forget cos they're sozzled.'

Alice sighed. 'We will go downstairs to the boot room and we will talk,' she informed him. 'And we will look at the boots – but first you will hold out your hands.'

He gave a muffled cry and stepped backwards.

Alice knew he was thieving. Grabbing his arms she pulled him forward. His hands were empty but there were two coins on the carpet behind him – a shilling and a six-pence.

'So that's it!' Disappointed she picked them up. She had always liked the lad. 'What have you to say for yourself, you foolish boy?'

His face crumpled. 'I was going to – I was only borrowing it...'

Alice resisted the urge to shake him. 'Come downstairs with me,' she told him. 'We're going to see the boots.'

Downstairs in the boot room, the gleaming shoes and boots were each tagged with the owner's room number. It was the work of a few moments to find the black boots belonging to the occupant of room thirty-one.

'So you stole some money and you also lied to me.' She felt a wave of anger at his stupidity. For the sake of a few coins he had risked a job in a decent hotel where he was well-liked. A job with the chance of small promotions.

He said nothing.

'Go to the office and wait for me outside the door.'

Alice wanted time to think. She wanted to ask Mr Warner if they could give the lad another chance — but was he worth it? Was this the first offence or had he been making a habit of stealing? If so he was being cunning. Never taking much so that the owner might not notice the loss or might at least be unsure. If it was a habit, then he would have to go. Which meant that they must return the stolen money and this in turn would allow the guests to see that the hotel's security was not as good as it should be.

'I don't need this!' she muttered, annoyed.

Following him to the office she found him in conversation with the new night porter and was cheered by the knowledge that so far he, at least, was doing well and had

221

earned one or two favourable comments from the guests.

To the boy she said tersely, 'Into the office!'

Following him in, she closed the door. Mr Warner wouldn't be on duty for another half hour so Alice sat Smith down and regarded him as sternly as she could.

'Mr Warner is going to sack you,' she told him. 'Unless I can persuade him to give you another chance. Have you done this before?'

'No, ma'am, I haven't. I swear I haven't.'

'You get paid. You have a roof over your head. You get well fed. Why steal?'

He stared gloomily at his feet. 'I owed someone.'

'Who?'

'Can't say.'

'Then you'd better go up and pack your things. Go on.'

He didn't move. Alice tried to think harshly but she reflected how easy it was to make a wrong move at any age. At his age it must be much easier. She herself had twenty-eight years of accummulated wisdom but she had made a serious mistake. Only Hester's intervention had saved her from an unhappy fate. Should she give this young man a chance?

'Smith! Did you hear me? I said go and pack. I'll give you a letter to take home to your parents explaining what has happened and why I can't give you a reference.'

There was another long silence and then she saw two tears drip on to his shoes.

He looked up slowly. 'I had a flutter on the horses yesterday. On the second race.'

'At the Roodee?'

He nodded. 'All the lads did.' He wiped his eyes with his sleeve. 'Simms got a hot tip from this geezer, see, who come in the bar. He said Sugarbaby was a cert! Simms said he must know because he's a bookie's runner. I didn't have enough so I borrowed three bob from him – and the horse came in last but one.'

'So you owe three shillings! That's a lot of money!'

'My Pa's going to wallop me!' His air of innocence had entirely disappeared to be replaced by one of deep apprehension.

'I hope so,' Alice told him. 'You deserve a walloping.'

More tears trickled down his face. He stood up. 'I'm sorry. That's all. I'm really sorry.'

Alice came to a decision. 'If you were to return the money, tell the owner what you did, and ask his forgiveness, we could see. If he forgives you – and it's a big if – I'll ask Mr Warner to give you a second chance.'

'Thank you, Mrs Meredith.'

'It hasn't happened yet so don't count your chickens. Now get back to the boot room and get on with your work. I'll send for you later.'

Later, when Mr Robbins came out of breakfast, he was invited into the office and stood in astonishment as Alice explained that the bootboy had stolen from him. After a short discussion with Alice, he agreed to see the boy.

Ten minutes later, in the office, Mr Robbins glared down into the cherubic face of the erring Smith.

'What's this I hear? You came into my room!' he roared angrily. 'You dared to come into my bedroom while I was asleep? You – you nasty sly little wretch!'

'I'm sorry, sir! I...' He stared up at his accuser.

'And you *stole* from my bedside table? You're nothing but a common thief and I know what to do with boys like you.'

'Please sir, I'm sorry! I never meant to...' Smith threw a terrified glance towards Alice but her face was stern.

Mr Robbins leaned towards the boy. 'Never meant to what, eh? Never meant to steal from me? Then how come you did?'

Smith swallowed hard and Alice saw that he was trembling.

Mr Robbins turned to Alice. 'Call the police!'

'Oh but Mr Robbins...' she said. 'I thought...'

'Call them. I won't be made a fool of by a tuppenny ha'penny kid! Let him rot in jail. Do him good. Teach him a lesson.'

Alice looked startled. 'But Mr Robbins, his parents will be broken-hearted. He comes from a good family.'

'Good family? What's good about a family with a thief for a son?' He poked a finger into Smith's chest. 'Eh? You! Tell me that!'

Smith looked very pale, as though he might faint at any moment. He glanced desperately towards Alice who looked stricken. 'Well, Smith, if Mr Robbins insists...' She shrugged and her hand strayed towards the telephone.

Desperately Smith turned back to Mr Robbins. 'I'm giving it back, sir. I'm giving the money back. Honest I am. Mrs Meredith has it.' He turned to her in a panic. 'Tell him! You've got the money...'

Alice reached into the desk drawer and drew out the two coins and handed them back to their rightful owner.

Mr Robbins stared at the money then slowly took it from her.

'Well ... Since I've got it back ... I don't know.'

Alice said, 'He's terribly sorry, Mr Robbins. It's his first and last offence. You do still have the money. Couldn't you ... Just this once ... ? I'm sure Smith has learnt his lesson.'

'Oh I have! I have!' The small mouth trembled.

Mr Robbins straightened up. 'Very well then. In this case I'll make an exception.' He looked at Alice. 'You can leave the police out of it.'

'Thank you, Mr Robbins.' She smiled nervously.

He glared at the boy, pocketed the money and said, 'Well get off to your work then!'

Smith, hardly able to believe his good fortune, dashed headlong from the room before Mr Robbins could change his mind.

After a second or two Alice and Mr Robbins exchanged smiles.

He grinned, 'Poor kid. He looked terrified – but then that was the idea, wasn't it? Your little plan!'

She said, 'I think we frightened him, don't you? You almost frightened *me* and I knew what was happening! Have you ever thought about a career on the stage?'

They both laughed.

'I'm very grateful to you, Mr Robbins,' she told him, 'for your understanding attitude. I'm giving him this one chance and I don't think he'll risk anything like that again. And he will be punished. He now has to earn the money he owes his colleague by doing extra jobs for me.'

Mr Robbins went off chuckling and Alice told Mr Warner what they had done. Busy on another matter, he nodded distractedly and Alice went in search of Simms.

'Don't ever lend money to the juniors,' she told him. 'It leads to problems. Please remember.'

Then she dreamed up several unpleasant tasks for Smith to do and went on her way with a lighter heart.

Later that afternoon Alice gathered all her courage and stepped into Holmes Bank in Eastgate Street. She joined a queue of people who were waiting to draw out or pay in money but it moved very slowly and she gave up and went to another desk where a bespectacled man was riffling through papers.

'Excuse me, but I—'

He held up a peremptory hand without speaking. Alice found herself staring at the top of his balding head.

'I wonder if I may—' she began.

Obviously exasperated, he tightened his mouth and sighed heavily. '*If* you would be so kind as to wait until—'

'But I have an appointment.' She hoped she didn't look as nervous as she felt. 'My fiancé has set up an account for me...'

His fingers became still. Slowly he looked up. 'And you are?'

'Mrs Meredith from the Mere. Mr Light-foot—'

His mouth opened and closed. In one fluid movement he dropped the papers, stood up and held out his hand. 'Mrs Meredith! Do forgive me! This is a pleasure! I'm Clarence Chard, the manager.'

His dazzling smile was apparently intended to offset his earlier neglect but Alice was not impressed. It seemed that if you were a nobody you could wait but if you were going to become Henry Lightfoot's wife, you would receive deferential treatment. After a fractional pause she allowed him to shake her hand.

'Do come into my office,' he purred. 'I shall explain the complexities of the system and give you any help I can.'

Alice followed him into a room which was half filled by a large desk. She seated herself in the leather armchair and listened while he produced a cheque book and paying-in slips and explained their use. Hardly 'complexities', she thought. Perhaps he imagined that women had smaller brains than men.

'I am going shopping,' she explained, 'and I shall need to pay by cheque.'

'Quite simple, Mrs Meredith. You simply fill in the cheque – date, signature, the amount and the name of the person or business you are going to pay. Some shops may ask for your address on the back of the cheque. That is quite in order. Just a precaution on their part and nothing to worry about.'

Moments later Alice was back on the pavement, breathing a sigh of relief.

'Now for the best part!' she whispered and set off cheerfully along the street.

Within the next hour and a half she bought a smart two-piece in heavy blue silk, a pair of buttoned shoes made of mushroom-coloured suede, some gloves to match the shoes and three pairs of fine stockings. Feeling rather light-headed, she went into a jeweller's shop and chose a pair of silver-and-gilt cuff-links as a wedding present for Henry. Carried away by the excitement she bought Hester a marquasite brooch in the shape of a curled feather. Suddenly exhausted, she remembered her baby and felt immediately remorseful.

'Henry said you must take care of yourself,' she reminded herself.'

Greatly daring, she found a taxi and rode back to the hotel in comfort and style. She was rapidly coming to the conclusion that she might find her future life very pleasant.

That evening Alice and Henry were shown to a quiet table in the dining room of the Grosvenor Hotel. Alice sat down and at once the waiter shook out her serviette and laid it carefully across her lap. Henry ordered champagne and the menus were placed in their hands. Alice studied hers with something akin to the panic that young Smith had suffered earlier in the day.

Henry said, 'The asparagus is good at this time of the year. Do you fancy that as a first course? Or something a little more satisfying?' He leaned forward and whispered. 'Eating for two, you know!'

She smiled. 'You won't let me forget it!'

'Why should I?' He reached forward and touched the hand which held the menu. 'I can't wait, Alice, for sleepless nights and walks in the park with the perambulator. I've waited most of my life for a little family and had given up hoping long ago. You have no idea how happy I am.'

Impulsively Alice leaned forward, brought his hand to her lips and kissed it. It was the first time she had ever wanted to kiss him and the realization burst upon her that she was beginning to love Henry Lightfoot. 'Love begets love,' her mother had often said and suddenly she knew it was true. This not-so-elderly man was giving her a second chance and she would learn to adore him.

'Alice!' he whispered hoarsely. 'My dearest girl!'

She smiled, shaken by her own emotions and his reaction to the small but loving gesture. We can make ourselves a wonderful marriage, she thought, dazed by the revelation. For a moment they had eyes only for each other and then the waiter interrupted them.

'Champagne!' he said, working the cork loose and filling their glasses.

When they were alone again, Henry said, 'To my dear Alice and our future happiness.'

Alice touched her glass to his and whispered, 'To our little family!' and they grinned conspiratorially before taking the first sip.

Henry said, 'You are looking very beautiful this evening, Alice. Is that a new outfit?'

She nodded. 'I went to the bank today. Rather unnerving but I managed and then I went a little mad! I bought some presents and these clothes. I feel like a princess!'

'Oh! That reminds me. Mr Lester popped in while you were out this morning. He brought you a small gift and asked me to give it to you. I'm so sorry. I quite forgot. And I asked him if he would care to give you away when we are married. I thought it would be good for him to feel needed now that he has no one – except his mother, of course.'

'I'm delighted,' Alice told him. 'I thought he was going down to London to see about selling his flat.'

'He's off first thing tomorrow morning but he'll be back in time for the wedding rehearsal. The vicar has asked to see us together for his little homily. I was wondering about our secret. Ought we to confide in him?'

Alice had never given it a moment's thought. 'I'll be guided by you, Henry. What do you think?'

He leaned forward. 'I think not,' he whispered.

'Then it's our secret.'

The evening passed happily. Henry ordered for them both – duck with all the trimmings followed by a summer-fruit compote with chantilly cream. When the taxi came to collect them Alice thought she had never been happier. As they rode back to the Mere, her head was on Henry's shoulder and her hand was in his.

First thing the next morning Alice found the handyman and led him to a corner of the lounge. Bob Olley was a carpenter joiner by trade but at the age of sixty had retired from his business and worked for the Mere part-time 'to keep his eye in', as he liked to tell people.

'This corner is going to be for the children,' she informed him. Seeing the look on his face she went on. 'I've cleared the idea with Mr Lightfoot and he's agreeable. All you have to do is put up three shelves, not too high, on which I can put a few books. We'll need room below the lower shelf for a large toy chest and room for the lid to open, of course.'

'Would that be square-edged shelves or moulded?'

'Ah. I hadn't thought about it. What do you think, Mr Olley? I want it to look attractive.'

'Moulded it is then, ma'am. Leave it to me.' His good natured face developed a slight frown. 'D'you want me to make the chest, too?'

'No. Just the shelves. I'm planning to buy a hessian chest with reinforced ends.'

'Will that last, Mrs Meredith, begging your pardon? A nice oak—'

'It's a question of safety, Mr Olley,' Alice explained. 'I don't want a heavy chest a small child could climb into and be suffocated. When it wears out we'll just have to replace it.'

After a few more moments discussion Bob Olley went off to find suitable wood for the shelves and Alice went to reception to meet Mrs Dymott.

Miss Maine smiled at her. 'Had dinner with your fiancé last night, I hear! Nice, was it?'

'Very nice. A bit posh but the food was delicious.'

'Better than our fish pie, then, I should think!'

Alice changed the subject. 'Have you seen

Mick Davies lately?'

Her face fell. 'Not since he left, no. I know he did wrong but he was fun. Used to make us laugh.'

'I really think you are worth someone better,' Alice told her earnestly. 'A man who could carry on that way ... We could have turned him over to the police. He'll be in real trouble one day, I'm afraid.'

Miss Maine shrugged. 'Still no word about poor Mrs Brightling. D'you think she really is dead?'

'I have to admit my hopes fade with each day that passes. All we can say is that we made her stay here as pleasant as possible. But she'll miss my wedding and that ... Oh! Here's Mrs Dymott.'

The two women spent ten minutes together discussing hotel matters and then Alice left her. She was off to the shops to buy the toys for Perdita's Box and had been looking forward to it. First she searched out Smith who was about to enjoy his mid-morning break.

'No time for a break, Smith,' she told him briskly. 'I need someone to carry all my parcels back from the shops.'

'But I haven't had my...' He looked longingly at the mug of tea and slice of buttered toast.

Alice hardened her heart. 'No time for that.' Bending down she whispered. 'You're about to earn your first sixpence. Mustn't keep Simms waiting for the money you owe him!'

With a martyred sigh, the boy followed her out of the staff dining room, watched by his sniggering colleagues, but he was greatly cheered by his first ever taxi ride.

When they arrived at the town centre Alice consulted the list she had made and they dived in and out of the appropriate shops. Jigsaw puzzles, beads to thread, snakes and ladders and ludo. Soon Smith was staggering along under his parcels. Alice stopped, out of breath.

'Is that the lot, then?' Smith enquired hopefully. 'My back's breaking!'

'Not quite but we can leave some to another day.'

'My arms are coming out of their sockets!'

'Nonsense. I'll choose a few books and then we'll find a taxi to take us back to the hotel.'

'I'm starving. I don't want to miss me lunch!'

'Stop moaning, Smith. You won't miss it.'

'I missed me break!'

She hurried into the next bookshop and picked her way along the shelves. *Animals of Africa, Boys Annual, Stories for Girls* and *My Favourite Bible Stories.*

By the time they were ensconced in the return taxi, Smith was red-faced with his exertions and looking forward anxiously to his lunch. He carried all the parcels into the lounge and Alice gave him a sixpence.

'You go straight to Simms and give it to him,' she warned the boy. 'Any nonsense and you'll be down at the police station before your feet can touch the ground.' She kept her face straight until he had gone then laughed. The fact was she had enjoyed his company.

Tired but happy she stowed her purchases in the big sideboard and made her way up to her room. Throwing herself on to the bed, she allowed herself to relax. Then her eye caught a note on the bedside table.

Dear Alice,
    I'm afraid Sergeant Flint brought bad news. A woman's body was washed up on the French coast...

'Oh no! Edith!'

    They think it is Edith Brightling. If so, it looks as though the so-called Dr Stewart might well be facing a murder charge. Do come and see me when you get back from your shopping. I'm so sorry, dear. I know you were fond of her.
    Hester

'Oh *Edith*! What did the wretch *do* to you?'

Tears ran down her face. In her mind's eye she saw Edith's saturated body floating in the sea, eyes staring, her soft grey hair tossed by the waves. Then she imagined the crumpled body abandoned by the sea, tossed on to weed-strewn sands ... or battered and broken among rocks. 'I hope they hang you, Albert Stewart,' she muttered fiercely. 'By the neck until you are dead!' Isn't that how the death penalty went? She tried to imagine the murderer dangling on the end of a rope and shuddered. Thank heavens they had him in custody.

Reaching for a handkerchief, she wiped her eyes and blew her nose. Then she washed her face and hands and hurried up to see Hester. It was a great comfort, she realized suddenly, to have the support of a family.

The next three days passed in a whirl of activity for Alice. Mrs Dymott was promising to become an excellent replacement and was able to take Alice's place whenever she needed time off – which was frequently. More fittings for her dress, shopping for shoes, good-natured arguments with Henry over where they should spend their honeymoon, a guest list to prepare with Hester and invitations to send out.

All as quickly as possible if not sooner!

thought Alice, aware of the child growing inside her.

On Tuesday she woke up with a feeling of dread. She had an appointment with Henry's doctor and he had insisted on accompanying her. She washed and dressed and took extra care with her hair. She put on a dark-blue skirt and crisp white blouse and a pair of her new stockings.

'Whatever shall I say to him?' she had asked Henry with a touch of desperation. They were going to confess to the pregnancy and Alice knew that the doctor would be shocked.

'Leave the talking to me, dear,' Henry told her. 'You just sit there and look beautiful!'

Beautiful? Alice stared at herself in the mirror. The morning sickness still plagued her and she looked pale and nervous but she had done her best. No matter how she looked she was still a pregnant, unmarried woman. A rush to the altar would never change that. She was going to have to live with it. She thought of the child when he grew up and started to ask questions. Would he, or she, work out the dates and discover the truth?

As she sighed guiltily there was a knock at the door.

She opened it to find Mrs Dymott there.

'I'm sorry to disturb you but there's a Mr

Symons with some chairs. He wants to know—'

'The upholsterer! He's early!'

'He says he has to go to a funeral later and is trying to get everything done before he goes.'

Downstairs Alice explained the rotation of the chairs and allowed Mrs Dymott to select the last five for renovation. Alice also mentioned the burned carpet in room fifty-one and Mr Symons said he might be able to mend it invisibly. While Alice was in reception they talked for a moment about the drowned woman in France and then Alice asked Mr Warner about Mr and Mrs Wittingstall.

'They left a few hours after the wife arrived,' he told her. 'She paid the bill and left a tip for the staff on top of what you had for the kiddies' toy box. Nice woman. I felt sorry for her. I gathered they were going straight home.'

Alice smiled. 'Funny isn't it?' she said. 'People come and go. We're given these tiny glimpses of their lives but we never know what happens after they leave. I wonder if their marriage will survive.'

'Women get too upset about the little things,' he said. 'A few drinks too many, a silly flirtation ... What does it really matter?'

Alice stared at him in disbelief. 'You can't mean that! It's a matter of trust, isn't it? His drunkenness and his philandering hurt her very much. It makes her unhappy and he *knows* it does. So how much can he care for her?'

He laughed. 'You would take her side! Women!'

'Would you behave like that to your wife?'

He hesitated, seeing the trap. Then he grinned and was about to say something else when they both noticed a middle-aged man who was pushing his way in through the door with undeniable arrogance. Mr Warner's grin faded and he muttered, 'One of those!'

The man strode up to the desk and banged three times on the bell even though Mr Warner and Alice were standing within feet of him, talking across the counter together.

Mr Warner moved towards him, his face a blank. 'May I help you, sir?' His tone was frosty. Alice hid her amusement. Mr Warner could be very *un*helpful when he wanted.

The man was slim and above average in height – probably in his late thirties or early forties, thought Alice, sizing him up with interest. It was rather early in the day for guests to be booking in at a hotel but perhaps he was simply making enquiries on behalf of someone else. His fair hair tended to be frizzy and his eyes were a very pale blue.

He said, 'One of the family. I'm here to see—'

'Have you made a reservation, Mr ... ?'

'No I haven't. Don't need one, do I? I've just told you that I'm—'

'I hope it's not for tonight, sir.' Being deliberately obtuse, Mr Warner flipped through the signing-in book with a sharply indrawn breath. 'Nothing here, I'm afraid.'

Alice was enjoying the small drama. She knew there were vacancies and she knew Mr Warner would suddenly 'discover' one – when he felt ready to do so.

The manager shook his head. 'Nothing at all. Now if you'd telephoned or written...'

'I tell you I don't need to book! If you would pay attention to—'

'You say your family is already here? What name would that be, sir?'

'It's Lightfoot, dammit!'

Alice was suddenly attentive. A member of Henry's family?

The man went on in hectoring tones. 'Your employer, Henry Lightfoot, is my uncle. Now *if* you would please let him know I'm here – that's Donald Lightfoot – I'd be forever in your debt.' His triumph was almost tangible.

Alice didn't know who was the most shocked – her or Mr Warner. They both looked at Donald Lightfoot and then glanced quickly at each other. Alice's first thought was that this must be the hated nephew but presumably he knew nothing of her existence. It seemed unlikely that he had received an invitation to the wedding. So why was he turning up without warning after all these years?

Mr Warner recovered quickly. Without altering his attitude he said, 'I'll telephone Mr Lightfoot and let him know you're here. Would you like to take a seat?' He indicated a nearby armchair.

'No I would not. I think we've wasted quite enough time already.'

He turned to glare at Alice as though keen to include her in his displeasure and Alice was aware of a frisson of delight. Donald Lightfoot was in for a nasty shock.

Mr Warner put down the telephone. 'Mr Lightfoot will be down presently.'

Delaying tactics, thought Alice. Henry was probably hurrying to see Hester and warn her of approching trouble.

'Why don't I just go on up?' Donald Lightfoot demanded.

Alice thought fast. 'Your uncle may be coming down the stairs. You would pass each other.'

The nephew turned to glare at Alice. 'Are you a member of staff?'

Mr Warner said, 'Mrs Meredith is our manageress.'

'Is she?' He sounded less than impressed.

242

'Then don't let me keep you, Mrs Meredith. I'm sure you want to go about your work.'

'I do indeed, Mr Lightfoot.' She smiled sweetly at him. 'But first I want a word with your uncle.'

'He'll be tied up, I'm afraid. We have a lot to talk about.'

'I'm sure you have.' She made no attempt to go about her work but maintained her smile and her air of politeness, which clearly puzzled him. In the background she saw that Mr Warner was relishing the situation.

At that moment Henry came into view round the corner of the stairs. There was a polite smile on his face but nothing that suggested a warm welcome.

'Uncle Henry! It's been an age, hasn't it?' Donald moved towards him and held out his hand.

Henry crossed the distance between them and the two men shook hands.

Donald said, 'Your manager was telling me there are no free rooms. You're doing well, then.'

'I like to think so. But don't worry. If you are planning to stay in Chester overnight I can find you a room in another hotel. I know many of the proprietors.' He smiled, half turning towards Alice. 'You haven't met my fiancée, have you? This is Alice Meredith. We are to be married in two weeks time.'

Alice stepped forward. 'Nice to meet you, Mr Lightfoot.' She held out her hand.

Donald stared at her, open-mouthed. 'Your *fiancée*!' He finally managed to shake the proffered hand. 'You mean ... Your *fiancée*? But that's ... I mean, when did this happen?' His face had paled. 'Mother didn't say ... Does she know?'

'She will shortly. The invitations are on their way.'

Alice watched the various expressions flit across the nephew's face. Shock, fear, anger. She turned to Henry. 'We mustn't forget our appointment but we have an hour before we need to set off. Shall I ring for tea for your nephew?'

Henry hesitated. 'I think we'll order tea and biscuits for four. We'll take it upstairs in Hester's room. It's sunnier than mine at this time of the day.' He smiled at Donald. 'Come on upstairs. Hester will be so surprised to see you.'

Oh no she won't, thought Alice, watching them go ahead, but she could see that Henry was tickled pink with the surprise he had given his unpleasant nephew. She asked Miss Maine to order the tea and then followed them upstairs.

Nine

Inside Hester's apartment Alice found her three relatives to-be sitting around the large coffee table. Donald had removed his jacket and a fancy waistcoat was much in evidence.

Hester said, 'Ah there you are, Alice. Come and sit here next to me. I've hardly seen you the last few days. I'll be glad when you've handed over to Mrs Dymott.' She patted the sofa and Alice joined her.

Donald said, 'So congratulations are in order, Uncle Henry.' He was trying hard to recover his former poise. 'My very best wishes to you both. Mother and Father will be very surprised. Very surprised indeed.' Unspoken but suggetsed by his expression was the extent of his confusion.

Henry laughed. 'I was surprised myself. A man of my age doesn't expect to be so fortunate.'

Donald gave Alice a weak smile and turned back to his uncle. 'And so soon after poor Aunt Marion's death.'

Hester said, 'I don't know why we all refer

to her as "poor Marion". She really had a very pleasant life. Some occasional ill health but she had everything necessary for her well-being. Henry was very good to her.'

'I hope I was.' Henry added.

'You were, dear.' Hester turned to her nephew. 'So what brings you to this part of the world, Donald? I don't think we ever expected to see you again. We parted on somewhat uneasy terms, didn't we?'

Donald flushed. 'I don't think ... It surely wasn't ... Just a misunderstanding. That's all. I realized the timing was all wrong. My fault entirely.'

Maggie came in with the tea tray and Hester filled and handed round the cups.

Donald said, 'So what are your plans, then, Uncle Henry? Are you leaving the Mere? I imagine you will want to live else-where now that you are to be—'

'Not immediately but maybe at some stage.'

'But you'll want to travel, I expect. See the world with your ... er ... new bride. I said to Mother that you must surely want to live a little while your health is still reliable. Switzerland is very bracing ... and Italy.' He turned to Alice. 'Have you ever been to Rome? Or Venice? You must persuade Uncle Henry to take you. I can make myself avail-able to take over here at any time. It's always been a dream of mine to share in the Mere while Uncle Henry is still alive rather than wait for his—'

Hester said, 'His death?'

Donald had the grace to look flustered. 'I didn't ... er ... didn't mean it quite like that but obviously eventually...' He smiled at Alice. 'Such a tragedy poor Aunt Marion couldn't give him any children.'

Alice took a bite from her biscuit and it went down the wrong way and made her cough.

Donald was still talking. 'I said to my parents, I'm making no plans until I've offered my services to Uncle Henry. I'm all he's got by way of an heir and I owe it to him.'

Hester was patting Alice on the back.

Henry said, 'So what are you actually doing at the moment – by way of a career, I mean? I seem to remember your father wanted you to go into the railways. Marvellous opportunities for advancement, I'm told. But it meant starting at the bottom and you weren't too keen.'

'It wasn't that, exactly. I ... er ... I had the chance to go to Australia and I took it.'

Hester looked up. 'Bit of a waste of time, by all accounts.' Her voice had sharpened.

'Wouldn't say that, Aunt Hester,' he protested. 'Travel broadens the mind, so they say.' He gave a nervous laugh.

Henry said, 'So when are we going to be

invited to *your* wedding, Donald? You must settle down sometime.'

Donald looked discomfited. 'That's partly why I'm here, Uncle Henry. The truth is that I have met a young lady. She's only nineteen and we're desperately in love. But ... her family aren't too keen. Impecunious, in their eyes. Me, I mean. I don't think they see me as a very good catch for Dulcie. That's her name. The thing is I always expected ... er ... hoped, rather, that I'd come into partnership with you, Uncle Henry. That's what I told her parents and they were quite impressed. Dulcie was ecstatic, of course.' He smiled at Alice. 'I'm sure you will understand her feelings. I told them it was just a matter of timing.'

Henry gazed at him and Alice saw compassion in his eyes. He said, 'I don't think I had planned on that, Donald. I did what I could for you, though. I put in a word for you with Simpsons, the auctioneers. That would have meant good career prospects. Must be almost seven years ago now. You weren't at all interested, I recall. Turned it down flat.'

'Fancied the hotel trade, didn't I? I thought...'

Hester said, 'We made it quite clear last time this idea was aired, Donald. We don't need another partner.'

'But who will inherit? You can't just die

and let the taxman take it all. I am your nephew and there's no one else.'

'But I shall soon have a wife.'

Donald hesitated. Alice could see him trying to decide how far he should go. How desperate was he, she wondered, to know his long term future was safe financially? Perhaps he had frittered away his chances over the years because he had relied on Henry needing him. She wondered what Dulcie was like and felt sorry for her.

Donald's face was reddening. 'Look, the thing is this ... I need to know something definite. I have to speak to Dulcie's parents next week. I need to tell them...' He looked from his uncle to his aunt and his mouth tightened. 'The fact is my parents feel you owe it to me. The money from grandfather ... You had more than a fair share. Father has always maintained that—'

Henry sat up suddenly and his expression had hardened. 'That was absolutely fair, Donald. Your father asked for his share early so that you could be sent to an expensive school and go on to Cambridge. Your grand-father wasn't ready. He had to sell a lot of shares to give your father that money. He sold when the shares were down and he lost a great deal of money. And all because of you, Donald. For you – to ensure your future. But what did you do? You wasted time, traipsing round the world in search of a good time.'

'That's not fair!' Donald shouted. 'Grand-father left you more money. A larger share.'

'Because I didn't ask for it when it wasn't available. I didn't ask for it at all. The money only came to me on his death, by which time the shares had matured as expected. I received what your father would have received if he hadn't insisted on having his money early to help you.'

Hester leaned forward. 'He did it out of love for you and he expected you to make better use of your expensive education. He expected you to work hard and get on. You're your own worst enemy, Donald.'

Alice kept her eyes averted. Donald's anger was painful to watch. He genuinely believed that he was being cheated but Alice could see quite clearly what had happened.

He swallowed hard and then tossed his head defiantly. 'What you mean is I'm being kept out in the cold until you are both dead. I mean all three of you … So then it's coming to me. Unless you're planning on leaving it to a dogs' home! So since you know it and I know it, why not let me in now?'

His manner suddenly changed as he realized how vulnerable he was and that antagonizing his aunt and uncle would do him no favours. In a softer voice he begged, 'Can't we let bygones be bygones? I really

250

do need to tell Dulcie's parents that I have prospects. That I can look after their daughter in the manner to which etc, etc!' At last he caught Alice's eye. 'Don't you have anything to say?' he demanded. 'Can't you see how unfair this is? Dulcie is the sweetest girl in the world and she adores me. I could very easily lose her.'

Alice said, 'That would be very sad.'

'Of course it would. Can't you, at least, say something to persuade Uncle Henry? I'm family. What do you stand to gain by seeing me shut out like this? Tell him he's just being stubborn. Tell him I'm entitled to...' He spluttered to a halt, overcome by his emotions and disappointed hopes.

Alice said quietly, 'I don't feel I should interfere. I'm sorry.'

He stared at her, struggling with his anger. 'Look Alice, the time will come when you and I will be left. They'll be gone. I don't wish it but it's a fact of life. You will have no children so it will just be the two of us. You and I ... we could run the Mere. You and I and ... er ... Dulcie. You could stay on here.'

Hester said sarcastically, 'How very generous of you!' She looked at Henry and narrowed her eyes.

Henry looked at Alice. 'May I tell him, dearest? Would you mind?'

Alice was startled. 'If you wish.'

251

Donald looked at their faces. 'Tell me what?'

'Alice and I are expecting a child.'

For a moment there was silence.

'You and ... A *child*? But you can't ... That's not possible.' He frowned, confused. 'A *child*?' he repeated. He blinked. 'I don't believe you.'

Hester said, 'It's true nonetheless. Alice is in the family way.'

'But you're not even married!' He looked at Alice. 'You and him?'

'Yes.'

'I thought ... er ... We all thought ... Because of you and Marion ... Oh *God*!' He covered his face with his hands.

Hester said, 'Donald! Please!'

'I'm sorry.'

Alice felt an unwilling compassion.

Hester said, 'I think you should be congratulating them. A baby at Henry's time of life. We're all delighted.'

Donald looked up. 'Hence the hurried wedding! I see it all now.'

He looked totally crushed. The emotion had drained from him leaving him spent. He sat back in the chair and surveyed them with scarcely concealed bitterness. 'A baby! Who'd have thought it?'

Hester said, 'A cousin.'

Donald groaned.

Henry said, 'When Hester and I are gone

252

Alice will run the Mere until the child is old enough to inherit. I'm sorry, Donald, if you expected otherwise.'

'That's it, then. I've lost Dulcie.'

Hester said, 'If she loves you she'll wait.'

'For what?'

'For you to find a job and start up the ladder. Give yourself five years.'

'Five years? You expect her to wait five years for me?'

Hester shrugged.

Alice said, 'You said she adores you, Donald. This will test her love. She's very young still but if she loves you...'

His eyes blazed as he swung to face her. 'You keep out! It's nothing to do with you. You're nothing but a jumped-up—' He stopped abruptly.

Henry looked grim. 'I'm glad you thought better of it, Donald. I shan't hesitate to throw you out if I see fit.'

His voice was cold and Alice watched him as he struggled with his anger. She had never seen him in this mood and she was glad she was not in Donald's shoes.

Hester said, 'Alice is right, Donald. If Dulcie loves you she will be willing to wait.'

He sprang to his feet. 'Very easy for you to say, isn't it? *If* she loves me. Well, she *does* but...' He breathed heavily. 'I can't stay here another moment. Between you, you've ruined my life. I hope you're satisfied!'

Henry rose to his feet. 'I think that's a bit strong, Donald. I'm sure you'll regret it later on when you've calmed—'

'Don't you dare patronize me!' White-faced, Donald glared round at them. 'You trick me out of what's due to me and then you dare to tell me to calm down! Well, damn you! You won't see me again. Don't send us invitations to your wedding because we won't be coming.' He straightened up and snatched up his jacket. 'Wait until I tell Mother. A baby on the way and you haven't even...'

Henry stepped forward, his face furious. 'Don't you say one wrong word about my wife-to-be ! Not one word, d'you hear me?'

'And if I do?'

'I shall knock you down, Donald.'

For a moment the two men faced each other but it was obvious Henry meant every word.

Donald hesitated for a few seconds then said, 'Your precious Alice is a gold-digger. I've met her—'

A blow from Henry's fist landed on the left side of Donald's jaw and he staggered backwards and nearly fell.

'I've met her sort!' he continued defiantly. 'You'll find out when it's too late. Gold-digger – that's what—'

Hester cried, 'Henry, don't!'

But Henry ran forward, white with rage,

and hit his nephew again. This time Donald flew backwards, hit the door and slid to the floor.

'Henry!' Hester screamed and rushed forward to help Donald up.

He pushed her away, his face crimson. 'Don't touch me!' He struggled to his feet and leaned back against the door, clutching his face.

They stared at each other. Alice, out of her depth, looked helplessly at Hester who, white-faced, was lowering herself back into her chair.

Alice stammered, 'You shouldn't have provoked Henry. He warned you...'

Donald felt his jaw. He seemed momentarily lost for words.

Henry was gasping for breath, visibly shocked by the extent of his own anger.

Donald straightened up. 'You've broken my jaw!'

'Broken your jaw? What rubbish!'

Hester cried 'Donald!'

Donald hissed, 'You *bastard*!'

Henry said, 'I won't have you using that kind of language in front of the ladies. Get out of my sight and don't come back.'

'With pleasure! But don't think you've heard the last of this. Marry this woman if you must but you'll regret it. You'll see what kind of woman she really is when it's too late and she's—'

He broke off as Henry stepped forward, pulled him free of the door and opened it. 'Get out of my hotel! I won't tell you again.'

Donald gave each of them a lingering look of real hatred then strode out of the door. 'I'll see you all in hell!' he cried and slammed the door behind him.

Hester muttered, 'That's right! Let the whole hotel know what's going on!'

Henry sank into a chair, still breathing with difficulty. 'I'm sorry,' he whispered.

Alice knelt beside him and took his hands. 'It doesn't matter, Henry,' she told him. 'Don't let him upset you like this. You'll make yourself ill.' She looked at Hester who was sitting with her head in her hands crying softly. 'Please, Hester. Don't let him do this to you. It's what he wants, don't you see?'

Henry said, 'I never liked him but I didn't expect him to turn on you like that. You don't deserve it. It's not fair.'

Hester wiped away her tears and swallowed hard. 'That's the sort of person he is.' She looked at her brother. 'Are you all right, Henry? You look like a ghost!'

'Say it, Hester. I know you're going to.'

'You shouldn't have hit him – but I'm glad you did. I wish it had been more of a tap and less of a sledgehammer though! I was frightened for a moment in case he hit you back.'

Alice said. Are you truly all right, Henry? You do look ... badly shocked.'

He smiled. 'I'm fine. Never felt better!'

They all laughed at the obvious lie.

Alice said. 'Thank you for – for protecting me.' She wished that he hadn't hit his nephew but she would never say so.

Hester said. 'A knight on a white charger!' and rolled her eyes. 'And Alice, don't blame yourself for what happened. Even without you, the meeting was bound to end with recriminations.'

'I shouldn't have interfered.'

Henry smoothed her hair with a shaking hand. 'Nonsense, my dear Alice. It was my fault. A vain old man, that's what I am. I couldn't resist telling him about the child.'

Alice put an arm round him. 'It doesn't matter.'

'It does. He's a jealous, spiteful...'

Hester shook her head. 'Thank heavens he had the decency not to hit you back! He must have longed to do so. I couldn't believe what was happening. Fisticuffs! It's just not like you, Henry.'

Henry had the grace to agree. 'It was stupid of me. I never did believe that violence solves anything but...' He shrugged. 'I was so angry, I lost control. I'm sorry ... And you, Alice? Are you all right? In your condition these upsets can't be good for you and the baby. Do forgive me, my dear.'

'Don't worry about me, Henry.' She was badly shaken but there was no point in making Henry feel any worse. He had apologized.

The silence lengthened until Hester stood up, suddenly brisk. She reached for the bell pull. 'A fresh pot of tea will do wonders,' she told them, putting away her handkerchief. 'Then you and Henry have an appointment, remember, with the doctor. You should ask him to check your heart while you're there, Henry. At your age...'

'I shall do nothing of the kind,' he interrupted, cutting her off in mid-sentence. 'There's nothing wrong with my heart so stop fussing.' He smiled at Alice. 'Ever since our mother died Hester has taken on the role of Mother Hen!'

Hester laughed and Alice tried to relax but in fact she was deeply shocked. The confrontation had alarmed her. Henry's violent reaction had taken her by surprise and Donald's hostility had left her with a feeling of deep unease. Where had he gone, she wondered and what would he do? It seemed unlikely he would oblige them by leaving Chester. He didn't seem the type of man to simply disappear into the sunset. Perhaps he would book into another hotel while he thought over his options. Surely he would want to retaliate. Firstly his hopes of advancement had been dashed and secondly he had been humiliated. She wished with all her heart that the ugly scene had never been played out – that they had tempered it somehow – but it was too late for regrets. Alice crossed her fingers and prayed that they would hear nothing more of the matter.

When Maggie put in an appearance Henry said, 'A pot of tea for two, please, and a large whisky.'

Hester forced a smile. 'We'll just forget the whole miserable business and enjoy ourselves. Donald Lightfoot? Who's he?'

'Never heard of him!' cried Henry.

Alice found it impossible to join in the attempted banter. She was quite sure in her own mind that they had not heard the last of Donald Lightfoot.

The visit to the doctor was much less stressful than Alice had feared. Henry had written to him explaining the situation – with the exception of the real father's identity – and if he was shocked, he hid it very well. His examination was thorough and as uncomfortable as Alice had known it would be but the verdict was reassuring.

'Mother and baby doing well.'

Drink plenty of fluids, he told her, and eat sensibly. Nothing too rich – except for a slice of wedding cake. The doctor and his wife had been invited to the ceremony and he congratulated the happy couple with real warmth.

'Never thought to see you enjoying father-hood,' he told Henry, 'but the fortunate child will be born into a happy home.'

Much more fortunate than you could ever imagine, thought Alice, remembering the dire prospects her child had faced such a short time ago.

When they returned to the hotel there was more good news.

Miss Maine waved them over excitedly. 'That drowned body wasn't Edith after all. Sergeant Flint came in with the news just after you left. It was a much younger woman. He doesn't know much except that it wasn't Edith but he said something about a French student who went missing from a beach picnic. Not murder at all. Probably a swimming accident.'

Alice brightened. 'So Edith might still be alive?' She glanced at Henry.

'Let's hope so.'

'You don't sound very hopeful.'

He shrugged. 'I'm afraid I'm not, Alice. I can't see any way for her to get off that ferry and not be seen. But we'll go on praying for her.'

Miss Maine said, 'Perhaps now they've got Dr Stewart they can make him confess to whatever he did. Then at least we'd know. Mr Warner thinks he may have had an accomplice.'

Alice went upstairs to change in a thoughtful frame of mind. Much as she wanted Edith to be alive she knew in her heart that Henry was probably right. It's the not knowing, she reflected sadly as she changed into her working clothes. And being unable to say goodbye.

Later that afternoon she was in the lounge impatiently watching Bob Olley putting up the bookshelves. The chest had been delivered and the toys she had bought lay in the bottom of it.

'They look so few,' she murmured. 'I still have some money, so I can buy more.' She had also decided to add some of her own money.

Bob Olley stepped back at last and together they admired his handiwork. He watched as Alice arranged the books.

'If you don't object to second-hand,' he said, 'I could bring you a few more books. My youngest, twins, are nearly nineteen. Well past the book stage – not that they had many, mind you. Not great readers but they liked the pictures.' He began to gather up his tools. 'They're both working, I'm pleased to say. Got one in on the river boats, taking the tickets. He loves it. The other's in a stable, mucking out, feeding the horses and such like. My wife's tickled pink. A few bob extra. It all helps.' He straightened up. 'I'll be off then. Time to clear out the gutters. Soon be autumn and the next lot of leaves'll be coming down.'

Alice thanked him and stood back to admire her project. As she did so she caught sight of Arthur Lester who was crossing the room towards her. He looked thinner, she decided. Probably not eating properly.

Alice held out her hand and he clasped it briefly. She said. 'Thank you for that beautiful candle you sent me. It has pride of place in my room but I don't know if I can bear to light it. It's so decorative. The ribbon effect is astonishing.'

'I wanted to give you something. You were so good to Perdita.'

Alice waved a hand to indicate the bookshelves and toy chest. 'This is my latest project. Perdita's Corner. I realized that we had very little to amuse the children on a wet day.'

'Perdita's Corner? Oh that's wonderful!' He swallowed. 'My mother will be touched by the idea – as I am.' He blinked rapidly and hastily covered his eyes with a hand.

Alice said, 'I wondered if we could have a likeness of her. I'd like to frame it and hang it above the shelves.'

'Of course. I'll look one out for you.' He was struggling with his emotions and Alice blamed herself for raising the subject. She should have given him more time.

To change the subject he said. 'And I'm the proud man who will give you away. When Mr Lightfoot asked me I was rather overcome by the honour.'

'It's kind of you to agree. Trust my brother to get into a scrape!'

He gave her a long look, about to say something – but no words came. Alice looked at him, puzzled.

She said. 'Are you sure you want to do it? I won't be offended if—'

'No! I do. I simply wanted to say...' He regarded her earnestly then glanced round the lounge as though to ensure that he wouldn't be overheard. 'I want you to know ... No. That's not right ... I'd like you to think of me as more than just a friend, Mrs Meredith. If you possibly could. I mean that I – and Mother – feel very close to you. I'd like you to feel able to turn to me if you ever need help of any kind.'

Surprised by the intensity of his words, Alice gave him an encouraging smile, a little unsure how to take them.

He went on. 'I'm sure you will be very happy with Henry Lightfoot. He's a good man and he deserves you. But ... Mrs Meredith...' He stammered, frowned then glanced away as though unsure how to continue.

Alice said. 'That's most kind of you, Mr Lester.'

'What I'm trying to say is that, dear Mrs Meredith, if you are ever alone – when you lose your husband – though God forbid such a thing! – I would hope you would turn to us for help. I'll be here in Chester. Waiting – to be of some service to you.'

Alice was becoming anxious. Should he be saying so much? Should she be allowing it? Surely he was overstepping the boundaries of what was proper. She understood how he felt and knew it was because of Perdita. Wasn't it? Her heart beat a little faster. Could it be something more? Suddenly she remembered that odd conversation with Arthur Lester's mother after the funeral. *He had noticed you, you know.*

As if reading her mind, he said. 'What a fool I am! I've gone too far. Please forgive me. Please forget everything I've said … Well, not everything but...' He closed his eyes, anguished.

Alice's heart was now racing uncomfortably. It was a declaration of some kind and she saw at once that it might threaten their comfortable friendship. She was surprised and confused but she was definitely flattered and admitted as much to herself. Arthur Lester found her attractive. Knowing that any man finds a woman attractive does wonders for her self-esteem. Alice, however, had enough presence of mind to see the dangers in the situation. There was no way she must encourage him but what on earth could she say that would cool the emotional climate? How on earth could she diffuse the situation without hurting his feelings?

She smiled quickly. 'How very sweet of you, Mr Lester. We do most definitely look upon you as a friend ... a valued friend. I'll remember what you have said and when the need arises – if it ever does – I shall certainly call on you and your mother for help.' She fancied she saw relief in his eyes.

'So you do forgive my ... my outburst? I really don't know what came over me. I should never have spoken so frankly on such a matter.'

'I do forgive you, Mr Lester, and I promise never to mention it again. Will that help?'

'Most certainly.' He smiled. 'You have saved me from a restless night!'

At once Alice had a mental picture of him tossing sleeplessly in his bed and she saw by his expression that he, too, considered the phrase an unfortunate one. They stared at each other, each at a loss for a suitable comment. The longer they remained silent, the worse it became.

He said, 'I think I'd better go before I say something I shall regret!'

Alice wondered if he had a mental picture of her in bed. With an effort she pushed the idea from her mind and said briskly.

'Well, I have things to do, Mr Lester. No doubt we'll bump into each other...' She stopped, appalled, as even this innocent phrase raised unwanted images.

They both began to laugh at the same time but stopped equally abruptly as Henry appeared. He at once slipped his arm fondly through Alice's and pulled her close.

'It's good to hear you laughing, my dear,' he told her. 'It does my heart good.'

His voice, Alice noted gratefully, was absolutely free from any suspicious overtones. Henry smiled at Mr Lester. 'I've decided to take my fiancée for a trip on the river. Do you know, Mr Lester, Alice has never been on the Dee?'

'I have never had time,' Alice protested. 'Or money to spare.'

Arthur Lester smiled. 'You'll enjoy it. My mother has always loved being on the water and Perdita...' He stopped abruptly and his expression darkened as the memories flooded back. 'I was going to say Perdita has taken after her ... Perdita *took* after her.' He glanced up with eyes that glistened. 'Sometimes I forget for a moment or two that she's gone. Isn't that terrible?'

'Not at all,' Henry said promptly. 'You need to forget sometimes, briefly. You mustn't feel guilty about it. Grief is a very aggressive emotion, very wearing. It will destroy you if you don't learn to control it.

Perdita wouldn't want you to make yourself ill. Try to think of it through her eyes.'

All three fell silent. Alice thought how well Henry had handled the moment – relieving the guilt and offering hope.

Henry glanced down at Alice. 'Well now, I've booked seats on the boat. Are you going to be ready in time?'

'I will!' she told him.

He patted her hand and looked at Mr Lester. 'Excuse us, won't you? If I don't take Alice away from the Mere she will never stop working.'

Alice laughed. 'I'll go and find something suitable to wear.'

Mr Lester said, 'It can be blowy on the water. Wrap up well, Mrs Meredith.'

'Thank you for the warning! I will.' She waved hastily and left the two men admiring Perdita's Corner. As she hurried breathlessly upstairs her heart was still racing. She felt as though she had stepped back from the edge of a cliff.

About this time, Martin Delby arrived at Chester town hall and asked to see one of the prisoners – a Mr Albert Stewart. There was no police station in the town and the police headquarters were based below the town hall and consisted of a number of cells, rooms where records were kept, interview rooms and office space for the police.

It was not ideal and the police complained regularly that they deserved better.

'I'm his lawyer,' Delby said. 'Sent to defend the blighter.'

The sergeant looked up from his desk where he was filling in a report form.

'Take a chair,' he said. 'I'll find someone to take you down.'

'I can find my own way if you give me a few instructions,' Martin Delby said helpfully.

'They all say that but they never do. It's a bit of a maze down there.' He rang a bell but no one answered it. 'Typical! I'll take you down myself if you hang on a minute.' He laboured on with a scratchy pen and an inkwell that needed frequent shakes to produce any ink. 'We're the poor relations,' he told Delby. 'Cramped quarters and undermanned but that's what comes of being City Police. Not part of the County Police. Not that we want to be but it's a question of money like everything else. All politics, this job. All red tape and filling in forms. Roll on my retirement!' He gave a bleak laugh.

Seven minutes later he pushed back his chair and crossed to a large board on the wall from which he took a large key. Delby followed him, ducking his head occasionally. He was a tall man and the basement area was low-ceilinged. Their footsteps echoed and Delby felt a frisson of apprehension. He suffered from claustrophobia and was thankful he was not incarcerated here, away from any glimpse of natural daylight.

The sergeant gave him a running commentary as they passed various cells, many of which contained inmates. 'This one's in for kicking a constable while drunk,' he announced, jerking his thumb at a closed door. There was a small flap in the door through which Delby presumed the prisoner could be watched from time to time. 'Old biddy of fifty-four!' He shook his head despairingly. They turned a corner and reached a cell from which screams and oaths emanated. He banged the door with his fist and shouted. 'Belt up, you two!' He glanced at Delby and said, 'Kids, would you believe? Two brothers. Proper little scallywags but when their ma arrives to collect them they'll be like two lambs! Ma's a bit of a bruiser. I wouldn't like to meet her in a dark alley!'

Delby said. 'Good gracious! I had no idea.'

'New are you?'

Delby nodded.

'You'll learn!' He turned another corner and poked his head round a door that was not a cell. 'Haven't you finished that yet?'

A voice said. 'Another ten minutes, Sarge.'

The sergeant sighed as he moved on. "Course, these are only pending cells, until it's decided what's going to happen to them. Which is after they've been to court. The old biddy will probably be let off with a caution ... This one in here – now he's a mad devil. Take a look!' He opened the flap.

Delby peered in and saw a young man slouched on a mattress on the floor. On seeing that he was being observed, the man leaped to his feet and waved his arms in the air so that his trousers, unsupported, fell round his knees. He also stuck out his tongue and rolled his eyes and began to jabber something unintelligible.

'Good Lord!' Delby exclaimed, backing away from the door.

The sergeant laughed. 'We've taken away his belt in case he hangs himself. Which he won't. He's as sane as you or me but he tries it on. They do. They want to plead insanity so they get let off but it doesn't wash ... Ah! Here's your chap.' He pulled open a door and said, 'On your feet, man. Here's someone foolish enough to try and get you off! Be nice to him.'

Delby stepped into the cell and heard the door clang to behind him. He stared at the prisoner and was relieved to see that this one appeared perfectly sane. He was actually holding out his hand and Delby shook it.

The cell was small – probably no more than ten feet by nine. The walls were made of bricks faced with white tile and the corners of the cell had been rounded off. Albert Stewart sank back on to his bed. Before Delby could speak the door opened again and a rickety chair was handed in. Delby sat down carefully. Without more ado he explained that he was going to speak for the defence.

'On the fraud charges,' he said. 'You know the murder charge has been withdrawn. The body they found wasn't Edith Brightling.'

Albert Stewart looked pale and shaken. His hair needed cutting and he hadn't shaved for several days. What showed of his shirt collar was grubby and his dark jacket was crumpled. 'If she *had* been murdered it was nothing to do with me! Nothing! I didn't lay a finger on her! I swear on my mother's grave! Do I look like a murderer to you?'

Not knowing what a murderer looked like, Delby shook his head. 'About these frauds,' he began. 'It might be better if you tell me—'

'I know I lied about not knowing her but I was in somewhat of a panic. If she'd disappeared then they were going to blame me. It's true we boarded together. We were going to spend a few days in Paris. Nothing wrong in that!'

'Of course not but I do feel we are wasting time, Mr Stewart. At least that is your real name, I take it.'

Stewart hesitated. 'One of them,' he admitted. 'We boarded and we went below deck and I found Edith a chair. She was tired and overexcited. A widowed lady like that on a spree with a younger man.' He smiled. 'You can imagine!'

In spite of himself, Delby wanted to know more so he smiled back. He leaned forward earnestly.

'I told her to relax and rest and I would take a turn or two around the deck. She seemed quite happy. When I went back down to see how things were she had gone. Her luggage was gone too. I thought she was in the lavatory so I waited and then I asked another woman to see if Edith *was* there. I thought maybe she'd been taken ill. Seasick. Something like that. She wasn't. No sign of her anywhere. I couldn't understand it. I thought it was odd but I was reluctant to report it. Afraid to draw attention to myself. Imagine my surprise when I left the ship and was arrested.' He wiped a hand over his forehead which was beaded with sweat. 'So that's it! Now you know.' He looked up with a trace of defiance.

Mr Delby drew a notebook from his pocket. 'Well, I appreciate you telling me but I don't have much time. Suppose you answer a few questions now about these other charges...'

Long after Alice's trip upriver had ended and she lay in bed reliving the experience, a solitary constable made his way along Hoole Road in the direction of the town centre. It was nearly midnight and he had been warned to keep an eye open for a pair of young villains who had committed a string of burglaries over the past fortnight. Ned Toller and Alfie Shaw, well known to the police, had so far evaded capture and Sergeant Flint was losing patience. The afternoon's briefing had been a miserable affair. The constables were told in no uncertain terms that the burglaries were an embarrassment to the force and must be stopped – 'Or heads will roll, my lads!'

Constable Pryor had only recently been transferred to Chester and he missed his quiet village station, tucked away in Dymchurch, in deepest Kent. He missed his mother's cooking, he was ribbed by his new colleagues and he hated Sergeant Flint. As he trudged along, the moon came and went among the clouds, the houses cast long shadows and the empty streets looked hostile under the lamplight.

A muffled crash made him jump and he snatched his truncheon from his belt in readiness for action. Peering into the bushes in the front garden of one of the nearby hotels he watched a tabby cat slither into the

273

shadows and cursed under his breath.

'Ruddy moggy!' he muttered. Relaxing, he prepared to move on.

But what had disturbed it? The hair on the back of his neck stood up suddenly and he drew in his breath. Ned and Alfie? That would be just his ruddy luck, he reflected. Two against one. Hardly an even contest if it came to a fight but if they ran he might collar one of them. As he crept forward in the direction from which the cat had sprung, he fancied he heard another sound. A scrape ... or a scuffle.

'Hells bells!' He whispered. If he could nab one of them it would be a feather in his cap. First month in the new station and an arrest under his belt! That would wipe the smiles from the faces of his new colleagues. He tried to remember what they'd been taught. *It's often better to stand and wait than to go blundering in. Let them make the first move.* That made a lot of sense. It would give him a chance to see how many there were. Cunning was required. Constable Pryor moved deeper into the shadow and waited, heart thumping.

He knew that another constable would be only a few streets away and would hear if he blew his whistle but that would be no good now. Frighten the beggars off, most likely. No, he'd whistle *after* he'd nabbed one of them. As his eyes became accustomed to the

274

gloom between this building and the one next door he tried to imagine what he might find round the side. Probably a store shed of some kind – or a pile of coke.

'Ah! I see you!' he whispered as a dark shape rose slowly from behind a bush. He saw an arm go back and then something was thrown up at the window. Whatever it was struck the side of the house and fell back to the ground. It sounded like a scattering of small stones. So was this one of the villains making contact with the other one? Was one of them already in the building? The dark shape now tried again and the constable decided to act.

'You comc here, my lad!' he shouted and rushed forward with the truncheon up-raised.

Halfway across the intervening ground he tripped over something and almost fell. As he steadied himself a dark hooded figure ran past him and set off down the street.

'Oh no you don't!' He set off after the fleeing figure, which ran much more slowly than he had expected. 'Come back here!'

He lumbered after the tallish lad running inexpertly along the pavement. In a very short time the constable had caught up with him and, reaching out, grabbed an arm.

'Got you, you young villain! Hold still, damn you!'

Somehow the figure twisted and tried

desperately to free himself. Suddenly he ducked his head and bit the constable's hand.

'Ouch! You nasty little tyke!'

Taken by surprise he relinquished his hold and his quarry took off again along the street.

'Strewth! It's a woman!'

The hood had slipped back and Constable Pryor had caught a glimpse of long hair. The terrified face also belonged to a female.

'Oi! You! Come back here!' He set off again in pursuit as she ran into the road. What was the world coming to, he asked himself as he reached out, grabbed a handful of hair and jerked her to a standstill. She was gasping for breath and the constable shook her hard to discourage any lingering idea of further escape. To his surprise she gave a sharp cry and collapsed on to the pavement at his feet.

'Jesus!' he cried. This wouldn't look good at all, he thought, staring down at her. He decided to blow his whistle.

While he waited for help, he knelt beside the fallen figure, took her pulse and was relieved to find her still alive. In the darkness it was difficult to see how old she was but she smelled unwashed and her clothes were dishevelled.

'A tramp lady!' he decided. She was lying in the middle of the road so he held her under her arms and dragged her to the pavement and propped her against the garden wall of the nearest house.

Constable Wardle arrived and together they discussed what they should do. It was a long walk to the police station and although they could carry her between them the idea held no appeal. Constable Wardle came up with the solution.

'She's coming round,' he said. 'We'll walk her as far as Colley's beat. Let him find her. He's a lazy blighter. Do him good.'

Constable Colley's beat was ten minutes' walk away. It didn't sound quite right to Chester's newest constable but he wavered. Hardly the correct procedure, he reflected nervously, but his colleague brushed away his muttered protest.

'Don't be so daft, Pryor. We do it all the time. Never bother with a drunk, Pryor. Dump him on someone else's beat. Then, come the dawn, the day shift gets to deal with him.'

'But this one's not drunk.'

'But she's a damned nuisance. We have to get rid of her. What's the problem? I mean she's not going to complain, is she? She's a vagrant. She's lucky we're not going to lock her up.'

A quarter of an hour later they settled her against a gate in full view of anyone going past.

'Suppose he doesn't see her? She might peg out.'

'She won't peg out. These old girls are as tough as old boots! You're soft, Pryor. D'you know that? Soft. Now get back on your beat and keep your mouth shut.'

Reluctantly Constable Pryor did as he was told but his conscience pricked him. Chester was a far cry from Dymchurch, he thought gloomily – and now he was getting a blister.

Ten

Next morning Alice cast a quick glance round the dining room, where the breakfasts were neatly laid out. Mrs Dymott crossed the room towards her.

'The window cleaner arrived just before you came down. I told him to leave the dining room till last. I didn't think the guests would want him peering in at them while they were eating ... Oh, and he brought in a bag full of clothes. He found it outside in the shrubbery as he came round the side of the house.'

'Clothes? How very odd.' Alice frowned. 'Could they belong to one of the guests?'

'Not very likely. The bag was very wet and the clothes...'

'What sort of bag? Where is it now?'

'One of those carpet bags. Mr Warner put it in the office. He said he'd make enquiries later.'

Alice left the dining room at a run and hurried into the office. The bag had been placed beside the desk and the moment she saw it she knew with a shock of recognition she had last seen it on the bed in Edith's room. Full of hope, Edith had been defiantly packing her clothes into it.

'Edith!' She murmured. Picking it up, she placed it carefully on the desk and opened it. 'Your favourite nightdress ... and your little velvet slippers!'

Mr Warner came in and Alice whirled round, the damp slippers in her hand.

'These are Edith Brightling's things! I recognize them, Mr Warner. I swear they are hers. I've seen her wear these very slippers ... How on earth did they get here?'

For a moment he looked doubtful. 'There must be hundreds of black velvet slippers,' he began.

'But this nightdress! And look!' She pulled out a small satin sachet. 'One of her lavender bags! This is definitely her bag! But what on earth does it mean?'

Mr Warner smoothed his moustache. 'You mustn't get your hopes up, Mrs Meredith. There might be a rational explanation ... although I can't think of one. Unless someone on the ferry stole her bag after she went overboard.'

Immediately crushed by this suggestion, Alice sank on to the nearest chair.

He was right. There was bound to be a logical explanation.

'But why bring it here? If you've stolen a bag belonging to another passenger you wouldn't know where that passenger lived, would you?'

'You would if there was a label on it.'

Alice looked. 'There isn't – but there might have been. There's a piece of string that might have tied it on … Oh dear! It seemed such a good sign.' She sighed. 'But at least it means that the bogus doctor didn't throw it overboard. Surely he would have done if he'd murdered Edith?' She stood up again. 'I'm going to report this to Sergeant Flint. He might have a few ideas on the subject. I can't simply let it go. Suppose Edith is still alive and was coming back to the Mere and then someone attacked her before she reached the front door?'

Mr Warner shrugged. 'A bit far-fetched, if you don't mind me saying so. But by all means report it. I admit it's odd. It's probably the right thing to do. There might be clues in there that would help to convict our charming doctor.'

Alice called a taxi and took the bag to the town hall and was directed to the police quarters.

A bored-looking constable nearing middle-age accepted the bag and its contents and listened to Alice without much enthusiasm. He made notes in between several large yawns.

Annoyed, Alice said sharply, 'I assume you

had a sleepless night?'

'You could say that.'

'Baby keeping you awake?'

'The baby's with my mother. She's nearly nine, bless her. It's the wife. She has bad rheumatics. Can't sleep with it and neither can I.' He reread his notes. 'This name Brightling rings a bell,' he said at last.

Alice, contrite, softened her tone. 'Yes. It's the woman who disappeared—'

'From the ferry!' His boredom vanished. 'This could be something. At least it's a start. A possible lead. I'll run it by our sergeant when he gets back from the hospital. He's got a body in their mortuary.'

Alice froze. 'Not a woman?'

'No. A young man. Drank himself to death. Practically pickled himself in alcohol. I don't see it myself. Horrible way to die. Liver rotted away.'

Alice said, 'If Edith Brightling is still alive she may have brought the bag back. I don't know why she didn't ring the bell. The night porter would have let her in. I think someone may have attacked her – or maybe she was ill. Could she be in the City Hospital? Could you check it?'

'I'm sure we will but it's best not to step on the sergeant's toes. It's his call, you see. He'll check it out. We'll alert all our beat bobbies. Now. Let's take a look in the bag.' He rummaged around but then shrugged.

'Not very promising. No address book ... No letters or envelopes ... We'll have to see what the sergeant makes of the stuff. In the meantime we'll tell the constables to keep a lookout for her. Better give me a description.'

Alice complied and then she asked, 'Who was on duty in Hoole Road last night? He may have seen something. He may have seen someone carrying the bag.'

He consulted a wall chart. 'Dan Pryor, that would be, but he's off-duty now. Fast asleep, I should think.'

'Then give me his address, please. I'd like to speak with him.'

'That's for the sergeant to do, Mrs Meredith. We'll follow it up, don't you worry.'

'But when will that be? It might be a matter of life and death.'

He smiled patiently. 'Hardly life and death but I take your point. You go home and leave this with me. We'll be in touch later on when and if we have any news.'

Alice left feeling very frustrated. Whoever had left the bag outside the Mere *must* know something of its history. Whoever it was might well be passing through Chester – might even be leaving the town as she waited irresolute, outside the police station. Suppose, just suppose, that by some miracle it had been Edith...

She retraced her steps. The middle-aged

man was no longer visible and she walked quickly along the nearest corridor until she came to a door marked PRIVATE. Knocking, she went inside.

A very young constable glanced up from his work. He looked about sixteen, thought Alice with amusement, and decided to take advantage of his inexperience.

'Can I help you, miss?'

'I have to deliver a letter to Constable Pryor by hand. I wonder—'

'Leave it with me. I'll see that he gets it.'

'In person,' she amended hurriedly. 'I have to deliver it to him personally.'

He shrugged and crossed to a wooden filing cabinet. Riffling through the files he pulled one out. 'Russell Street, near the canal. Number eight.'

'Thank you.'

'No trouble, miss.'

He smiled and Alice felt a pang of guilt which she quickly smothered. She hurried back up the steps, left the town hall and set off in the direction of the canal. She found the street without any problem and was soon lifting the knocker on number eight. A woman came to the door with her hair in curling rags.

'Yes?'

'I need to speak to Daniel Pryor. Are you his mother?'

'His *mother*? Bloomin' sauce! Do I look old

284

enough to be his mother? I'm his landlady. What's it about?'

'I need to speak to him and it's rather urgent. If he's asleep I'd be grateful if you would wake him.'

'Urgent? How d'you mean, urgent? He's on nights and—'

'It concerns an elderly lady, a friend of mine, who might be very ill. She's gone missing and they told me at the station that Constable Pryor was on duty in the area where she was last seen. So you see...' She left the sentence unfinished.

The woman's expression changed. 'Gone missing? What? Lost her memory, has she?'

'We don't know but we have to find her.'

'You'd better come in.'

She left Alice in the hall and went upstairs to rouse her lodger. He followed her down a few minutes later tucking his nightshirt into his trousers.

Alice explained and as she did so she saw his face. He was clearly feeling uncomfortable with the situation. For a while he said nothing. His landlady, tired of waiting, said, 'Well do you or don't you know about this?'

He swallowed. 'Now you come to mention it, we did see an elderly woman in that vicinity, around midnight, it was, but ... but we couldn't make head or tail of what she was saying and—'

'*We?*' Alice asked.

'Another constable happened to be nearby and...' He paused, biting his lip anxiously. 'She was determined to keep walking and she didn't want to be arrested. We thought she was a vagrant. Last we saw of her she was in another constable's area and we assumed she was going home. She smelled of – of gin.' He shrugged.

His landlady looked at Alice. 'All right? They tried to help her but she wanted to go home. Good of them not to arrest her at that time of night.'

'Ye–es.' Alice wasn't at all satisfied and the description of a vagrant hardly sounded like Edith. 'Was she carrying a carpet bag by any chance? I work at the Mere Hotel and we found a bag outside in the front garden.'

'A bag? So *that*—' He stopped. 'I didn't see a bag. She wasn't carrying anything. She was a bit rough. Bit my hand, in fact, when I—'

He stopped again.

The landlady prompted, 'When what?'

'When I tried to hold on to her. She was sort of wild and tried to run away.' He looked at Alice. 'Does it sound like your friend?'

'Not really. I can't imagine her biting anyone.' Disappointed, she said, 'May I leave my address with you, in case you think of anything else that might help?'

Dan Pryor agreed reluctantly and a scrap of paper and a pencil were found. Thanking him and apologizing once more for interrupting his sleep, Alice made her farewells and left. She walked back through the town so that she could think. Someone in Chester had dumped Edith's bag on the hotel forecourt in the middle of the night. The mystery vagrant might or might not be connected but someone out there knew something and that person had to be found.

Arthur Lester walked through the churchyard, a posy of violets in his hand. His wife's favourite flowers. Every year on the anniversary of her birthday he and Perdita had brought a posy to the grave. Today he came alone, a sad pilgrimage, and stood, posy in hand, and stared at the headstone.

Beloved wife of Arthur Lester.

Beneath the inscription a new one had been added.

Perdita Marie Lester
Beloved daughter
Rest In Peace.

Arthur sighed deeply, thinking of the few short years his small daughter had lived. And the fewer years that she had shared with her mother. He thought about his daughter's birth, her first steps, her first days at school, her birthday parties – especially the last one.

'Courtesy of Alice,' he murmured. 'She made it possible.' He often spoke to his dead wife. 'Alice was very good to us. She's a good woman.'

He often spoke Alice's name when he was alone. It seemed to shorten the impossible gulf between them. He thought of their last conversation and his face burned. He had said far too much.

Arthur picked up the small vase, walked over to the water tub and filled it. He slipped the raffia tie from the violets and arranged them carefully. Next week he would bring some brighter flowers for his daughter – she loved marigolds.

Stepping back he took a last long look at the spot where his wife and daughter were buried and thought of the small coffin.

'Goodbye, my darlings,' he whispered. 'God bless and care for you.'

At least they were together, he thought, with something approaching envy. As he turned to retrace his steps he noticed an elderly woman sitting on the nearby seat. For a moment their eyes met and then she lowered her gaze. She was dishevelled and dirty. Her shoes had once been dainty but were now soiled and scuffed. Matted hair clung to her face which was shiny with perspiration.

Arthur sighed. Another lost soul. Another wretched human being.

She glanced up at him and he saw with surprise that once she had been beautiful, with large brown eyes and a good complexion. Probably ill, he thought, noting her pallor.

Impulsively he smiled at her but she at once looked away as if ashamed.

Probably lonely. Arthur touched the brim of his hat. 'Another hot day!'

Startled, she nodded.

He waved a hand to indicate the churchyard. 'It's always so peaceful here.'

Another nod.

Was she hungry, he wondered. Should he give her a shilling or would she spend it on drink? Many vagrants did. Impulsively he turned and hurried away to the nearest shops. Ten minutes later he was back in the churchyard, relieved to see that the old woman was still where he had left her.

He approached her carefully, afraid she would dart to her feet and scurry away.

'I hope you don't mind,' he told her gently. 'I bought you a little picnic.'

Before she had fully understood, he placed a brown paper bag in her lap and walked swiftly away. At the corner he turned to see her already devouring the iced bun. There was also an apple in the bag and a bar of chocolate. Smiling to himself he continued towards his mother's flat. He would come again tomorrow and if she was there he would buy her something else. A little warmth crept into his heart. At least he could make somebody happy.

It was nearly four o'clock that afternoon when Alice and Smith returned to the Mere with another selection of toys and books. Smith was duly rewarded with a sixpence which he immediately took to Simms. Alice, watching him go, hoped that her strategy was working and that he would never again wander from the straight and narrow. Too early to say, of course, but she felt fairly confident that he had learned a hard lesson while he was still malleable.

As she went towards Perdita's Corner she was thrilled to see two little boys delving into the chest with cries of excitement. A woman she presumed to be their mother sat nearby reading a magazine with a cup of coffee to hand.

One of the boys looked up at Alice. 'Look what I found – it plays music and it dances.'

He was holding a clockwork clown who turned on his base and waved his arms to the music. The boy's face glowed with delight and Alice was reminded of her unborn child. Would she one day have a son who would look up at her with the same innocence? Or a daughter – she thought of Perdita's expression as she looked at her birthday cake. Her child would be able to play with the guests' children, which would be good for an only child. It was an appealing thought and she smiled.

The second boy, older and with a serious expression, gave her a brief smile as he turned the pages of the animal book.

'I've brought a few more things for the box,' she told them. 'Perhaps you two boys would like to unwrap them for me.'

As they began to undo the parcels their mother spoke to Alice. 'The toy box and books are a lovely idea. The receptionist told me the story behind it. At least she will always be remembered, poor little soul.'

The two women chatted for a few moments. The family were staying for three nights and then moving further north to visit family friends. Alice excused herself and crossed to reception to take a look at the signing-in book. As she closed it again Mr Warner handed her an envelope.

'Chap brought this in earlier,' he told her. 'Wouldn't give his name but was most insistent you should get it before six thirty.' He gave her a long look before smiling.

'Thank you. I wonder who...' She took one look at the handwriting and faltered. It was from Sebastian. Afraid her surprise might

show in her face, Alice hurried upstairs to
her own room.

It was terse and to the point.

Dear Alice,
   I must see you. I'm in Chester for one
night. Meet me at eight under the Eastgate clock. If you're not there I shall
come to the Mere and ask for you.
   Seb

Alice sat down on the edge of the bed and
stared at the familiar writing as panic seized
her. Whatever happened, he must not come
to the hotel – which meant she would have
to meet him as directed. But how could she?
It would still be daylight at eight o'clock and
she might be seen and recognized. If only he
had put an address on the letter. Then she
could have replied that she was sick and
unable to meet him.

'Why, Seb?' she asked. 'What do we have
to talk about?' Unless it was nothing to do
with her but to do with Eddie. Had something happened to him?

Another thought struck her. 'Oh no!'

Hester had suggested that the two of them
had dinner together in her room to go over
the list of invitations. These had already
been sent out but Hester wanted Alice to
know who the various people were. Three
wedding presents had already arrived and

the senders would have to be thanked. They also had to arrange place settings.

'How do I get out of that?' she muttered, frowning unhappily. She was fond of Hester and hated the thought of lying to her – but she would have to meet Sebastian. Thank goodness there was still little indication that she was pregnant. He must never know that.

Stuffing the letter under her mattress, Alice made her way to Hester's room and knocked on the door.

'Come in.' Hester was sitting at her desk, surrounded by scraps of paper. 'Oh it's you, dear. Come and look. I've written all the names on strips of—' She frowned. 'You don't look very happy, Alice. Is something wrong?'

'Only that I feel so dreadfully tired, Hester. Would you mind if—'

'You've been doing too much! I told Henry he should insist that you stop work. I shall—'

'Would you mind if I don't come along this evening? I'd like an early night.'

Hester's obvious concern doubled Alice's guilt.

'Of course I don't mind. I'll sort it all out and we'll go through it together tomorrow. And don't get up at the crack of dawn, Alice. Mrs Dymott is coping very well. She's going to make an excellent replacement.'

Back in her room, Alice fought down a

growing excitement. She was going to see Sebastian again and she knew she must keep her feelings for him hidden. He must believe that she was totally in love with Henry Lightfoot – which she was, she reminded herself. Or would be eventually. But what would Sebastian think when he saw her again? If she were honest, Alice did want him to regret abandoning her. She wanted him to be bowled over by the sight of her and to compare her very favourably with his wife. It was a matter of pride. So what would she wear? Dare she put on the new clothes she had worn when she went out to dinner with Henry?

For the next hour she agonized over her wardrobe, trying on skirts and blouses, dresses and jackets and rejecting them all.

'Like a love-sick fool!' she told herself sternly.

Suppose he took one look at her and breathed a sigh of relief, telling himself he had made the right choice after all.

'Oh *Lord*!' she cried, surveying the heap of clothes on the bed. 'What does it matter? Why should I dress up for a man who threw me over for another woman? I'll wear my workaday clothes...'

That evening, wearing her *new* clothes, Alice slipped out of the hotel by the side door, crossed the forecourt and turned left towards the town centre. Breathing a sigh of relief that she had met no one on the way out, she walked briskly along with her head held high. She had finally convinced herself that if she looked good she would be more in control of the situation.

'Keep your distance, Alice Meredith, and your dignity.'

As she neared the town centre she avoided other people's gaze and prayed that she would not meet anyone she knew. When she came within sight of the Eastgate clock she stopped and looked for Sebastian. What would she do if he were late, she wondered anxiously. She dared not loiter. Dressed in her finery she would certainly attract attention. Moving slowly forward she searched the faces without seeing him.

She gasped as two strong arms went round her from behind, holding her prisoner.

A familiar voice said, 'Guess who this is?'

So much for keeping your distance, she thought, struggling to free herself. Turning, she searched for a scathing comment but it was already too late. He pulled her close and kissed her with an intensity that momentarily swept away all her reserves. She found herself not only allowing the embrace but returning the kiss for a long dizzying moment. A mocking whistle from a passer-by shocked her into sanity and she pushed him away breathlessly.

Sebastian was looking at her with an expression that was all she had hoped for but now she knew she had made the wrong decision. She should have worn the sober workaday clothes.

'Alice! *Alice!*' he murmured. 'Is this elegant creature really you?'

He looked exactly as she had remembered him. The slim figure, bright hair, blue eyes, eager, boyish expression. He wore pale grey trousers with a grey and black striped blazer and sported a rose in his buttonhole. He looked every inch the young man about town and Alice suddenly realized that he had made a big effort to look attractive. But why go to so much trouble, she wondered. And why was Sebastian looking at her with undisguised admiration? Alice was puzzled.

He linked his arm through hers but she quickly withdrew her own with a nervous glance around her to see if anyone was watching them. She gave Sebastian a warning look and he shrugged as they began to walk and turned into Frodsham Street.

'Don't, Seb,' she pleaded. 'Don't do this to me.'

'Don't do what?'

'Don't carry on as though nothing has changed.'

'Has anything changed?'

'You know it has. You are married to Nellie and she is expecting a baby. I am engaged to

Henry Lightfoot. I call that change even if you don't.' Keep your distance, she thought frantically as she gazed up into his eyes. He smiled, the familiar mocking smile that had once melted her resistance and threatened to do so again. 'Please, Seb, just tell me what you have come about and then let me go. No one knows I am here with you...'

He raised his eyebrows. 'Are you a prisoner, then? Is he keeping you under lock and key?'

'Of course he isn't but he would be hurt to know I was seeing you.'

'So he knows about me?'

'Yes he does. And before you ask he is a very understanding man, very kind and ... and I love him.'

'Does he know everything about us?'

Alice hardened her heart. 'He knows you said you loved me and then abandoned me. Yes. He knows that and he isn't impressed.' She realized with embarrassment that her voice was rising. 'So what is this about? I can't stay long. Is it Eddie?'

'You're in a mighty hurry to get rid of me. I thought we might find somewhere to have a drink and a chat. We're old friends, after all. Where's the harm?'

'I've no time for a drink, Seb. Just tell me what's happened to Eddie.'

'Nothing's happened to him – but something's happened to me.'

Fear clutched her. Sebastian was ill. 'Oh no!' she whispered. 'What is it?'

He stopped abruptly and turned to face her. 'It's my turn to be abandoned.' Before she could speak he went on. 'Nellie left me. She said she only married me because she was expecting the baby but she doesn't know if it's mine or Eddie's and—'

'*Eddie's?*' Alice stared at him. This couldn't be true. Eddie and this Nellie woman?

He nodded and his eyes had darkened. 'She said she wanted it to be his but when she told him he denied it all and so she told me it was mine. Like an idiot I jumped at the chance to marry her. I was besotted with her.'

'You didn't know about her and Eddie?'

'Not then.'

Alice's heart was thumping. 'But *you* married her.'

'Yes. But it didn't make any difference. Eddie changed his mind and she upped and left me. Gone back to her mother until Eddie can find a room somewhere. Seems she'd rather live in sin with him than stay married to me.' He sighed. 'So much for true love!'

Alice's heart went out to him but a small, mean part of her was glad. Now he knew what it was like. He was staring past her and she turned to see what he was looking at.

He frowned. 'I thought I saw someone

following us but he's gone. Pickpocket most likely.' He shrugged. 'So you can laugh as much as you like...'

'I'm not laughing, Seb. I know what it feels like, remember?'

'I need a drink, Alice. Come with me. I'll buy you a lemonade and—'

'No. I have to go ... So you came all this way to tell me that. Were you hoping for sympathy?'

'I was hoping you'd forgive me and – and come back with me.'

'I forgive you. Now I must go.'

'And come back with me,' he repeated. 'I know I've been a fool, Alice, but at least I—' He took her hand.

'How *can* I come back to you?' Alice cried and frustration lent an edge to her voice. 'Have you forgotten? You're married and I'm engaged to be married. If you're expecting me to abandon Henry and run off with you...' For a brief moment she wondered if she wanted to do exactly that but it was quite impossible and her common sense came to her rescue. 'Firstly, I love him dearly. Secondly, even if I didn't I wouldn't hurt him the way you hurt me and thirdly, for better or for worse, you're married to Nellie and the child might be yours.' As mine is, she reflected angrily. 'You have a duty to Nellie. You should be trying to persuade her to come back to you. You're her husband and you are the child's legal father.'

'And if the child is Eddie's? What then? Your precious brother—'

'Don't blame me for what Eddie has done. If it *is* his child then he should have married her but if the two of you...' She rolled her eyes. 'What a hopeless mess!'

They glared at each other while Alice's mind whirled furiously. She had dreamed so many times of the day when Sebastian would come to her, begging her to marry him. Instead all he could offer was to live in sin with him while Nellie lived with Eddie. Suddenly she felt unbearably weary of the situation. Serve them all right, she thought.

Seb took hold of her hand. 'Listen, Alice, I don't care a fig for what's happened. Just say you'll give me another chance. That's all I ask. I can be different. I've learned my lesson.'

'But I can't, Seb. The truth is I don't want to marry you. Even if I did I'd never trust you. I'll always remember you with ... affection but I'm going to marry Henry. That's what I want. Someone I can trust. You go back to Nellie and talk to her again.'

'But she loves Eddie. She won't listen.'

'She's married to you! She should give it a chance.'

Sebastian stared past her again.

'What is it?

'I could swear … Oh who cares? If he tries to steal from me he'll regret it.'

Alice could see no one who looked remotely suspicious. She said, 'I'm going now, Seb. Let's wish each other well and part as friends. If Nellie doesn't come back you'll have to divorce her and then you'll meet someone else.' She smiled suddenly. 'You still have great charm!' Reaching up she kissed him but before he could hold her she had slipped away and was hurrying back the way she had come.

'Don't look back and don't cry!' she whispered. 'He's not worth it and you're well out of it. What a ghastly muddle – and his friendship with Eddie will never survive. Oh Nellie, whoever you are, you have done a lot of harm to those two.'

She reached the hotel and let herself in by the side door. Once upstairs she undressed quickly and slid between the sheets – and not a moment too soon, for Hester then arrived to see how she was and to bring her a cup of cocoa.

Eleven

Long before Alice had arrived back at the Mere, Sebastian was in Northgate Street, propped against the bar in the Pied Bull, drowning his sorrows with a mug of beer and brooding on the disaster that had overtaken him.

'Another, please,' he told the barman.

A young man slid on to the stool beside him and ordered a bottle of champagne. 'And two glasses.' He smiled at Sebastian. 'Care to join me? I hate to drink alone.'

'I won't say no!'

The man thrust out his hand. 'My friends call me Don.'

'Sebastian. Mine call me Seb.' They shook on it.

Sebastian was intrigued. In his experience it was very rare for young men to want to share champagne with total strangers. Perhaps things were different in Chester. He said, 'Live round here, do you?'

'No.'

'Me neither. So what are you celebrating?'

Don grinned broadly. 'Let's just call it a

bit of unexpected luck. A plum!' He glanced upward. 'Someone up there loves me!'

The champagne arrived, the cork was popped and the two glasses filled. Sebastian finished his beer in less than a minute.

Don asked, 'So what brings you to this bonny town, Seb?'

'The usual. A woman.'

'Ah! Women. God bless them all!' Don grinned at Sebastian who stared at him gloomily. 'You don't agree?'

'They're all tarred with the same brush.' Sebastian sighed heavily. 'My wife's run off with my best friend, damn her.'

'How terribly unoriginal. I'm sorry. Here, drink that up.'

When Sebastian obliged his new friend refilled the glass. 'So is that what you're doing here? Trying to get her back?'

'Not exactly.' Sebastian didn't know whether he could be bothered to explain the complexities of the situation. The champagne was mingling with the beers and he belched loudly. 'Sorry.'

Don drew his brows together. 'Didn't I see you in Eastgate Street? By the clock.'

Sebastian nodded. 'I was waiting for someone.'

'The woman from the Mere?'

He nodded again then frowned. This chap seemed to know a lot about him.

'Mrs Meredith?'

Sebastian sat up a little straighter. 'You know her? Well, I'll be damned. Small world.'

Don nodded and his expression changed slightly. 'Seems she's snared my old uncle! Henry Lightfoot. Talked him into marriage. Lord knows how!'

Sebastian's head felt thick with the beginnings of a headache but he was intrigued and tried to concentrate. 'So what's this uncle like?'

'A stupid old fool, in my opinion. Going soft in his old age.' He refilled the glasses. 'Drink up, Seb!'

Dutifully Sebastian drained the glass once more. Confused he studied his new friend. Who was this man exactly?

Don went on, unable to conceal his bitterness. 'Henry Lightfoot. A wealthy man. And it'll all go to her. You have to hand it to her. She's landed on her feet, as they say. What woman in her right mind would turn down an old man if he's got plenty of money? It talks, doesn't it?' He stared round the bar then lowered his voice. 'How d'you know Alice Meredith?'

Sebastian hesitated. Something warned him not to say too much but his mood was changing from grief to anger. Alice's rejection had hurt him. Women. They were the very devil. Give them half a chance and they'd ruin your life. He was in the mood for

304

some sympathy and this man seemed willing to listen.

'We were sweethearts once,' he began. 'Not so long ago.' It seemed only yesterday. If only he hadn't let himself be dazzled by Nellie, he and Alice might be wed by now … He closed his eyes and his thoughts wandered to Nellie and then to Eddie and his jaw tightened. Every way he looked he'd been outsmarted. He wanted to go on with the story but needed to put himself in a good light. He did not want to come across as an idiot who had messed things up.

While he was considering his next sentence Don was regarding him with friendly concern. 'To men!' He grinned. 'Down with the women!'

'I'll drink to that!'

He realized suddenly that his stomach was churning and he excused himself and staggered to the gents, where he was sick. When he got back to the bar his new friend was nowhere to be seen. The barman shook his head. 'He didn't say,' he told Sebastian. 'Legged it the moment you'd gone. Odd sort of bloke. Bit la-di-dah!'

'Did he say he'd be back?'

'Didn't say a word.' He reached for the empty champagne bottle and held it up. 'Didn't pay for this, either, mate, so it's down to you!'

It was after lunch on the following day that Henry received the letter. Alone in his flat he read it through with growing disbelief. It was from Donald and full of hate. He sat down and tried to reread it but his hand shook too violently and the words blurred in front of his eyes. Desperately gulping in air, he felt again the pain in his heart which had troubled him since Donald's visit; a pain he had hidden from Alice and Hester. Now it began to frighten him and he was seized by a cold panic.

'Hester!' he murmured. 'I must find Hester.'

Struggling to his feet he stumbled to the door, still clutching the letter. Somehow he made his way to Hester's door. If she were out, he knew he would be in desperate trouble but fortunately she was at home.

He knocked and called out, 'It's me!'

'Come in, dear!'

He tried to open the door but his fingers wouldn't close around the doorknob. Instead he knocked again. After what seemed an interminable time she opened the door.

'Henry!' she screamed as he fell into her arms. 'What is it? Oh dear God!' With an effort she prevented him from falling and half-dragged him to the sofa.

'You're ill!' she told him. 'I must send for the doctor. We must—'

'No! *No!* Not yet, Hester,' he begged,

clutching her hand to keep her near. 'You must read this letter first.'

'But you look so pale.'

'It's the shock, that's all.' As though to disprove the words, he doubled up, clutching his heart. Moments later he was breathing normally again. 'I shall be all right shortly,' he insisted. 'Hester, you must read this letter from Donald. About Alice. I can't believe it but ... but he challenges me to ask her if it's true.'

'Ask her what?' Hester snatched the letter from him, reached for her spectacles and read it for herself. Slowly she sat down. 'But that's impossible. A tissue of lies! How could he have seen Alice meeting this fellow – Sebastian? Alice was tired and she went to bed early. I took her a mug of cocoa. I *saw* her in bed.' She looked up. 'He's making it up to frighten you, Henry. Don't you see? It's Donald's way to revenge himself. He wants you to lose faith in Alice so that you don't marry her. So that *he* gets the hotel instead of her. He's crafty, I'll give him that much.'

'Do you think so, Hester?' Henry stared at her with desperation. 'I do so want to believe it but ... it has the dreadful ring of truth about it.'

'Look dear, he wanted to upset you and he's doing exactly that. He's making you ill, Henry. The wicked, vicious little ... Oh!

Words aren't bad enough for him.'

A spark of hope flared within Henry and he struggled to sit up on the sofa.

'Read it to me again, Hester. Maybe you're right. Maybe it *is* all lies.'

Hester began.

' "You think your fiancée is so wonderful but you don't know her at all. It is as I thought – she has hoodwinked you. I saw her yesterday meeting a man under the Eastgate clock at eight o'clock. ..." '

Hester frowned. 'Eight o'clock.' She looked at him, frowning.

Guessing the direction of her thoughts Henry asked, 'When did you take her the cocoa? Could she have been there? Is it possible?'

'About nine or a little later. She could have...' She looked at him. 'If she did meet him, Henry, she must have had a good reason. She *must* have done. I won't believe – are you all right, dear? You keep screwing up your face. Are you in pain?'

'It's nothing. A few twinges, that's all. Go on with the letter.'

' "They embraced. I followed them and they talked together for quite some time. After they separated I followed the man into the Pied Bull and we drank together. His tongue loosened, he told me they had been sweethearts, that they still loved each other but he had been a fool and married someone else who has now deserted him ..." '

Henry said, 'So now he is a free man.' A cold fear was creeping through him. Alice and Sebastian. She had been with the man who was the father of her child but he could never tell that to Hester. They mustn't mention it in front of her. The true name of the child's father was a secret he could only share with Alice. The terrifying question was – had Alice shared it with Sebastian? If he knew he had made her pregnant he might never give up trying to win her back.

'A free man? Of course he isn't a free man! He is *married*, Henry. His wife may have left him but he is still married to her.'

'Oh yes, so he is.' He put a shaking hand to his head. 'I'm in such a state I can't think straight at the moment. Finish it, please, Hester.'

'We should show this to Alice. She can explain it, I'm certain of it.'

'We'll send for her in a moment, Hester. First finish the letter.'

' "I'm sure you are trying hard not to believe what I say. My advice to you is – ask Alice. She will either admit it or lie to you. If she denies the meeting, you will never be able to trust her again. Poor Uncle Henry. I think you have made a big mistake but after the way you've treated me I can still find it in my heart to forgive you ..." '

Henry put a hand to his heart. 'I won't believe it of her. Alice is true to me. She *is*.'

'Of course she is, Henry.'

He watched his sister fold the letter, trying not to wince as a fresh pain pierced his chest.

Hester said, 'We must find Alice and show her the letter. I'll go in search of her myself.' She stood up. 'Wretched man! Spiteful wretch. And then he has the audacity to offer to forgive you! Alice will soon put an end to all this nonsense.' She reached the door and paused, turning back to face him.

'When I find her, Henry, I shall send her up on her own.'

'Oh, do you think so, dear?' He tried to hide his relief.

'Yes I do. It is a matter for the two of you to resolve. You don't need me. Alice will talk more freely with you. She doesn't want a third person hovering in the background.'

'Thank you, Hester.' Henry was deeply moved. Hester could be very irritating but she always had his welfare at heart.

As soon as she had left the room he put his legs down to the floor and straightened up. He didn't want Alice to see a frail, frightened old man. He didn't want her to compare him with Sebastian. The situation required him to be strong. As he tried to compose himself another pain gripped him, causing him to double up with a cry of pain.

'Hester!' he cried although he knew she couldn't help him. No one could.

The following pain was so intense it rendered him speechless and seconds later he felt himself losing consciousness. The last thing he knew was that he was falling forward and then all was dark.

An hour later Alice followed Hester into the ward in City Hospital where Henry lay in bed flanked by a doctor and two nurses. His face was paper-white, his hands on the blanket pale and thin. The doctor, a young man with curly hair, was reading the chart that he had taken from the end of the bed. The nurses listened intently to everything he said. One of them was the ward sister, the other a nurse.

Hester waited silently until the conference was over then stepped forward to speak to the doctor.

'I'm Mr Lightfoot's sister,' she said. 'How is he? What exactly is the problem?'

The doctor gave her a thin smile. 'We're keeping him stable at present,' he assured her. 'It was a heart attack.'

'But it's over?' She lowered her voice. 'I mean, he will recover, won't he?'

'From that one, yes, but I don't want to raise your hopes too high. There's no guarantee that there won't be another.'

'Mrs Meredith is his fiancée and she

would like to speak to him.'

'Ah!' He glanced at Alice. 'I'm afraid not. Only next of kin.'

'But they are to be married shortly. Please. Just for a moment or two.'

He hesitated. 'Very well but it's most important that he doesn't get excited. He has to be kept calm.' He turned to Alice. 'Can you guarantee that you won't upset him in any way? It could be dangerous.'

'I promise. I might be able to do him some good.'

'Five minutes at the most. The nurse will keep a discreet eye on you. If she says you should leave, you should do so.'

'I understand.'

A few moments later Hester was outside the ward and Alice was standing alone beside Henry's bed, holding his hand. He smiled weakly at her and she leaned over to kiss him.

'Please listen to me Henry,' she said gently. 'I can't let you lie there worrying. This is what happened. Sebastian wrote to me saying that if I didn't agree to meet him he would come to the Mere. Of course I didn't want that to happen because I didn't want you to be upset. I thought it might be about my brother Eddie and it was in a way. Seb's wife has run off with my brother.'

Henry gave a slight nod. His eyes never left Alice's face.

She said, 'He doesn't know about my baby and he never will.'

'Do you still love him?'

'No. I told him so. I could never trust him again. He wanted me to go with him but I refused. I told him I love you, Henry, and I do.' She squeezed Henry's hand. 'I didn't embrace him, Henry. He embraced me. There's nothing between me and Sebastian any more. His journey to Chester was wasted. That's why he was so depressed. That's probably why he drank too much and told everything to Donald. I had no idea Donald was still in Chester and no idea he had seen us together.'

Henry smiled. 'So how's our little boy – or girl?'

'Very well, Henry. Before too long he or she will be kicking me!' She smiled.

He said, 'If I die, Alice—'

'*Henry!*' She stared at him, appalled. 'Why should you die? Don't talk like that.'

'But if I did ... Would you marry Sebastian?'

'Never! Not even if he were to divorce his wife.' She gave a wry smile.

'It's ironic, Henry, isn't it? The woman who took my place is now hoping to become my sister-in-law!'

Henry managed a faint smile.

Alice said, 'I almost pity her!'

The ward sister appeared round the

curtain. 'I'm sorry, Mrs Meredith, but Mr Lightfoot has to rest. You can come in again tomorrow. He will be in good hands.'

Alice leaned down and kissed Henry.

He said, 'My dearest girl, say you forgive me.'

'For what?'

'For doubting you.'

'I forgive you. And do you forgive me for giving you all this pain and unhappiness?'

'I love you, Alice.' He whispered.

'And I love you,' she said.

And as she walked away down the ward, her eyes were full of tears. Donald Lightfoot had a lot to answer for, she reflected. He had come perilously near to killing the man she loved.

As she left the ward she passed Sergeant Flint and they both stopped in their tracks and turned.

'Mrs Meredith?' he said.

'Sergeant Flint!'

'What are you doing here?'

Alice explained that Henry Lightfoot had had a heart attack. 'And you?'

'They've admitted an elderly woman and knew I was looking for your missing guest – Edith Brightling.'

Immediately Alice's spirits took a turn for the better. 'You mean you've found her?'

'I don't know. We've found somebody but the stubborn old thing refuses to speak.

Therefore we don't know who she is. She was brought in yesterday in a bad way. Malnutrition, mainly, but she also seems to have lost her memory. Or else she's pretending to have lost it. The ward sister thinks she's pretending.'

'Edith is, or was, an actress.' Alice's hopes were rising.

'Exactly. She fits Mrs Brightling's description, so I was going to contact you at the hotel but seeing as you're here ... If you have a moment you might like to take a look at her.'

Eagerly Alice agreed and, quickly explaining the situation to Hester, it was decided that Hester should return to the hotel and finish wrestling with the place settings for the wedding breakfast.

'We must think positively,' she told Alice. 'Henry will want the wedding to go ahead as planned. We'll see how he is nearer the time but in the meantime we'll ensure that everything is ready.' She turned to go. 'And don't walk back. Take a taxi, Alice. We've all had a shock and you must take care of yourself.'

The sergeant led the way towards the ward reserved for elderly patients. It was a sad place although Alice appreciated that the staff did their best. Men and women shared the long high room, which smelled of sickness, polish and disinfectant. Most of the patients were in bed although one lone man sat in his dressing gown with a dazed expression on his face. The air was full of sounds, sighs, grunts and snores while a steady unintelligible mumble came from one of the patients. The sergeant stopped midway down the ward and indicated a patient who was half-hidden by the bed-clothes.

He said loudly, 'You've got a visitor.' There was no response. He stepped forward and tugged at the bedclothes.

Alice stared. All she saw was lank grey hair and a face buried in the pillow.

'I don't know,' she said. 'It might be.'

'Apparently when they brought her in she smelled terrible.' He poked the blankets. 'You! Wake up and show yourself!'

Perhaps not, Alice reflected. Edith had always been so vain about her appearance. Rarely had Alice seen her without her stage make-up carefully applied. Rouge, mascara, lipstick. This ruined creature could not be the Edith Brightling she remembered. She moved to the head of the bed and said sternly, 'Edith, is that you? This is Alice Meredith.'

Grunting, the woman slid further down in the bed like a small burrowing animal trying to escape the light.

Sergeant Flint tugged again at the blanket. 'She's playing with us,' he told Alice. 'These old women, they get very cunning. Probably wants to stay here for the free board and lodging.'

Alice leaned over the bed. 'Edith. Please speak to me. I've been so worried. Whatever's happened we can sort it out. We found your clothes – in the bag. I know it's you.' She knew nothing of the sort but thought it worth a try.

The sergeant muttered something under his breath then said aloud, 'I haven't got all day, Mrs Meredith! Is it her or isn't it?'

'I think it may be,' Alice hedged.

Impatiently Sergeant Flint made a grab for the blankets but whoever it was gave a startled scream and clung to them more fiercely.

Alice said, 'Why don't you leave her with me? I might be able to coax the truth out of her.' Bullying won't succeed, she thought. 'If it is her, I'll ask the hospital to notify you.'

He took out his watch, studied it and returned it to his pocket. He gave the hidden figure an angry look then nodded. 'You're welcome to her. I've got better things to do with my time.'

When he had gone Alice pulled up a chair. 'Edith!' she said. 'It's me, Alice. Do please talk to me. I shall stay here until you do.'

After a long pause the figure crept up to the top of the bed and frightened eyes appeared. Alice drew in a deep breath. It *was* Edith. But not the Edith she knew.

Gone was the animation. Gone too the spark of intelligence in her eyes. She looked dull and uncaring. Edith without the soul, thought Alice, stricken. She leaned forward and patted a shoulder. 'We all thought you were dead,' she told her. 'We thought Dr Stewart had thrown you overboard!'

'Alice?' The voice was a mere whisper.

'Yes, it's Alice Meredith. Now sit up and talk to me, Edith, or I'm leaving.'

After what seemed an age, Edith slowly emerged. Without her makeup she looked years older but Alice was in no doubt as to her identity. The large brown eyes and the voice gave her away. Edith dragged herself into a sitting position and stared at Alice. 'I came to the Mere and tried to rouse you,' she whispered. 'I was throwing some little stones up at your window when this stupid constable arrived. He chased me.'

'Oh you poor thing!' Alice, genuinely shocked, took hold of her hand.

'Mr Lester saved me. He gave me some food. He called it a picnic.'

'Mr Lester did?' It seemed unlikely. Alice shook her head doubtfully. Poor Edith. They were wrong about her. Her memory really *was* failing her.

A nurse passed down the ward and blinked in surprise as she saw Edith sitting up in bed conversing. Alice winked at her and after a moment's hesitation, the nurse passed on.

Edith's eyes filled with tears suddenly. 'I've got nothing, Alice,' she whispered. 'That wretch took all my money. I can't come back to the Mere. I can't go anywhere. I'm too old to get a job...' She began to cry in earnest. 'What's to become of me? I've been so foolish. I've only myself to blame!'

'No job?' Alice thought quickly. 'What on earth do you mean? I've got a job for you. I've been waiting to find you.'

'What sort of job?' Edith regarded Alice with suspicion.

What sort of job? A good question. Alice thought frantically. What on earth could Edith do? 'I'm going to need help,' she told her. 'Once I'm married. Henry is absolutely determined I should have a maid. Someone to help me dress, someone to help around the flat.'

'A *maid*?' Edith appeared unimpressed.

Alice bit back a sharp comment. It was a good sign that the old Edith was still in there somewhere. 'Not exactly a maid, Edith. More a ... a personal help. Henry and I intend to start a family and I don't know how I could manage alone with a child to bring up. I should need to engage a nanny ... unless, of course, you were there.'

Alice allowed the idea to sink in. Edith had never had a child. Maybe the thought of a baby to care for would appeal to her maternal instincts.

Edith frowned. 'You and him? But...'

'I'm not Marion, am I?' Alice hoped this bluff would work.

To her delight Edith seemed to accept this. She sat up a little straighter and tucked back a few stray wisps of hair. 'You'd never manage a baby on your own,' she told Alice.

Alice hid a smile. 'Exactly,' she said. 'I shall need someone to help me in lots of ways. It could be a very interesting job for the right person.'

'I suppose I could help out ... for a while. See how we get along.' The colour was creeping back into her face and the dull look had left her eyes.

Alice nodded. 'You could have your old room, in lieu of wages, and your meals ... and a little pocket money.' She would have to speak to Henry, she decided. As soon as he was well enough.

She leaned forward. 'Can you tell me what happened, Edith?' she asked at last. 'Can you bear it? Dr Stewart was arrested on suspicion of your murder.' She explained briefly how Edith had been seen embarking in Folkestone and missed disembarking in Boulogne.

Edith covered her face with her hands and for a moment Alice thought she had pushed her too far but at last Edith looked up.

'That man would never harm a hair of my

head,' she insisted. 'Although I know now he was no good. He took my money ... No, even that's not true. I gave it to him, Alice. I trusted him. It was so wonderful at first. Like a dream.' She began to pick fluff from the blanket. 'For a few wonderful days before we left England...' She swallowed hard.

Alice said nothing.

'Then he suggested Paris and of course I jumped at the chance. We went aboard and he came downstairs with me so that I could find a seat and rest.' She smiled wistfully at the memory. 'Everyone was watching us. Or I imagined they were. Because of Bertie. He was such a natty dresser!' Her smile faded. 'He said he'd take a few turns around the deck and I said I'd go up in half an hour after we'd left port.' Her face crumpled and tears ran down her cheeks. Alice lent her a handkerchief. One of the nurses looked concerned but Alice gave an almost imperceptible shake of the head. She thought Edith should get it all off her chest now that she'd started. Then hopefully they could put it all behind them.

Edith went on. 'Suddenly I changed my mind. I wanted to go round the deck with him and I wasn't that tired. So I went up on deck, taking my bag with me. I didn't want anyone to steal it. When I went up on deck he wasn't there. The ship was still in port but I knew we'd be leaving the harbour very soon. Then I saw him. He was in the bar with another woman. A very young, blowsy sort of woman. He didn't see me and I watched him. It was horrible. *Horrible*. He had his arm around her waist and she was smiling up at him as if he was saying the most wonderful things to her.'

'Edith! How ghastly for you!'

Edith nodded. 'At first I couldn't quite believe it was happening but then I saw him whisper in her ear and she put a hand to her mouth and gave him a look that told me he'd just suggested something ... something saucy! You know what I mean...'

'What a pig!' Alice shook her head. 'I think I'd have strangled him!'

Edith gave a long ragged sigh. 'That did it, Alice! I was sickened. That's the only word for it. So shocked and hurt and ... and humiliated. I didn't have the nerve to confront them. I thought that she'd laugh at me. I turned away before they saw me and all the time I was wondering how I could endure the rest of the crossing. And how could I ever trust him again? That was the worst part.'

There was a long silence. Alice longed to comfort her but there were no words powerful enough to undo the pain Dr Stewart had inflicted on poor Edith. He had shattered her confidence albeit without knowing it.

Alice thought bitterly that she knew exactly how it felt to be passed over by someone you love. Sebastian had treated her to the same agony of mind.

She poured some water into Edith's glass and handed it to her. Edith sipped it dutifully then continued. 'I made up my mind then and there that I couldn't go through with it. I had to get away. To get off the ship before it sailed. I ran back to the gangway. I must have been the only one leaving! One of the crew asked what was wrong and I said I couldn't face it. I pretended I was afraid of the sea.'

Alice nodded. 'So that explains what happened to you. They thought you'd gone overboard and then a woman's body ... But never mind all that. It doesn't matter now!' She began to smile with happiness and threw her arms around her friend. 'Dear Edith! You can't imagine how glad I am to have you back!'

Twelve

Henry was delighted that Edith had been found alive and as well as could be expected. She was discharged from the hospital on the Saturday and safely installed in her own room at the Mere once more.

'Edith cried,' Alice told Henry that evening at the hospital. 'And so did I. Tears of joy, of course. Neither of us ever expected to see her there again. She has nothing, Henry, apart from her personal belongings and a few clothes.'

He squeezed Alice's hand. 'You must help her, Alice. Do things discreetly. She mustn't feel that it is charity ... What has happened to Dr Stewart now that she has been found?'

'They've dropped the murder charge but he is still in custody in Chester. I think the charges are various. Fraud, non-payment of bills, theft, deception.' She shrugged. 'He'll certainly spend a little time in prison.'

'Serves him right! We shall never know how many unfortunates he has ruined. Edith has suffered but compared with some she may have had a lucky escape. She has a good friend in you, Alice.'

He lay back on the pillow, exhausted by the effort of conversation, and Alice was once more aware of a growing unease. It was July 22nd and the wedding had been planned for the following Saturday. Was Henry going to be well enough, she wondered, and decided to talk to Hester about it. Better to postpone the ceremony until he was fully able to enjoy it.

'You look tired, dearest,' she told him. 'Are you getting enough rest?'

Henry put a finger to his lips and beckoned her closer. 'Not as much as I would like.' He pointed towards the man in the next bed. 'Mr Collins is a garrulous soul. On and on until my head spins. He's asleep at the moment, thank goodness.'

'Couldn't they move you?'

Henry shook his head. 'He would only trouble someone else. No, I put up with him. He means well. I think he believes he's cheering me up!' He smiled. ' "Keep your pecker up, gaffer!" That's his favourite phrase. It's quite an experience, being in hospital. You meet all sorts.'

'I'll go and let you rest. I'll see you again tomorrow.'

To her surprise he made no protest but as she leaned over to kiss him he clung to her suddenly.

Alice studied him with growing alarm. 'What is it, Henry? You seem distracted somehow.'

'Distracted? Do I? I can assure you I'm not. Just a little weary. The staff are wonderful but I do long to be home again. My recovery ... I thought it would be speedier.' He smiled. 'Forgive me, Alice. I'm an impatient wretch! I'll see you tomorrow.'

Outside the ward Alice hesitated then went in search of the ward sister.

'I need to know when Mr Lightfoot will be discharged,' she explained. 'We are to be married in a week's time and I don't...'

The sister looked at her unhappily. 'Dr Hewitt has asked to see you,' she said. 'He is rather worried about your fiancé. He doesn't want him to leave the hospital too soon. Come with me and we'll find him.'

With a sinking heart Alice followed her along the corridor and into a small office. Dr Hewitt rose to his feet and shook Alice's hand. To Alice he still looked too young to be a qualified doctor. More like a student...

'Do sit down, Mrs Meredith.'

She sat as directed and braced herself for bad news. They were going to have to postpone the wedding. Poor Hester. She had lavished so much time and energy on it.

'Mr Lightfoot's condition is giving me some concern, Mrs Meredith,' the doctor told her bluntly. 'I don't wish to alarm you but we expected him to make better progress.'

'I thought he looked tired.'

He nodded. 'The truth is he seems to be getting weaker instead of stronger. He has been with us since Thursday but—'

'That's only two days!'

'Indeed, but despite all our efforts he is showing no signs of recovery – at least not the signs we would expect. It was only a mild attack, you see. The fact that he isn't returning to normal suggests that he might be heading for another one.'

Alice gasped. This was not the bad news she had expected. This was much worse.

Dr Hewitt continued. 'We are monitoring him as well as we can but I felt you should be prepared for the worst.' His smile was apologetic. 'I know you have your wedding planned but I do think you should consider changing the date. The stress of the preparations ... all the excitement. It can't help, Mrs Meredith. Mr Lightfoot really needs hospital care until he shows some definite signs of improvement.'

'I see.' Alice sat in a stunned silence. Her happiness at Edith's return had been totally undermined by this unexpected warning. Another attack? 'Does this mean ... Would another attack be worse than the first one? Is that what you're saying?'

'Not necessarily. It might be *as* severe or

less severe. It's quite common for people to have a series of small attacks.'

'Instead of a major one.' She was desperate to find a gleam of hope. 'Is that what you mean?'

'No–o. The series might be followed by a major attack. It might not. There's no way of knowing, I'm afraid. I don't want to give you false hope, Mrs Meredith. As far as I am concerned the signs are not promising.'

'Does Henry – Mr Lightfoot – know this?' She thought it might account for his apparent distraction.

'Not yet. The news itself might upset him. We don't want to make matters worse but we must err on the side of caution.'

Alice nodded. 'Thank you for being frank with me. I'll go home and speak with his sister. We'll delay the wedding and –' she shrugged – 'and wait and see. When will you tell Mr Lightfoot?'

'Probably tomorrow. You have to understand, Mrs Meredith, that Mr Lightfoot won't be feeling any better so he may be worrying about how he will cope with the wedding. It may come as a relief to him to know he has more time in which to prepare himself.'

They shook hands and Alice walked from the room crushed by worry and disappointment. Poor Henry. He would be devastated when he knew.

Hester was out when Alice reached the hotel but returned an hour later and they took an early supper together in Hester's flat. She received the bad news with an immediate panic.

'He's going to have another attack? Dear Lord!' She stared at Alice wide-eyed. 'But that's ... That might be fatal. Oh Henry! *Poor* Henry! He can't die! He's so *happy*!'

'The doctor said it might be less severe.' Alice couldn't bring herself to paint the worst scenario. Not yet. Later Hester might have to know. 'The point is we have to put off the wedding.'

'And poor you! Oh Alice, my dear, who would have thought it would come to this? Everything was going so well.' Hester laid down her knife and fork and stared down at her salmon salad. 'I've quite lost my appetite,' she murmured. Then her face darkened. 'This is Donald's fault. How I hate the wretch! If he hadn't come to the Mere ... If he hadn't provoked Henry the way he did ... and that terrible letter he wrote...' She leaned across the table and seized Alice's hand. 'But don't you worry, Alice. Henry is stronger than they think. He's got an iron will and that's what matters. Will power! He'll pull through, you mark my words!' Her face fell. 'But suppose he doesn't? Oh dear God!'

'We still have time to notify the guests.' Alice tried to distract her. Hester was older than Henry and Alice didn't know how *she* would stand up to the strain of the situation.

'The guests? Oh yes of course.' Forgetting her lost appetite Hester applied herself once more to her meal. 'We can't write to them all by hand but I'll ask the printer to run off some cards. We'll say a new date will be sent later. Oh!' A forkful of salmon hesitated halfway to her mouth. 'But the baby! I'd forgotten.' She stared at Alice. 'How long can we wait? People will be able to work out that ... Well dear, you know what I mean. It really is essential that the wedding goes ahead as quickly as possible ... And suppose Henry were to have another minor attack before the *next* date.' She bit her lip in frustration.

Alice hadn't given the problem any thought and was equally nonplussed. 'Does it matter if everybody knows – or thinks they know?' she asked. 'Do we care?'

'We certainly *ought* to care, Alice.' Hester gave her a prim look then began to eat once more. 'Let's just think about this. The wedding was planned for a week today. We could make it...' She counted on her fingers. 'We could make it August the fifth but that only gives us an extra week. Suppose we say the twelfth? We've lost nearly a month but...' She shrugged. 'It may be the best we can do...' She sighed heavily. 'Poor Henry. He must feel so helpless. He'll be fretting and that's not going to do him any good.' Now she pushed her half-finished food away. 'And there's the accommodation. People will have to cancel and hope they can re-book later. It won't be easy with the holiday season. Many of the best hotels will be full for August. We certainly are – barring cancellations. Which reminds me. Four more parcels arrived for you and Henry. Wedding presents no doubt. One rattles – I think it's broken.' She sighed. 'Maybe you could spend an hour or so with me this evening, helping me address the envelopes.'

Just before seven that evening Alice slipped into Edith's room on her way up to Hester's. In her hand she carried a bag full of coloured fabric scraps.

Edith was already wearing her night-clothes but she was sitting beside the window. A few hearty meals and she had made a surprising recovery. Almost her old self, Alice thought with affection.

'I've brought you some scraps,' she told Edith. 'I had very little but Hester found some oddments for you.' She produced some from the bag. 'A coloured handker-chief, some yellow wool, a handful of beads and a length of red ribbon. Will they do?'

Edith seized them with delight. She had

decided to make a rag doll for the toy box. 'I could plait the wool for her hair ... and cut the handkerchief in half and then gather it up for the skirt.' She looked up eagerly. 'The beads could be re-threaded. They're a bit big but it doesn't matter. And that velvet can be two shoes. Look!' She held up what looked like a small circular cushion. On it she had already embroidered an eye with long eyelashes and a rosy cheek. She said, 'One more eye and cheek and the face is finished. Then I can stitch on the hair.'

'No eyebrows?'

'Oops!' She laughed. 'And eyebrows. Good thing you mentioned that.'

Alice admired it. She was pleased that Edith had found something to take her mind from the miseries of the past few weeks. She told Edith about Henry and the wedding delay.

'Don't you fret,' Edith told her. 'They don't know what they're talking about. Of course Henry will be all right.'

'Edith! How can you say that about the hospital? They looked after you, didn't they?'

'I wasn't ill. Only tired and a bit hungry. I never was one for hospitals and my mother wouldn't set foot in one. Not even when she broke her leg. Henry's not going to have another heart attack. Hospitals always look on the black side so that when you're cured they can take all the credit. I was taken ill once when I was in a play at the Royalty. I was playing a lady of the night.' She rolled her eyes at Alice's reaction. 'A great part!' She lowered her voice. 'I had to seduce a nobleman. All very naughty. I can see myself now in that costume. Red velvet and a fur collar. I looked wonderful although I do say it myself. Anyway I fainted on stage in the middle of my speech.'

'Edith! What was it?'

'We never found out. They carted me off to City Hospital where the doctors all shook their heads over me. Said they'd better prime my understudy for the next evening but I wasn't having that. I was up and out of there first thing in the morning. And back on stage for the matinee! We gave them some free tickets.' She laughed. 'I reminded them of that last week when I went back in but the nurses were all too young. They said Matron might remember but I daren't ask her ... No, you take it all with a pinch of salt, Alice,' she advised. 'Henry will be fine.'

'I hope so, Edith. I do hope so.'

Henry opened his eyes, awakening from a dream which lingered in his mind with a faint sense of menace. He'd been walking along a sandy beach with sand dunes behind him and a single narrow path leading through them into unseen territory. In the dream he had walked nervously, keeping a watchful eye on the rough waves which crashed on the shore and roared hungrily across the sand, higher and higher, closer and closer. Soon the waves were breaking across his feet and he turned back in search of the single path which would take him to higher ground. Water crashed over him and he stumbled. Just as he reached the path he was horrified to see water pouring down it towards him. It knocked him down...

He cried out, wide awake, his pulse racing and stared round the dimly lit ward. A dream. Nothing more, he told himself. Breathing more easily, he settled down again. A nightmare ... But there was a slight pain in his chest. Something he had eaten, perhaps.

'Too rich!' he muttered, trying to convince himself that this was nothing more than indigestion. Yes, that was it. A bit of discomfort in his chest. A twinge ... He screwed up his face and waited to see if it would go away. Then he could go back to sleep.

The ward was dim at this time of the night although an occasional light glimmered reassuringly in the darkness. By the light he could make out the two rows of beds, each with a sleeping figure huddled beneath the blankets. At least most were sleeping. Henry could hear muffled sobbing from further up the ward and, from the opposite side of the

334

room, a whispered gabble that might have been a prayer. Beside him Mr Collins snored intermittently. At the nurses' station the two uniformed figures whispered together and rustled paper.

Henry concentrated on his own problem. Was the pain going to go away? It didn't. It came again. Was it indigestion?

'What have you eaten?' he asked himself. Certainly not cheese ... At lunch he had been given 'a light diet' of boiled fish and mashed potato followed by rice pudding. Nothing indigestible there. Tea was a glass of milk and two slices of bread and jam. Supper ... He couldn't remember. Biscuits most likely. So maybe it wasn't indigestion.

Sweat poured from him and now his breathing was difficult. Pain started over his heart and spread to his left arm. He was having another heart attack! Panic swept through him, making his symptoms worse. In desperation he tried to reach the bell on his bedside table but instead he knocked over the water jug and it crashed to the floor. He tried to cry out – no sound came but the crash had woken his neighbour, Mr Collins. In the gloom of the ward, Henry saw the man raise himself on one elbow and peer across at him.

'You all right, gaffer?'

Henry tried to answer but the pain was much worse and he was breathless.

'Want me to call someone, do you?'

'Plea—' The words came out as an untelligible croak but his neighbour went into action.

'Nurse!' he hissed loudly. 'Come, quick! Mr Lightfoot here's in a bit of trouble!' When there was no response he raised his voice. 'Oi! You lot! The gaffer's in a bit of trouble!'

Henry thought that the sound of the nurse's shoes on the linoleum was the most welcome sound he had ever heard. Help was at hand. They would know what to do. He tried to thank Mr Collins but his mouth was bone dry and his lips no longer moved so he gave up the struggle and closed his eyes.

As the nurse arrived, Mr Collins warned her, 'Mind the glass. He knocked over his water jug. I heard it go. That's how I knew. In a bit of a state, isn't he, poor old devil.'

Henry opened his eyes. In a daze of pain he watched the nurse turn on the personal light and heard her kick the shards of glass under the bed. Then she leaned over him.

'Mr Lightfoot? *Mr Lightfoot!* Can you hear me?'

There was a note of urgency in her voice.

Before Henry could manage an answer, Mr Collins leaned over to get a better view. 'Not gone, surely? Not just like that! I mean, he was fine and dandy before he went to sleep. Well, hardly dandy but—'

The nurse turned on him. 'Please Mr Collins. Go back to bed.'

Henry gasped, 'Chest ... arm.'

The nurse plumped up his pillows, wiped his brow and gave him a sip of water. 'I'll fetch Sister Wood,' she said and disappeared into the gloom.

While he waited for them to return Henry felt the pain creep up into his left jaw and fought down his panic.

Mr Collins materialized beside him. 'You'll be fine, gaffer. You just hang on. They'll be sending for the doctor, you'll see.'

Henry felt the warmth of the man's hand on his shoulder and tried to smile.

Then the sister arrived, her expression calm, her manner efficient. Henry felt safer. He was in good hands. She sent Mr Collins back to his bed, took Henry's pulse and his blood pressure and wrote on his chart. As she turned to smile at him the pain doubled and his mouth opened in a silent choked cry of protest. The sister's expression changed to one of urgent concern and then a black mist came down and the last thing he heard was the sister saying, 'Oh doctor, you're here! Just in time. Mr Lightfoot has...'

In reply to a worrying phone call from the hospital, Hester and Alice arrived shortly before ten and were immediately ushered into the consultant's room and invited to sit down.

'Mr Frayne will be with you shortly,' the nurse told them and left them alone. Alice's own heart was behaving very badly. It seemed faster than normal and echoed in her ears like warning drums. Clasping her hands tightly in her lap she avoided Hester's eyes, which were as frightened as she guessed her own to be. The room was small and cluttered. Filing cabinets, bookshelves, piles of bulging cardboard files on every surface. A dead plant withered in a vase on the window sill and there was something about the room's impersonality that made Alice nervous.

Hester said, 'Men! They're untidy creatures!' and gave Alice a weak smile. The curtainless window was closed, the walls were bare. The large desk and hardback chairs took up most of the space. But what did it matter, thought Alice. The bad news she was expecting would not be lessened by a bowl of expensive lilies or a Gainsborough.

The door opened and the consultant joined them. Mr Frayne was a small dapper man in a dark brown suit. His shoes were highly polished and his watch chain gleamed against the dark waistcoat. He wore wire-rimmed spectacles low on his nose and regarded Hester and Alice over the top of them. Alice thought he looked more like a bank manager than a consultant. In her ignorance she had expected a white coat and a stethoscope.

'I'm sorry to greet you with bad news,' he said, 'But Mr Lightfoot had another attack during the night.'

Hester clutched Alice's hand but said nothing.

Alice said, 'You mean ... a more serious attack?'

'I'm afraid so. He really is very poorly and he needs total rest. The problem is he is afraid he is going to dic and is determined—'

'And is he?' asked Hester, her face pale. 'Is he going to die? Is that why we've been sent for?'

Alice clutched the edge of the desk to steady herself. Henry was going to die. She prayed desperately. Please, God, don't let this happen. Henry is a good man...

'No, no!' Mr Frayne gave her a less than reassuring smile. 'At least we hope not. He has a good chance of making a recovery but it will be a very slow business. He understands this—'

Alice stood up. 'I must see him,' she said. 'I can't just sit here and ... I want to see him.' She glanced at Hester who took hold of her hand and gently pulled her back on to her chair.

Hester asked, 'Is my brother conscious?'

'Good gracious, yes! This isn't a stroke. And his mind is quite unaffected. He has made up his mind that he wants to be married this afternoon and nothing—'

'This afternoon?' The words came in unison from Alice and Hester.

Mr Frayne nodded. 'This is why I thought I should have a word. We've done our best to dissuade him in his own best interests but he seems to consider the wedding an urgent matter. Very urgent, in fact. Those are his words.'

He glanced at Alice but his expression was unreadable. Despite this she felt herself blush. Poor Henry. She saw only too clearly that her proposal to Henry had led to this moment. Hester no doubt felt equally guilty.

He continued. 'Above all we need to keep him calm. Arguing against the idea simply made him very anxious, almost angry, and we mustn't upset him. We mustn't do anything that will speed up his heart. You do understand that, I hope.'

Hester nodded. She looked woefully out of her depth, thought Alice. Mother Hen! She remembered Henry's words.

Alice said, 'Is it possible? To be married in the hospital? If that's what Henry wants and—'

Hester looked at her. 'But the wedding

340

gown, all the guests, the wedding break-fast...?'

'We can do without them. I don't mind. It's Henry we have to think about.'

The consultant nodded. 'To be frank with you both, Mr Lightfoot has had a very painful experience and a terrible fright. He thought he was dying. He might have died – I won't pretend to you. It was fortunate that I had been called from my bed to see another patient so I was still on the premises when the call came. He wants to marry, Mrs Meredith. Even if he were to die tomorrow he wants to die a married man. That's how he put it.'

Alice felt tears pressing against her eyes and blinked frantically. 'We could ask the Reverend Tanner to come to the hospital.'

Hester said, 'You could wear your wedding gown. Henry would love that. And we could bring his clothes...'

Mr Frayne shook his head. 'We won't be able to dress him. He mustn't be moved. Absolute bed rest, I'm afraid. But he won't mind being married in a hospital gown. He simply wants to make you his wife, Mrs Meredith. Then I think the peace of mind will be beneficial to him.' He smiled. 'Arrange it with the ward sister. I can tell you the staff are already looking forward to it. Also the other patients. A bit of excitement for most of them – but as little

excitement for Mr Lightfoot as possible!
Strictly no visitors. As few people as possible. No champagne. Just a very short
service. We have to arrange for the minimum exertion on the patient's part.' He
stood up and held out his hand to each
in turn. 'Put his mind at rest, Mrs Meredith.' He smiled. 'Soon to be Mrs Lightfoot.'

He left them with instructions to wait for
a nurse to call them to the ward.

After a hectic few hours back at the hotel,
Hester and Alice returned to the City
Hospital by taxicab in some style. Passers-
by turned to stare as Alice stepped down
wearing her wedding gown and carrying a
small bag which contained Henry's shaving
brush, soap and razor. She had no idea
whether or not he would be allowed to shave
himself but Henry had insisted.

Hester followed wearing the skirt and
jacket she had bought for the wedding and
carrying a large cake which the chef had
somehow produced in the short time available. Lastly but not least, the Reverend
Tanner descended wearing his robes and
clutching the appropriate books. Fortunately the day was fine with hardly a breath of
wind. Hester had the two wedding rings in
her purse.

The little party made its way into the

hospital and up to the ward where Sister Wood came hurrying to meet them. To Alice's relief she was smiling broadly.

'Everything's ready,' she told them in a loud whisper. 'Mr Collins is going to give you away and will be one of the witnesses – we couldn't talk him out of it, I'm afraid! Mr Lightfoot said it was the least we could do since he had raised the alarm last night and probably saved his life. I'll be the other witness.' She listened to Alice's request that Henry could be shaved. 'Oh dear no! A few bristles won't matter at a time like this. I did tell you. He can speak his words of the service and kiss the bride but that's about all. Now...' She put a flustered hand to her head. 'Oh yes! One of the cleaners is going to play the wedding march on the mouth organ but no hymns, I'm afraid. We do have to keep it simple and get through it as soon as possible for your husband's sake. Also, we don't want Matron to descend on us. She agreed to the ceremony but with obvious reluctance.'

Hester said, 'We brought a cake for you all to share. Chef was determined. It's only a sponge but he managed to ice it and stick on a few cherries.'

Alice thought fleetingly of the elaborate three-tiered cake which had been ordered from the best confectioner in Chester. Hester had decided they would go ahead with it

343

and send out small boxed portions to all the guests who would now have no wedding to attend.

'Wonderful!' said Sister. 'I think we'll have to make room for it on the nurses' station.'

As soon as Henry was declared ready the musical cleaner was sent for. She was a large Irish woman by the name of Marie and she gasped with delight when she saw the bride.

'Well now, if you don't just look the most marvellous creature!' she told Alice. "Tis a pleasure to play for you, dearie!' She produced a small mouth organ, beamed at everyone and began to play a very inaccurate version of the wedding march.

Mr Collins, wearing a faded dressing gown and slippers, had pinned a daisy to what would have been a buttonhole. He drew back Henry's curtains with a flourish and Alice and Hester began their progress through the ward. Alice thought of the church and the aisle and Arthur Lester who was going to give her away and Edith and Maggie who were upset not to be present. She was sorry to have disappointed them but Mr Frayne's orders had been quite clear.

'You look a treat, ducks!' Mr Collins told her.

She thanked him with a self-conscious wave and there was a sudden chorus of approval and sporadic applause.

'God bless you both!' someone cried.

'Thank you.'

'He's a lucky man!'

Henry watched their approach with a broad smile on his face but as they drew nearer, Alice could see tears glistening in his eyes. He was propped against the pillow with Sister Wood standing beside him. He looked very weak and paler than earlier in the day. Was this little ceremony really going to put a strain on his heart? She forced the dark thought to the back of her mind and returned Henry's smile.

The Reverend Tanner was standing on the left side of the bed and he motioned Alice forward until she stood beside him.

'Now look at that!' Mr Collins cried. 'Mr Lightfoot, I congratulate you. You've picked a winner there. I reckon—'

The vicar said, 'Hush, Mr Collins! For the time being this is God's house.'

'Sorry, I'm sure.' He looked affronted. 'I was only saying as how—'

Sister moved round the bed, took him firmly by the arm and moved him back a few paces. She put a warning finger to her lips and he rolled his eyes.

'Women!' he muttered.

'We are gathered here in the sight of God...'

Alice's gaze was locked on Henry's as she tried to concentrate on the vicar's words.

Henry had insisted on this for the sake of her and for the child. She would be forever in his debt and somehow she would repay him for his goodness. If God granted him a reprieve she would make him the happiest man alive.

The vicar turned the page with a practised flick of his finger. 'Do you, Henry Albert Lightfoot, take this woman to be your lawful wedded wife? To love and to cherish...'

'I do,' he said.

'Do you, Alice Meredith, take this man?'

He looked at her for her response but she was still staring at Henry, praying for God to grant him a future.

Hester prompted. 'Alice!'

'I'm sorry. Yes, I do.' She wanted to add, 'I do love you, Henry,' because she did but this was not the place.

'Who gives this woman to be married ... ?'

Mr Collins stepped forward, his face pink with pride. 'I do.'

The rings were exchanged, the final words pronounced and Alice leaned forward to kiss her husband. He smelled of cheap soap but his face was radiant.

'I love you, Henry!' Alice whispered. 'I always will.'

'And I adore you.' He lowered his voice. 'And our child. Take good care of him, Alice. Don't let him forget me.'

'Henry! Don't talk like that. You'll be with

us. We'll...' Choked she stared at him through tear-filled eyes.

He gave her a tired smile. 'I'll try,' he said. 'I promise you I'll try.'

Epilogue

July 1909

Hester and Alice walked slowly along the path, watching young Henry as he skipped ahead of them, a small posy of flowers in his hands. The Reverend Tanner came towards him, the breeze whipping at his black vestments.

'Ladies! Good morning to you.'

'Good morning, Reverend,'

'I see young Henry is full of beans,' he said with a smile. 'Quite recovered from his mumps, I see. He's a fine lad. Very sturdy. Looks more like his father every day!'

Alice glanced away. She still worried sometimes about Henry's reputation as well as her own. Henry's sudden death had made it glaringly obvious that the child had been conceived out of wedlock. Naturally no one except Hester knew that the boy was Sebastian's child. In fact Henry's untimely death seemed to have spared her the humiliation of gossip and they had heard no more from Donald.

Hester nodded. 'My brother would have been so proud of him.'

Alice said, 'We've come to put some flowers on my husband's grave. Henry likes to do it himself. A little weekly ritual. A little link with the father he will never see.'

'Such a tragedy.' The vicar shook his head at the memory. 'Still, Mr Lightfoot did marry you. He was determined about that.'

Alice sighed. She would never forget that Henry's determination to do the right thing for her and the child had hastened his death. After the little ceremony he had quietly passed away in the night and Alice had found herself a widow less than twenty-four hours after becoming a wife. But Henry had seen to it that they were secure. Henry's share of the hotel had passed to her and the child. When Hester died her share would pass to the child.

Young Henry came running back along the path and Hester said, 'Walk, dearest child. Never run in a churchyard.'

'Why not? Nanny Brightling says I may.'

'I'm sure she doesn't, Henry. That was a little white lie, wasn't it?'

'Yes, Aunt Hester.'

'So what do you say?'

'I'm sorry.'

He looked up at her. 'But why can't I run?'

'God doesn't like it.' She took hold of his hand and they walked on ahead of Alice and the vicar.

The Reverend Tanner said, 'I spoke to Mr Lester this morning. The date is finalized. The first banns will be called next Sunday. I was saying only last week to my wife that I am very happy for you. The boy needs a father and, if you will forgive my familiarity, Mr Lester is a very lucky man.'

'Thank you.' She smiled her surprise at the compliment. 'We're hoping young Henry will have brothers and sisters to grow up with. A real family.'

They parted on this happy note and Alice hurried to catch up with her son. Hester was gathering up a few stray leaves from around Henry's grave while young Henry struggled to put the posy into the small stone vase.

For a moment Alice stood in silence with her head bowed and her eyes closed. Sometimes when she came alone to the grave, she fancied her husband could hear her thoughts and felt sure that he would approve of her forthcoming marriage.

Hester put an arm around her shoulder. 'See how well it has all worked out,' she said softly.

Alice opened her eyes. 'How *well*? But Henry *died*!' The anguished words seemed to utter themselves and she was as surprised as Hester as they hung in the air between them.

Hester took both Alice's hands in hers. 'He would have died, Alice. The doctor told us that, remember? His heart was damaged and nobody knew. Henry would have died a sad and disappointed man but instead he was happy and in love. *And* a father-to-be! You gave him that and it was wonderful for him.'

Dear Hester, Alice thought. She had been so supportive through the past few years. Impulsively Alice kissed her.

'Alice!' Hester beamed at her. 'What was that for?'

'For being the mastermind!'

Quick to understand, Hester laughed. 'You didn't have to say yes – and neither did Henry. I think it was meant to be.'

Alice smiled. 'You are a great comfort to me. Always there when I need you.'

'And why shouldn't I be? You and little Henry are my family now.'

Alice slipped her arm through Hester's.

'Let's go home,' she said and, with a cheerful heart, held out her hand to her son.